Poppy's Christm

Annette Hannah is a Liver Bird who relocated to leafy Hertfordshire in the 1980s and now lives near a river with her husband, two of their three grown-up children and a crazy black Cocker Spaniel. She writes romantic comedies in settings inspired by the beautiful countryside around her and always with a nod to her home town.

She worked in marketing for many years as a qualified marketeer, which she loved as it tapped into her creative side.

As an avid reader, she began to review the books she read, became a book blogger and eventually plucked up the courage to fulfil her lifelong dream of writing a book.

For four years she was a member of the Romantic Novelists' Association's new writers' scheme, during which time she wrote a book a year. After signing a two-book deal with Orion Dash in 2020, she graduated to a full member of the organisation and is also their Press Officer.

She loves long walks along the river, travelling to far-flung places and spending time with her friends and family.

You can follow her on twitter @annettehannah
www.sincerelybookangels.blogspot.com
www.annettehannah.com

Poppy's Christmas Wishes

Annette Hannah

First published in Great Britain in 2021 by Orion Dash,
an imprint of The Orion Publishing Group Ltd.,
Carmelite House, 50 Victoria Embankment,
London EC4Y 0DZ

An Hachette UK Company

3 5 7 9 10 8 6 4 2

A CIP catalogue record for this book is
available from the British Library.

ISBN (Paperback) 978 1 3987 1058 0
ISBN (eBook) 978 1 3987 1001 6

Typeset at The Spartan Press Ltd,
Lymington, Hants

Printed in the UK

MIX
Paper from
responsible sources
FSC® C104740

www.orionbooks.co.uk

To Jake, Damon and Lydia,
my very own three perfect wishes come true.
I'm so proud of you.
Always remember to follow your heart, work hard
and never give up on your dreams.
All my love, Mum x x x

Prologue

Breathlessly, they pulled away from each other. He exhaled loudly, adjusted his clothes and helped her dismount from the table.

'So that's the kitchen christened, which I believe is a full house.'

'Oi, cheeky.' She slapped him playfully on the arm and slipped back into her robe, her heart still racing. 'I don't think we've done it in the airing cupboard yet,' she laughed.

He gave her a cheeky wink and kissed her on the cheek, raising his arm behind her to check his watch as he did so. 'I've probably got time for a quick coffee before I head off.' He patted her on the bum on his way past to get his overnight bag.

Poppy had been hoping for a bit of an afterglow moment before normality kicked in, but she knew he needed to get back to Liverpool as he was back at work the next day. She filled the kettle and rinsed out his flask.

'I wish you didn't have to go back. It's so unfair, we should have been moving in together.'

'I know, I'm sorry, but it just couldn't be helped; they need me up there for just a little while longer. But it's only a few weeks and it'll fly by.' He pulled her over to the living-room window and cuddled her from behind, kissing her cheek. 'Look at that view of Market Square and the amazing fountain.'

'It is gorgeous, isn't it? The quaint little shops, a pub on the doorstep, just a stone's throw away from the river … and so handy for the station so I can get the train home whenever I want to.' She laughed. 'I'm beginning to sound like the estate agent now, extolling the virtues of the historical market town of Bramblewood.'

'I think you're going to be very happy here.'

'Don't you mean *we?*' she replied.

'Yes, of course.' He walked away from the window, gulped down his coffee and got ready to go.

Poppy's heart sank.

'I'm going to miss you.' She wound her arms around his shoulders and lifted her face to him. He kissed her passionately.

'You too. Good luck with the new job.'

'Thank you. Well, it's the training course first in London. I'm a little bit nervous but I'll be counting down the days until you join me and then it's Christmas in New York here we come. I'm so excited about that, it's going to be amazing.'

'You'll be great and I'm sure the time will fly. Bye then.' He kissed her and went to walk away but came back and pulled her into his arms. 'I do love you, you know. Always remember that, no matter what happens.'

'Are you OK?' she asked.

He took a deep breath as though he was about to say something important but then shook his head. 'I'm fine. Apart from the fact that I'll miss you a lot.'

'Aw, I'll miss you too. Bye then, have a safe trip and text me when you get home.' After closing the door, she went into the main bedroom, picked up the framed picture of the two of them from the bedside table and hugged it to her chest as she curled up on the sofa to watch a film.

A few days later, after completing the training course,

2

she arrived at the office bright and early following a short bus ride from Bramblewood. A lady called Tania showed her to her desk and introduced her to a young man called Dan; the three of them sat next to each other in the corner of the office. Tania showed her where the facilities and the stationery cupboard were and Dan got her a coffee. Poppy had spoken to them both on numerous occasions when she worked at the Liverpool branch, so it was good to finally meet face to face. As she unpacked her bits and pieces into her desk and drawers, she felt that she might like it here after all. She would miss her best friend Layla, with whom she'd worked for years and who had cried buckets when Poppy had left, but she'd promised she would visit lots.

'I can't believe it's lunchtime already,' said Poppy, as Tania invited her to the canteen.

'Hopefully that means you're enjoying it so far then if it's going quickly.' Tania handed Poppy a tray. 'So, what was it that made you move two hundred miles away from home?' she asked as they moved their trays along the counter past displays of sandwiches and glass screens showcasing various hot meals.

'Oh, my boyfriend Ed was offered an amazing job opportunity down here that was simply too good to turn down. It was a huge promotion. He'd been bypassed for the directorship at our branch which he'd been working towards for years, so he was really disappointed about that – devastated, in fact, as it was his dream job. However, this job was a close second. He wasn't keen on moving but asked me to come with him. I wasn't so sure as I loved my job and have great friends there. But he eventually managed to persuade me, especially when he told me about the New York proposal he had in mind. He suggested this job, so I applied for it and, lucky for me, I got it.' She placed an egg and cress sandwich

3

on her tray and a cup under the spout of the drinks machine, which after a bit of fiddling around with, soon filled with coffee.

'Oh, that's worked out perfectly for you then,' said Tania. 'So, when's he moving down?' She chose a jacket potato and thanked the lady behind the counter for adding tuna.

'Well that's just it, he was meant to move down the same time as me, but his job was delayed until the new year. So as soon as he breaks up for Christmas, we're off to New York to get engaged and then after Christmas, he starts his new job here.'

'What lovely news and how exciting for you,' replied Tania.

'I know, I can't wait, in less than a month I'll have a fiancé and we'll have moved in together.'

'What's his new job?' asked Tania as she paid for her food.

'He's going to be the financial controller,' Poppy said, her heart bursting with pride.

'No, he's not,' interrupted a woman who pushed Poppy's tray along the shelf whilst she searched for her purse in her bag. Poppy only just managed to catch the tray before it fell off the end of the counter. The unsmiling woman continued. 'David Bimble is the new financial controller; he starts next Monday.'

'Well, that's not true. You must be mistaken?' said Poppy, her voice caught in her throat as a feeling of nausea washed over her. 'I was only with Ed the other night; he was saying how much he was looking forward to moving in with me.' *He did say that, didn't he?* She wracked her brains to see whether he had said anything of the sort and realised he'd actually worded his answers very carefully.

'I can assure you if it's Ed Casey you're talking about then he turned the job down last minute and caused me a lot of extra work in admin.'

'But why would he do that?' she asked, more to herself than this smug woman.

'I heard he had a better offer.' She pushed past Poppy and paid for her food.

'I'm sure it's just a misunderstanding,' said Tania, shooting the woman a look as if to say shut up.

Poppy gathered her tray up along with her feelings of confusion and joined Tania who was waiting for her by the till.

'Britt likes to cause problems; watch out for her as she's not the nicest. Are you OK? You look a bit pale.'

'I'm not too sure,' answered Poppy honestly as prickles of unease crawled down her back.

Chapter 1

Three weeks later

Poppy expected the weather to be much colder at the top of the Empire State Building, especially this late in December. But the sun was joyful, beating down, caressing her skin and bathing her in a warm glow of happiness. She looked down at Ed as he knelt before her holding the most beautiful ring. Sparkling rainbows dazzled her as the sunlight danced on the exquisite diamond. Her heart thumped against her chest as she was about to hear those special words she had waited so long to hear.

'Poppy Kale, will you marry me?'

This was it; this was the moment. Her heart was singing.

'Yes,' she replied and held out her perfectly manicured hand to her new fiancé.

As he tried to place the ring on the ring finger of her trembling left hand, he accidentally dropped it on the floor, and they could hear it rolling away.

'Oh no,' cried Poppy as she got down on her hands and knees to join Ed in the search.

'It's OK, I've got it,' shouted a man from behind them.

Eyes shining with relief, her hand on her chest, Poppy turned to the man to thank him. On closer inspection, she realised it was her grandad. How thoughtful of Ed to invite him to the proposal, she thought. The old man smiled lovingly at her and closed his hand tightly around the ring. Poppy had a strange feeling that something wasn't right, but she couldn't quite grasp what it was. She turned back to Ed when she felt him tugging on her hand and was astonished to see him pushing a doughnut on her finger; it wasn't even a ring doughnut – it was filled with jam and was now looking quite messy. Suddenly everything went dark, the sun wasn't shining anymore, and she felt shivery.

That's when she realised what was wrong: her beloved grandad had died two years before. She could hear a buzzing noise and her mind felt fuzzy. She tried to eat the oozing doughnut, but her hand couldn't seem to find her mouth, it looked so delicious but so messy.

There was that buzzing noise again, it vibrated through her head. She slowly opened one eye and then the other and with a sinking heart she realised it was her doorbell that was making all the noise. She wasn't in New York enjoying a Christmas proposal from the love of her life. Instead, she was alone in her tiny flat, no grandad, no boyfriend, no ring and no bloody doughnut. She whimpered as the events of the last few weeks came flooding back to her.

It was an understatement, but life for Poppy wasn't exactly going to plan.

After the high of looking forward to an exciting new start down south with her boyfriend Ed, she had fallen back down to earth with not so much a bang but more like a head-on collision without the protection of an airbag.

The dream had really knocked her, especially seeing her grandad again. He had looked so well but it tore her heart apart to wake up and realise all over again that he wasn't here anymore.

Her grandad had never liked Ed, although it was more a distrust than a dislike, but he always said it was important to let Poppy make her own decisions in life and he supported her in her choices, no doubt hoping that Poppy would eventually come to her senses and realise that Ed simply wasn't good enough for her. She wished she'd listened to him.

She had never seen herself as one of those girls who crumbled without a man in her life. Yet whenever she thought about the break-up, tears of humiliation stung her eyes, and her stomach sank. He had driven her mad with frustration, being dishonest, ignoring her calls and uprooting her life. She thought after all that, he would consider her worth more than this.

After the conversation with Britt, she'd left messages on his answerphone, and it was only when she'd threatened to get the train back up to Liverpool that he'd eventually called her back.

'I'm so sorry, Poppy, I wanted to tell you, but I felt so bad.'

'You felt bad,' she shouted, her body tensing. 'How do you think I felt when some strange woman told me that my boyfriend isn't in fact coming down to live with me despite moving me away from my home, my job and my friends for him. But he has changed his mind and didn't think I was important enough to be told.' Her lip quivered and her voice shook with a mixture of anger and despair.

'Poppy, please don't get upset. I was all set to join you but then the guy who beat me to the director's job got sacked – he couldn't hack it apparently. Harvey offered it to me, and I just couldn't refuse. Even though he's made it quite clear that his expectations are sky high. It's a hell of a lot of pressure but it's also what I've been working towards my whole life.'

'Your whole life, your job, your relocation, it's all you, you, you. What about me? You persuaded me to give up my job

8

that I was very happy with, and I had prospects and I gave it up for you. Well, more fool me.'

'Look, I'm really grateful that you gave up your job but try not to be so negative. Look on the bright side – it might be good for you to have a change of scenery, you always said that you wanted to do something exciting, and it is a beautiful place. I think you'll love it there.'

Poppy felt she would burst as the blood rushed to her face. 'Try not to be so negative,' she repeated. 'Who even are you? Why can't you relocate the director's role – I'm sure you could do it from down here.'

'You know what Harvey's like, he likes his team around him and I really tried to get your job back for you, but it was too late. It's all happened so quickly.'

'But when will you come down next?'

'Well, that's the thing, Poppy, it's going to take up all of my time and every ounce of energy I've got to prove myself in this role. And, well, the thing is I just don't see how a long-distance relationship will work. I think we need to take a break.'

'What?' she shrieked. 'Are you serious? But what about New York? We're supposed to be getting eng—' she hesitated as her mind went into overdrive. 'Oh wait, I get it now. That was just a ploy to persuade me to move away with you. Wasn't it?'

'No, it wasn't. I *was* going to propose but it's all about priorities. This job will take everything out of me. Maybe one day in the future when I've made a success of it we can get back together again?'

'But I want you now, not in the future.' She felt deflated.

'I feel like an absolute bastard and a coward for what I've done, but I hope we can still be friends.'

★

9

She'd never forget those words. How could she when they were etched on the inside of her eyelids? They couldn't have hurt her more if they were engraved on her heart with a Stanley knife. But he was a coward and he was a liar. She'd given him everything and the only thing he'd given her was a fully paid-up membership of the broken-hearted club.

She fitted the bill perfectly, ticking off the requirements one by one on an imaginary list: shoulders slumped, tick, surrounded by empty chocolate bar wrappers, tick, mascara all over face, tick, watching boxsets of *Sex and the City* alone every night, tick (although she had to admit that she did that anyway as it was her favourite programme), feelings of shame at having been so foolish, big tick.

She had really thought that Ed was the one; he was tall and handsome and quite arrogant with some people but not with her and she got butterflies in her stomach whenever she saw him. He had a great job at Recharge Accountancy Ltd and was really going places. He was also her boss and as inter-office affairs were frowned upon, they'd had to sneak around to see each other for the first few months of their relationship, until it became serious and Ed had okayed it with one of the partners.

Those first few months were thrilling and naughty, all secret smiles and winks. Touching hands slightly whilst passing each other in the corridor would send tingles through every nerve in her body, not to mention the sheer indecency that took place in the stockroom every now and then. Ed made her feel so special and wanted.

The only little niggle she'd had about him was his reluctance to spend; he was a typical accountant and liked to take care when it came to relieving himself of any cash. He was ambitious though and knew exactly what he wanted. He'd filled Poppy's head with hopes and dreams of what saving up could achieve: the huge house in the countryside filled with children, fancy holidays and anything else she wanted. Poppy didn't really mind as she saw herself as an independent woman who was earning a good living so didn't think anything of paying for the odd meal. Poppy didn't care about material things, so this hadn't bothered her whilst they were together. It would wind her best friend Layla up whenever she told her about it, though, because she thought Poppy deserved so much better.

She would have done anything for Ed, which is why she hadn't hesitated to apply for the job down south when he asked her to. Knowing that he would be joining her soon had filled her heart with happiness.

When Ed had driven her down to Bramblewood with all her possessions, they explored the small market town and loved it. The flat was situated in the market square above a characterful little shop called 'Odds'n'Sods'. The name had made them laugh at first, but they quickly came to realise how apt it was, as the owner Mr Ives sold practically everything you could possibly need. He and his wife would ensure that if they didn't have something you needed, they would order it in. The market square was surrounded by other quaint shops, cafés and restaurants, a small B&B and The Flamingo's Leg, a pub which backed onto the river with tables and chairs outside.

The historic market town of Bramblewood featured shops that were hundreds of years old with original black Tudor beams peeking out through white exteriors. The other buildings were a lot more modern but had been built in keeping with the original architecture.

A beautiful working fountain stood resplendent in the centre of the square, which was lit up at night. According to

Mr Ives, market stalls would fill the area every Monday and attracted quite a crowd.

The River Bram, which meandered through miles of beautiful countryside and eventually flowed into London, was on their doorstep. A large village green, a church and a charming old, converted signal box all hundreds of years old added to the quaintness of the town. The place was picturesque. They'd spent the weekend exploring it together but now that Ed wasn't coming, it had all dulled for Poppy. The enchanting brightly coloured lanterns that were strung up along the shops in the high street and round the market square were a welcome sight for most people, including Poppy when she'd first arrived. They'd heralded the fact that Christmas would soon be here, but now they were a sad reminder of the Christmas she should have had.

The doorbell rang again. Poppy jolted awake from the half-asleep state she was in and rubbed her eyes. Feeling more disappointed that the doughnut wasn't real, rather than the proposal, she flumped down the hallway of her tiny flat in her onesie and fluffy bunny slippers. She opened the door to a flurry of shopping bags, the sound of bottles clinking together, a bright purple suitcase and a very excited best friend wearing a sparkly red Santa hat with a flashing bobble on the end of it.

'Merry Christmas,' Layla sang, as she kissed Poppy on both cheeks. 'I'm so glad I'm here at last – what a long journey. I had fun on the tube, it was like a party, everyone squished up against everyone else. A hot guy insisted I wore his hat and I thought you said no one talks to each other? Practically the whole carriage was singing Christmas songs, it was a lovely atmosphere.' She dropped her bags in a heap on the living-room floor, shook off her coat and threw it over the arm of the worn leather armchair. She looked around the cosy room.

'Hey, where's your tree? Where are your fairy lights? You love fairy lights. I thought you were joking about cancelling Christmas, but you must be serious if you haven't got fairy lights. Oh, come here, give us a hug.' Layla stopped to draw a breath and Poppy allowed herself to be swallowed up in a long-awaited cuddle.

The soothing arms of her friend caused her to have a mini-meltdown. Poppy wept huge hot tears into Layla's shoulder, leaving mascara trails on her expensive cream top, whilst wailing about how lonely she'd been and what a double-crossing bastard her ex was. Layla let her get it out of her system until eventually Poppy took a deep breath and offered to make her a nice cup of tea.

Layla shook her head, 'Look, a cup of tea might solve everything in the soaps, but this is real life and it's a celebration.'

Poppy put her hands over her ears and squeezed her eyes shut. 'No celebration, I told you I'm not doing Christmas.'

'Who said anything about the C word? The celebration is because I'm here and I've brought your favourite rosé, and some flavoured vodka.' She smiled as Poppy opened her eyes wide. Layla grabbed Poppy's wrists and gently pulled her hands away from her ears. 'Come on, you've been working all day and I've travelled two hundred miles to be with my bestie, it's time to partay! Let's crack open this bottle.' She waved the gift bags which contained the bottles. 'Right, which way's the kitchen?' Poppy led the way and took two wine glasses out of the cupboard. Layla filled them with the pale pink liquid. Before picking them up, she took Poppy in her arms and hugged her again.

'It's so good to see you, Poppy, but I can't wait to see that

13

gorgeous smile of yours again.' She held her at arm's length and looked into her face. 'If I looked up "melancholy" in the dictionary, I swear it would just show me a picture of your eyes as they look right now. Wait. Oh no, you've had that dream again, haven't you?'

Poppy nodded. 'I wish it would stop.'

'It will stop, I promise, babe, it's just because this was the time it should have happened. One day you'll be so glad that it didn't happen. You know what they say?'

'Shitty things happen for a reason,' they chorused together.

'Seriously, Layla, I don't know what I would have done without you on the other end of the phone and my computer screen these last few weeks; I wish I'd never applied for this stupid transfer. What was I thinking?'

'Don't be blaming yourself, you trusted him and weren't to know what a sneaky shit he really was.'

'Oh, I suppose it wasn't really his fault – it was his lifelong ambition to get that job.' Even though they had split up, Poppy felt guilt claw at her insides for slagging him off.

'Don't go feeling sorry for him, Poppy, he's not worth any of your tears.' Layla's mouth was pursed in disgust and her expression reminded Poppy of when she'd accidentally put her finger in poo whilst cleaning out her cat Misty's litter tray. She understood Layla's loyalty to her, but she didn't want her to hate Ed too much in case they got back together one day.

'You're so much better off being rid of him. Anyway, enough about him, he always puts me in a bad mood. Happy C word to you.' Layla's ability to brighten the mood along with her contagious smile gave Poppy the lift she so desperately needed.

Poppy felt a little more like her old self as she danced round the living room to Christmas songs whilst they demolished a couple of bottles of wine and half a bottle of her favourite chocolate orange vodka shots. She whipped the Santa hat from Layla's head so fast that the static caused her usually perfect straight blonde hair to have that 'dragged through a hedge backwards' sort of look. This just made her look even more sexy than she normally did, with her big baby blue eyes and slender figure. Layla Rose was gorgeous and a lovely, caring person too. Poppy's hair was a mass of jet-black unruly curls and she had always been envious of Layla's completely kinkless locks.

'You know what, Layla, you are the only one who can ever get my hair straight. I've spent hundreds of pounds on hairdreshers and they never do it like you do,' Poppy slurred. 'I love you so mush and you're my bezzie mate in the whoooole world.'

'Oh that reminds me.' Layla stopped mid-dance during Mariah Carey's 'All I Want For Christmas Is You' and jumped off the rickety little wooden coffee table that had been her stage for the last half an hour. She grabbed her purple leather handbag and rummaged through it until she found two shiny gold envelopes. She thrust them into Poppy's face.

'Here's an early Christmas pressie to help cheer you up.'

Poppy ripped open the envelope eagerly, but the alcohol prevented her eyes from focusing properly on the words printed on the card. Layla explained that she had booked them both into a local spa the following day for massages, manicures and pedicures.

'Oh Layla, that's lovely, but how can I let anyone touch this body. I mean, look at me.'

'You're beautiful, Poppy, curvaceous with that hourglass figure. If anyone deserves pampering it's you – and me, of course.'

Poppy kissed her friend's cheek for being so kind. She

could do with a release from all the homesickness and stress of a new job and of being dumped.

She opened the second envelope and her stomach churned as she saw what was inside. She shook her head.

'No, Layla, I told you, as far as I am concerned Christmas is cancelled. Why on earth would I want to celebrate anything when my life is in bits? All I want to do is to curl up in bed with a couple of bottles of wine and eat at least my body weight in chocolate until this so called "season of goodwill" is over. Layla, I am not going to the office Christmas party – I told you I didn't want to go.'

'I know you did, my love, but I ordered the tickets anyway because we need to find the fun-loving Poppy that I know and love again. So, you need to listen to Auntie Layla, and do exactly as I say because tonight, I am going to be your fairy godmother.'

She cupped Poppy's chin in her hand, squashing her cheeks comically as she lifted her face to look at her.

'Now repeat after me: I, Poppy Kale, shall go to the ball.'

'I, Poppy Kale, shall go to the ball,' she mumbled through misshapen lips that were still being squeezed by Layla's hand.

'Good girl,' said Layla and kissed her on the forehead.

Poppy woke the next morning with a tongue like a Brillo pad and a head that felt like an axe was sticking out of it. She sprang out of bed when she remembered her friend was in the spare room. Unfortunately, she then had to lie down again as the blood rushed to her head far too fast but after a few minutes she padded out towards the kitchen to make strong coffee and bacon rolls. She'd even pinched some brown sauce sachets from the canteen at work for Layla as she only ever had ketchup at home.

'Remember I'm a veggie so only two slices of bacon for me,' shouted Layla as soon as she heard the bacon sizzle.

Poppy laughed; she knew that Layla would be trying her best not to think of it as an animal but after drinking the night before, she simply couldn't resist.

'Oh my, this is heaven,' Layla groaned five minutes later as she bit into the thick, juicy bacon.

'You sound like Meg Ryan in *When Harry met Sally*,' Poppy chuckled before biting into her own.

Layla banged her hand on the table with every subsequent chew, which made Poppy laugh again.

It didn't take long to clear up the mess from the previous night, numerous empty bottles and pizza boxes were hurriedly tossed into the recycling bin. Poppy felt it would take a lot longer to clear up the mess that her life had become but she was grateful for Layla, who never let her down. She felt she owed it to her to try and have a good time despite everything. Both girls showered, dressed and headed off to Hailey House spa for their pampering sessions.

Chapter 2

The time for the dreaded party had arrived. After hearing the taxi beeping outside, Poppy and Layla necked their vodka shots for Dutch courage and raced down the stairwell of the flat. They had siphoned the rest of the vodka into two smaller bottles which were hidden in their handbags.

In the back of the taxi, Poppy folded her arms to let Layla know she would not be taking part in any joyous shenanigans. Layla grabbed her perfectly manicured hand and gave it a little reassuring squeeze.

'Come on, you're gorgeous, and we're going to have a ball tonight just like old times.' Layla paused. 'Look, I was saving this for Christmas Day, but I have a little good news to cheer you up.'

Poppy's ears pricked up, 'What good news? Has Ed broken his leg skiing or something?'

'No,' Layla replied, 'I've applied for a job in your branch and I have an interview in January.'

Poppy smiled and hugged Layla as tightly as she could despite the resistance from the seatbelts restraining them.

'Oh Layla, that's amazing news! You can come and live with me here and everything will be so much better. I can't wait and I think that deserves another shot, yippee.'

They both took a swig from their stowed away bottles and clinked them together in celebration. Poppy wasn't going to be lonely anymore.

The taxi eventually pulled into the gate of the stately Belvedere Manor. Nestled deep in the countryside about half an hour away from home, the grounds were entered through a long winding driveway edged with fir trees adorned with twinkling lights. Views of the gardens on both sides were enhanced with subtle lighting and as they got closer to the building, the centrepiece took Poppy's breath away and she could tell that Layla was equally as enamoured as she squeezed her hand.

'That bandstand looks so magical and look at its reflection in the lake, it's so beautiful, it's made me feel quite emotional.' Her eyes filled with tears as she gazed at the intricate dome and marvelled at how many sparkling lights had been entwined around the columns.

'Aw I know what you mean, I'm feeling quite emosh myself. Must be the vodka 'cos even I have a little tiny tear in my eye.' She laughed and undid her seatbelt. Members of staff in smart red and black uniforms opened the car doors to escort them and the other arrivals to the grand entrance. The weather outside was crisp and Poppy pulled her coat tighter to protect her from the Siberian chill in the night air.

The arched doorway opened to a spacious reception area with cream marble floors, partially panelled walls and a number of heavy dark oak doors, each with a gold sign engraved in black lettering with the name of the room. Once inside, Poppy's eyes were drawn to the focal point, an elaborate fireplace filled with burning logs and guarded by giant nutcrackers who stood to attention on either side. Garlands decorated with oranges studded with cloves and bundles of cinnamon sticks tied with ribbon draped luxuriously from the mantelpiece and ornate gilded mirror above. The prettiest Christmas tree towered in the corner, the star on the top skimming the ceiling, red and gold ornaments dripping from every branch as fairy lights twinkled around them.

Poppy drew in a deep breath. 'It smells amazing in here, like mulled wine and my grandparents' house. Cosy and warm and, I suppose, Christmassy.' She smiled at the memory of the stripy pillowcase she would lay at the bottom of her bed every Christmas Eve. The excitement of leaving a carrot and mince pie out for Rudolph and Santa. The trying to squeeze her eyes shut as tightly as possible as she knew if she didn't sleep, HE wouldn't come. She never actually remembered falling asleep, but she always did obviously and before she knew it the morning would have arrived. The look of delight on her grandparents' faces as she dragged the bulging sack of presents into their room flashed in her mind. One year she had got a nurse's outfit and still had a picture of her wearing it, smiling her toothless smile and holding her nana's hand. That was the year her grandad had taught her the song 'All I Want For Christmas Is My Two Front Teeth'. Christmases were the best times, and she treasured the memories with her grandparents, who had brought her up after her mother had died.

'I'd almost forgotten how much I love Christmas,' she said, nudging Layla affectionately with her elbow. 'Thanks for helping me remember.'

'At last, that's just what I've been waiting to hear. Oh, I'm so pleased I've got my Poppy back.' Layla grabbed Poppy's hand and made a beeline for the nutcracker soldiers, pulling her phone out of her bag on the way.

'We've got to have a selfie with Ben and Jerry!'

'Who?' asked Poppy.

'Our dates for the night, that's who.' She draped Poppy's arm around one of the nutcrackers and put hers around the other, then lifted her phone up so she could get them all in the picture. Poppy linked her arm through Layla's and threw her head back laughing when she saw the picture of Layla wide-eyed with her lips on the soldier's face. 'OMG I didn't realise you were kissing your one.'

'Oh yes, well, Ben is very handsome, but you can't talk, look at you all cosy, cheek to cheek with Jezza.'

'Right, enough of your leading me astray shenanigans, we need to find out where we're supposed to be,' said Poppy, still chuckling.

'Ah here we are,' said Layla, pointing to a large notice board with the names of all the companies that had booked their Christmas parties there. 'Recharge Accountancy' was one of five companies listed and the sign told them they should be in the Young Suite. They obediently trotted off in the direction of the room, high heels click clacking, giggling and holding onto each other for dear life as they tried not to slip on the beautiful shiny floors.

A few of Poppy's colleagues had already arrived and stood by the bar awkwardly. She still didn't know many of them, but she got on really well with the two who sat next to her in their busy office. Dan, a trainee accountant, was in his early twenties, whereas Tania, PA to one of the directors, was fifty five. She was originally from Latvia and still had a strong accent. Poppy, at thirty, was pretty much in the middle, age-wise, and enjoyed their company as they tended to have a bit of a spark about them and good humour. Poppy introduced Layla to Dan and Tania.

The long table was lavishly set to seat fifty people; bottles of red, white and sparkling wine were arranged down the middle, and each placemat had a Christmas cracker and party accessories on it. They chose their places at the end of the table quickly so they could sit together, Dan and Tania sitting opposite Poppy and Layla. The hum of multiple conversations filled the air in the elegant room, and the faint sound of Christmas carols could just about be heard in the background. Waiting staff in black and white uniforms served a mouth-watering three-course meal. The wine flowed freely, and Poppy finally began to relax and much to her surprise she found she was enjoying herself.

The accessories on the table were a huge hit. Dan had an elf hat with huge sticky out ears on it, and Tania wore a girly elf hat with two long white plaits and slightly smaller ears. Layla had a sparkly silver masquerade mask and Poppy had a fluffy white-feathered angel halo on a headband. They giggled a lot; Dan told his unfunny jokes but the way he told them with that cheeky glint in his big brown eyes just made them laugh anyway.

Tania told stories of her rich ex-husband's sexploits and the various times she had caught him literally with his trousers down.

'The last time was in a hotel we were staying in and he was in flagrante with a commis chef called Ingrid. He had been trying to persuade her to make us sandwiches even though room service had finished. When I walked in and saw them together, I sprayed his bare bum cheeks with the fire extinguisher that was next to them. They both ran out looking like they'd been through a carwash in an open-topped convertible by the time I'd finished.' They shrieked with laughter.

'Layla and I had such fun on our nights out in Liverpool. We got up to so much mischief and sometimes we'd be out so late, we'd get the first bus home the next morning. I can't even remember where half the places were, but I remember one place called the Yankee Clipper and I'm still trying to work out if it was a real boat or a dream,' said Poppy.

'The nightlife in Liverpool is fantastic. We could just fall out of one club and trip into another next door. Always with our vodka in our bags, especially when we were younger and didn't have much money. If we ever had any unwanted attention from men, we would just put our arms around each other and pretend we were a couple to get rid of them and it worked every time,' Layla laughed.

'Except for the weirdos whose eyes would light up at the thought of it,' added Poppy, her face wrinkled in disgust. 'One time a guy dressed as a killer clown tried to grab me during part of a show, and I panicked and knocked a whole table full of drinks over in my bid to escape. It was hilarious.'

'The most annoying thing about that was that we had only just doubled up on drinks for happy hour so that did not make us happy. So many great memories, Poppy.' Layla smiled at her friend who was still giggling.

'Well,' said Dan as he jumped to his feet, his tie loosened and shirt hanging out of his trousers. 'It's time to make some more. Come on, let's go, the Cuban entertainment is about to begin next door and then the dancing. All grab a wine bottle each.'

The main ballroom was beautifully ornate with wooden panels around the lower walls painted a subtle shade of powder blue; pale lemon wallpaper, delicately patterned with powder blue flowers, covered the upper parts of the wall. Blue hummingbirds in gold-embossed birdcages decorated tall vases which stood either side of an opulent mantelpiece. Heavy tapestry drapes in gold with swirls of peacock blue adorned the floor to ceiling windows. Circular tables were placed around a marble dance floor in front of a stage which had a heavy oak bar next to it. A DJ played Christmas songs as glamorous guests spilled from myriad doors. As the main lighting dimmed, coloured lights reflected around the room and onto excited faces.

They chose a table near the stage and not too far from the bar. The disco music changed to the distinctive beat of rumba and two beautiful women appeared on the stage in red and gold shiny costumes, more like bikinis, complete with huge tail feathers and sparkly showgirl headdresses that shimmied as they danced. The show was spectacular as they sang and swayed in time to their musician's drumbeat. Poppy heard the loudest roar of laughter from another table and did a double take as she saw the most drop-dead gorgeous man moving in time to the music. His dark hair was gelled back to one side and his chiselled jaw was finished off with a dimple in his chin. His body was perfect, not too muscly but taut enough to make Poppy's imagination run wild.

'OMG, Layla, look at him! He's gorgeous!' Layla spun round in the general direction and shrugged her shoulders.

'Mmmm, he's not bad but he so loves himself, he would spend longer getting ready to go out than you would. You'd be better off with his mate; he looks lovely and what an incredible laugh, it's absolutely contagious.' She then put her finger under Poppy's chin and gently pushed up to close her mouth as she continued to gawk at the sexy love god.

Poppy turned her head to see who the Adonis was with and saw he was talking to another tall guy.

'Oh, he's cute, more drop-dadbod gorgeous than drop dead. With those lovely sparkly eyes he looks far more approachable than the other one ... but what's with the moustache and goatee, I wonder.' He glanced over and caught her looking, so she quickly turned away. Layla tapped her on the shoulder and whispered in her ear.

'You need to kop off with someone to take your mind off the other fella.' Poppy was feeling the effects of the wine and giggled.

24

'But I've already got my lovely Jezza. He's the only man I want right now!' she laughed. 'Seriously though, I'm right off men now but maybe you should.'

'No, I really can't be arsed. The ones I meet are idiots.'

As the limbo started, Poppy continued to ogle her new fancy man and noticed he wasn't a smiler whereas his friend would burst into deep belly laughs as he watched his friends taking their turn under the limbo stick; she couldn't help but join in the laughter. He looked at her and this time she didn't look away. His eyes locked onto hers, stirring up an emotion she didn't recognise. She felt a magnetic pull towards him from the centre of her chest. He laughed again as one of his friends collapsed backwards and grabbed his arm, and she laughed too. He had an aura about him that almost glowed.

It was obvious his friends loved him by the way they touched him and laughed with him. Their faces lit up like the shine of a thousand buttercups when he spoke to them. One of the men in his crowd who'd just been kicked off the limbo competition put a hand on each of his cheeks and kissed him full on the mouth. Poppy felt quite voyeuristic and reluctantly turned away. The band kept playing and people queued to take part in the limbo competition. Dan was instantly disqualified for trying to lift the stick with his hands. He was now wearing the dancer's headdress and was shaking his own tail feathers whilst dancing on the bar.

Eventually there were only two people left in the competition: Tania, who wore Dan's tie like a sweatband around her head to keep her wild ginger curls at bay, and the guy with the goatee. They appeared to be having a fun time, surrounded by people clapping and singing 'how low can you go.' Mr Goatee was a whole lot more flexible than he looked and managed to beat Tania, but he graciously handed her the bottle of champagne he won and gave her a kiss on the cheek.

Tania came to join them and handed the bottle of champagne to Poppy.

'This is from the guy with the goatee. He asked me to give it to the beautiful girl with the blue dress and the sad eyes.' Poppy blushed, looked over to him and smiled. He smiled back and raised his glass to her.

As the band played the last of their songs, Dan, still wearing the feathered headdress, started the conga by holding onto the waist of one of the Cuban girls who was now wearing his elf hat. They were closely followed by the other Cuban girl and Mr Fancy Man. Layla followed in front of Tania and Mr Goatee, who grabbed Poppy by the arm on the way past.

He laughed his deep, booming laugh as he moved her arms to his waist and high-kicked from side to side. Soon she felt clammy hands on her waist and looked round to see 'Burger Breath' Brian, one of the directors, wearing Tania's discarded elf hat on his sweaty, bald, but for a few grey tufts, bonce. In order to distance herself from Brian, she found she was moving closer to Mr Goatee until her arms were quite a way round him and embarrassingly, she found herself practically cuddling him. She rested her face on his back with her cheek on his soft black shirt and found it soothing just being carried along by the rhythm. The wine on top of the vodka had gone straight to her head and she nodded off for a second or two. The next thing she knew he was gently trying to disentangle himself from her. Much to her embarrassment she realised that the conga had finished, the disco was now blasting eighties tunes and she was cuddling him like he was her pillow at home.

'Oh my God, I'm so sorry, I got a little bit too comfortable there,' she said as she freed him from her embrace.

'I'm certainly not complaining. Fancy a dance?' He looked at her, seemingly amused by her embarrassment and she couldn't help but grin back at him and his friendly blue eyes. She joined him in throwing some shapes on the dance floor, this guy could really move, and he was obviously a born entertainer. She laughed as he thrust his arms and hips in perfect John Travolta style before swiftly and seamlessly moving into a comedic routine that David Brent would have been proud of. Poppy had to hold her sides, which ached from laughing. Tania and Layla had joined them along with most of his party and the dance floor was heaving. Mr Fancy Man was doing a slow dance with one of the Cuban girls and Dan was last seen creeping under the table with the other. Mr Goatee leaned over and shouted in her ear, nearly bursting her eardrum.

'Hey sleepy girl, my name's Gabe, what's yours?' His deep sexy voice vibrated in her chest as he stared into her eyes, and she felt that strange pull again.

'Ooh, Gabe, that's a posh name. My name's Poppy, nice to meet you.'

'Ah I haven't heard that accent since I used to watch Brookside,' he replied in a perfect exaggerated Liverpool accent.

'I used to love that programme,' replied Poppy.

'Me too, they should never have stopped it. Hey, you do realise with a name like yours we could never get married, don't you?'

'Well I'm never getting married, I'm through with men and relationships but go on, tell me why. I'm intrigued.'

'Me too, I know that feeling very well; my surname is Sellers, get it? Poppy Sellers.' He laughed his deep booming laugh again, which resonated in her heart and she couldn't help but join in.

As soon as the last song was finished, the dance floor had emptied rapidly. Poppy thanked Gabe for the dance and he kissed her hand. She was amazed to see that it was gone 1 a.m. There were a few people left milling around, waiting for taxis. She headed over to Layla and checked her mobile phone to see a few missed calls and a text from the taxi company.

'Oh no, Layla, the taxi driver has taken another fare who told them we'd gone. We'll have to wait for ages now. They've said it will be at least an hour.' Layla couldn't have looked less bothered as she was singing and dancing around the glorious Christmas tree in the reception area.

'Come and join us,' shouted Layla, 'these are the baddies, I mean "BADS", Bramblewood Amateur Dramatic Society.' She gestured with her hand for Poppy to join her and her new friends. Poppy recognised some of Gabe's group and said hello. She glanced over to see Gabe talking to Mr Fancy Man who was even more gorgeous up close. She noticed he had his arm draped around the Cuban girl but at least she was wearing a coat now. She felt a wave of envy as she saw them walk off together. Gabe looked in her direction and walked over to her.

'Well, that's my ride cancelled; Mr Loverman is taking Eliza home in his nifty little two-seater instead of me.'

They were interrupted by a loud voice shouting that they were very sorry, but everyone needed to wait outside as the staff were locking up. This statement was greeted by groans from the remaining ten people as they wrapped up in their coats and braced themselves for the frosty night.

Poppy's heart leapt as she stepped outside and saw the bandstand in all its majestic glory. Twinkling lights glowed against the midnight blue sky and the moon reflected on the lake beyond. She felt the cold air brush her face as she ran to it. After almost losing her footing on the steps, she felt the warmth of strong arms grab her and hold her until she was steady again.

'Careful, Sleeping Beauty, you were almost a goner there.' Gabe's voice had a calming quality about it that made Poppy feel as though everything would be OK. 'Oh, thank you for saving me, I didn't fancy a moonlight swim.' She gestured to the lake that she'd almost toppled into. 'Isn't it just beautiful here? I love it.' She moved to the centre of the bandstand and twirled around, her arms out to the sides. 'I just want to dance all night long.' She shivered and Gabe pulled her close to him. 'Come on then, let's dance.' She felt tiny in his bear hug of an embrace. 'But there isn't any music,' she said.

'Well, that's strange because I can hear music when I look at you,' said Gabe. She laughed and slapped him gently on the arm. 'You're such a smooth talker, I can see why everyone loves you.'

'What's not to love?' he laughed. 'OK, you want real music, here we go.' He searched through the playlist on his phone and the soothing tones of George Michael singing 'Last Christmas' filled the frosty air. Gabe held his hand out to her, which she accepted gracefully, before he twirled her round then masterfully pulled her towards his chest.

'Wow, I can tell you're a professional dancer.'

'Not really, but I can get by.' They swayed rhythmically and she snuggled into his warmth.

'Come on then, I'll keep you warm and you can tell me why you're off men now.'

'No, that's boring,' replied Poppy. 'How about first you tell me why you have a goatee.' She covered her mouth up. 'I'm so sorry, I was meant to just think that bit. I've had an itsy bit too much to drink.'

'What, this thing?' he said, rubbing at his bristles. 'Well,

I've got to say I'm sure you will have never heard this excuse before, but I'm currently playing a genie in a play inspired by Aladdin and other fairy tales, it's called *Three Wishes*. Some bright spark decided to shave my head and made me grow this incredibly annoying goatee and moustache. I was also encouraged to eat an extra burger or two for the lead-up to the show as genies are apparently rounded as well.'

'Ah that's amazing, a genie! I love that. And I love that you've really made an effort to get into character.' She smiled, contemplated whether to tell him her story and decided he had a good honest face.

'Wait, my feet are killing me. Shall we sit down with the others?' She had been so engrossed in dancing with Gabe that she hadn't noticed their friends had joined them and were huddled around the edge of the bandstand.

'Poppy, you forgot this.' Layla held a bottle of champagne out to her.

'Oh great. Thanks for this, by the way, Gabe.' She popped it, wincing as she did so as she was terrified the cork would take her eye out. Everybody cheered at the universal sound of celebration. Poppy filled the glasses of those who'd brought theirs with them. She then sat back down again and huddled into Gabe, swigging from the bottle and passing it to him to do the same.

'So where was I up to?' Gabe was about to answer but she remembered. 'Ah yes, well the reason I've gone off men is because my ex dumped me uncereno ...' she faltered, 'I mean uncero .. nomously ...' She tutted. 'What I mean is he dumped me very rudely in a strange place with a new job when he was meant to be moving down here too.'

'Do you mean unceremoniously?' asked Gabe, a twinkle in his eye.

'Yes, that's what I said. Basically, I was stitched up and I took a demotion so am not even enjoying my job. Everything has gone horribly wrong; in fact, I wish you were a real genie,' she said, suddenly feeling sorry for herself.

'Why would you wish I was a real genie? And in fact, how do you know I'm not?'

'Because if you were, you could grant me three wishes and then my life would be perfect,' she simpered.

She shivered and he cuddled her into his warmth.

'Well, it is Christmas so let's just pretend for one night only that I am a real genie. What would your three wishes be?'

'Well, we would need a lamp first, silly,' she replied.

'OK,' he said, smiling, as he noticed a rusty old watering can by his foot on the floor of the bandstand. He dragged it over to her and she smiled and rubbed it with her coat sleeve three times.

'My first wish would be to have a love like my grand-parents used to have. But first I need to get fitter, I've been eating rubbish and exercise has gone well and truly out of the window.'

'Well, I think you are pretty perfect as you are but OK, and do you have anyone in mind?'

'Well, yes, I want my ex, Ed, to fall in love with me again. He broke my heart; we were so much in love. In fact, we … well, I mean I still am and I'm sure he will be when he comes to his senses. I think he just panicked because he'd uprooted my life and felt bad.'

'Well, I think he's an absolute fool to let someone like you go. Beautiful, talented, a great dancer and a genuinely lovely person from what I've experienced.' Gabe's kind words made her feel as warm on the inside as his body was making her feel on the outside. His voice was smooth and rich. His eyes twinkled in the moonlight and seemed to stare deep into her soul. She nestled further into his warmth. It surrounded her and reminded her of the Ready Brek glow she had seen on TV adverts. She felt protected by him as if nothing could hurt her. She wanted to keep looking at him, he was so mesmerising. Her eyes fluttered every now and then with the effort of trying to keep them open, but wine always made her sleepy and they slowly closed.

Layla had overheard some of the conversation and piped in, 'She fancies your mate, but I've told her he loves himself.'

'Layla.' Poppy's eyes pinged open and she tried to cover her giggling friend's mouth. 'Well yes, I do like Mr Fancy Man, but he went off with the belly dancer and didn't even notice me.' Poppy blushed furiously. Thank goodness it was dark, she couldn't believe she had said it. How desperate did that make her sound? She tried to change the subject. 'But anyway, like I said, I'm finished with men for ever. As long as I've got my friends like Layla, my fairy godmother, and now you, my gorgeous genie, then that's all I need.' She linked her arm through his.

'I can understand that completely, some men can be horrible,' he replied.

'You know you sound like someone…' She searched her brain for the name of the singer who he reminded her of, his voice was hypnotic. It came to her, and she tunelessly sang in as deep a voice as she could manage, 'Can't get enough of your love.'

'Barry White, you mean. It has been said before, I must admit.'

'Yes,' she replied sleepily, 'you sound just like him. Do you like belly dancers?'

'Thanks, I take that as a huge compliment. Well technically she wasn't a belly dancer, she was a Cuban dancer but what the hey, I get your drift. In answer to your question, it would depend on whether the belly dancer had a nice personality, I suppose.' He shrugged, causing her to open her eyes and blink a couple of times before closing them again.

'My second wish,' she yawned, 'is to be happy in my job. I'm bored of working in an accounts office – there has to be more to life than that surely. I want to do something I'm passionate about. I love to cook and create new dishes, and I want to be my own boss. Then my third wish is ... oh I don't know, I'm so ordinary I would just for once in my life like to do something extraordinary. I was supposed to be in New York right now being proposed to.'

'Wow, New York. I'm sorry about that darling but maybe you've had a lucky escape with this guy.'

Poppy shook her head. 'He chose a stupid job over me, but he will come round, I know he will, once he realises what he's missing.'

'I'm sure he will, so as every good genie says, your wish is my command,' Gabe boomed. 'As from this moment I will endeavour to make Poppy's Christmas wishes come true.'

'Wait a minute though.' Poppy took another swig of champagne and held the bottle for Gabe to have some. 'What about you? What do you wish for? It can't be all about me.'

'What do I wish for? Ooh there's a question, now let me think.' He stroked his goatee with his finger and took another swig of champers. 'Well actually my wishes are pretty similar to yours apart from the *love* one. I've finished with relationships, once bitten and all that. But I could do with getting fitter and I've had a brilliant idea of how we can both do that.'

'I can't afford a gym membership though if that's what you're thinking.' Poppy wanted to ask him about his relationship but could tell from his body language that he didn't want to talk about it.

Gabe shuddered. 'I definitely wasn't thinking about the gym. No, I've got a much better idea than that, but I'll need to sort something out first.'

'Ooh that sounds exciting, I can't wait. What else?'

'Well, my day job is boring as hell so I would like to leave that behind.'

'What is it that you do?' asked Poppy.

'I work in customer service for an energy company, so I just deal with people moaning, sometimes rightfully but nevertheless moaning all day long and the negativity is soul-destroying.'

'That sounds so bad. You seem like such a positive person so yes, we need to get rid of this crappy job. What is it you really, really want to do?'

'I'd like to be a screenwriter.'

'Oh that sounds amazing and so exciting! Have you written anything already?'

'Well yes, you know the play I was telling you about?' He rubbed his goatee, 'The one I grew this thing for.'

'Yes, *Three Wishes*, wasn't it?'

'That's right. Well, I wrote that, and I've got so many other ideas on the go too. I've got stacks of scripts at home that have never seen the light of day.'

'Well, we simply can't have that. Maybe I should be your fairy godmother.' She picked up a stick. 'I could wave my wand and you could become a famous screenwriter. It's easy, you'll see.'

Gabe smiled, showing his perfect white teeth and Poppy couldn't help but smile back. Like a sunflower to sunlight, she felt drawn to him and he lifted her heart.

'Ah I don't know, it's such a tough business to get into but at the end of the day I enjoy writing them.'

'I can promise you this: that one day I'm going to come and watch your plays and films and whatever else you write.'

'You should try it, it's quite cathartic. Writing saw me through the worst of times, I can totally recommend it after a shitty break-up. I did some of my best work after my ex dumped me. But anyway, let's not get miserable. Tonight is a celebration and I'm celebrating meeting my new friend Poppy.'

'Hold on, mister, you've still got one more wish left,' said Poppy after they'd both had another swig from the bottle.

'There's only one thing I can think of for my third wish and that's to dance with you to my favourite Christmas song.' He put the song on his phone, stood up and held his hand out to her. She allowed him to pull her up and laughed in delight as he spun her round to 'All I Want For Christmas Is You!' Poppy felt as though she were in a beautiful dream as all their friends joined in the dancing and snowflakes began to drift from the sky.

'Well, that was an easy wish to fulfil so we're on a roll,' Poppy laughed as they sat down again and huddled for warmth. 'I just hope we can remember the others.'

'Let's type them into our phones so that we don't forget them,' said Gabe, 'and I'll see what I can do.'

She handed him her phone and he typed the three wishes in the note section for her with his freezing cold fingers.

'Make sure to swap numbers too,' Poppy yawned.

As he typed, a bright shooting star flew across the inky black winter sky. Much to the enjoyment of the remaining partygoers who were cuddled together amicably for warmth, giggling hysterically as they sang rude versions of carols such as 'Good King wet his pants' and 'Rudolph the red knobbed reindeer'.

Poppy drifted into a deep drunken sleep and found herself

35

snuggling into the warmth of Gabe's body. She thought she had never felt so comfortable in her whole life, it was as though their hearts were hugging. She had never had a connection like this before with anybody.

'You know, you are so cuddly like a bear. You are my Genie Bear Friend, my GBF, I love you,' she managed to whisper.

'And you are my little miss narcoleptic sleeping beauty,' he replied, before entering his number on her phone and saving as GBF.

Chapter 3

A couple of days later Gabe was spinning his frayed office chair from side to side in his day job. In between irate customer calls, he thought back to the Christmas do and wondered how Poppy was feeling now. It was nearly 4 a.m. before the taxis managed to get back for the rest of the crowd, who were still huddled together in the bandstand. Gabe had carried a then snoring Poppy to the taxi accompanied by a sleepy Layla. He then asked the taxi driver to wait whilst he carried her up to the first-floor flat.

Once inside, he'd laid her on her bed where she immediately snuggled into the foetal position, still wearing the angel halo and with a false eyelash stuck to the side of her nose. He almost screeched when he saw it as he thought it was a huge spider, which he was terrified of. He said goodbye to Layla, who thanked him with a hug and a kiss on the cheek before bolting the door behind him as he left. He hadn't got home till gone five and slept most of the next day.

He'd had a great night as usual with the BADS crew who were always good fun and that was the last night off they would have for a while as the pantomime was in full swing and each performance was usually a sell-out.

On the stuffy bus ride home later that day, Gabe's thoughts drifted back to the night out and he laughed to himself thinking about Poppy wishing that he was a real genie. She was such a lovely girl and it saddened him to think that she was so heartbroken. He had found that she'd occupied quite a lot of his thoughts lately. She was beautiful and funny with a sense of vulnerability about her which played on his protective instincts. He wasn't ready for a relationship, even if she had been interested in him but, he thought, as the saying goes, you can never have too many friends. Her friend Layla said she fancied Marco, but he knew that would only bring her more misery; Marco wasn't someone a girl could rely on and her ex sounded like a right shit.

He pulled his phone out of his pocket to read her wishes again. As he read, he began to realise that this could be the kick up the arse he needed to get himself out of the rut he'd been in for far too long. Feeling buoyed up about himself for the first time in ages, he sent Poppy a text.

'Hi Poppy
Are you ready for operation Poppy's Christmas Wishes?
As I'm ready for you
Love your very own GBF x'

P.S. Check your notes folder just in case the champagne
obliterated your memory.

His stomach flipped at the sheer bravery of contacting her but told himself his heart was safe as, after all, she had friendzoned him immediately and that seemed like a good place to be.

Chapter 4

Poppy had not long been home from work and was tucking into the veggie lasagne that Layla had made for them.

'Oh, this is scrumptious. I'd forgotten how good Layla's legendary veggie lasagne was,' she managed to say between mouthfuls. 'I love coming home to the delicious smell of cooking in the flat. It reminds me of getting back from school to Nana and Grandad and being loved.'

'Well, you are loved very much and don't you ever forget that,' replied Layla.

'It doesn't feel like it when your future fiancé can't stand the sight of you so moves you two hundred miles away just to get rid of you.'

Layla's face screwed up, her expression spewing contempt at the thought of her best friend's ex. Poppy swore she heard her growling as she bared her teeth.

'He is just one big loser and totally doesn't deserve you and as soon as I get back to work, I'll be telling him to his face. He's nothing but a gobshite and you're so much better off without him.'

'I'm so glad you're here for Christmas, Layla, I don't know what I'd do without you. Just knowing I've got someone who has my back is a good feeling.'

'I've always got your back, just like you've always got mine.' She winked.

Poppy smiled, feeling comforted. 'Are you sure your mum

and dad don't mind you not spending Christmas with them this year?'

'Oh, don't worry about my mum and dad. We kind of had a falling out but it'll all blow over, I'm sure.'

'Well, I do hope so. I hate to think of anyone upsetting you.'

'No, I'm fine, honestly, you know what my dad's like; he gets all holier than thou sometimes.'

'Oh yes, I remember the time he caught your brother drinking on the allotment and made him work on it for months as a punishment.'

'Yes, but Stu is really good at growing cucumbers now,' said Layla. 'And his pumpkin won first prize in a Halloween competition.'

'Oh, you always know how to cheer me up, Layla,' Poppy laughed heartily.

'I'm not even joking,' Layla laughed.

'OK, if you're sure. Sorry to go on about me again but I can't believe I was supposed to be spending Christmas in New York with that idiot and even worse that he was going to propose. Do you know he never even offered me my share of the cost back from when he cancelled the trip?'

'What, he made you pay for your own fare? But he earns so much more than you – I thought he was treating you.'

'Nope.' Poppy shook her head.

'Listen, you are so much better off without that prick. Don't even give him another thought,' continued Layla. 'And about the refund. Well, the thing is . . .' she hesitated.

Poppy looked at her and stopped chewing. 'What is it?'

Layla cleared her throat and paused as if she was struggling to find the right words. 'The reason he hasn't given you the money back is because he didn't cancel the trip.'

'What do you mean he didn't cancel the trip?' Poppy asked with her mouth full. For a split second her heart soared. Could this mean he was going to come back to her, and the holiday was still on?

'He's gone with Randy Mandy.' Layla spat the words out quickly as she didn't know how else to deliver them without hurting her best friend.

Poppy nearly choked on a piece of garlic bread and her heart plummeted back down to earth. She looked like she was about to burst, her face a curious shade of purple. She grabbed her glass of red, gulped it down to clear the bread from her throat and spluttered, 'What the ...'

Layla tried to calm her.

'Look there was no easy way for me to tell you this. Believe me, that stupid big-headed Ed tried to persuade me not to tell you but he is seeing her now, although he says it only started after you two had broken up.

'I only found out because she accidentally on purpose announced it to the whole office that she was being whisked off to New York by her boyfriend. I looked at Ed and his guilty, terrified face just said it all. They are trying to keep the "relationship" a secret.' She made quotation marks with her fingers as she said the word relationship.

Poppy could feel a huge lump stuck in her throat and this time it wasn't the garlic bread. Her bottom lip trembled as she tried her hardest not to cry.

'Oh no, why did it have to be Randy frickin Mandy? I can't compete with the likes of her; she has a body to die for and a face that belongs on a magazine cover,' she spluttered.

'She's not all that, especially compared to you. I could see you on the cover of a magazine.'

'Oh yes, which one, *Gardener's World* or maybe *Wildlife Weekly*? I feel like I should just hide away under a rock or something.' She looked at her reflection in a spoon. 'I mean just look at me, I'm hideous.'

Layla took the offending item of cutlery from her. 'Everybody looks hideous with a spoon face, look.' She put her arm round Poppy, pulled her towards her and held the spoon like a phone as though she was taking a selfie. 'Say cheeeese.'

Poppy had to laugh at their misshapen faces. Layla grabbed her phone and took a picture of their spoon reflection and sent it to her. 'There, that will help you realise whenever you feel bad about yourself that even Randy Mandy would look bad in a spoon.'

'Randy bloody Mandy,' she spat through gritted teeth. 'But, but surely Ed wouldn't be so stupid as to mess round with her. She's the boss's daughter. I've known Harvey to sack people for far lesser crimes than this. Not only that, but she was always nice to me and emailed me lots when I first moved away. Are you telling me that all this time she had her painted talons stuck firmly into my Ed's back?' Poppy had jumped up and paced up and down the room, her wine swirling around like a fine brandy in the glass of a connoisseur. 'She must have been laughing the whole time she was acting so concerned about me. She's such a bloody slapper and of course he went off with her – who wouldn't? I hope he gets sacked.'

'Don't worry, she's so high maintenance that I think he will soon get fed up with her. Listen though, the other thing is she is really friendly with a girl you work with as I've heard her on the phone giggling. I think her name's Britt!'

'Uuuuuuuurgggh!' Poppy half screamed, half growled. 'She always looks me up and down when I see her, and it was her that told me he didn't have the job. I hate them all.'

As the girls curled up on the couch together and chatted about the situation, they were in no doubt that Ed had been cheating on her, even though he had promised her that there had been no one else and in fact had tried to say he was depressed and needed time alone. He was a liar. Funny how it was too late to cancel Poppy's transfer but not his. It made her wonder if he had ever intended to move down south or the whole thing had been a ploy to get her out of the way.

'The thing is, Layla, you know me and if someone doesn't want me in their life, I would never force myself on them. If he wanted to split up, he could have just said and although it would have been hard, I would have gotten over it. But this way I've ended up moving hundreds of miles away from my home and my bestie just for him.'

'I know you would, honey, but I think he's just a huge coward and if there's one thing I know about you, it's that you're brave and strong.'

'Isn't that two things?' Poppy winked at her.

'OK, Mrs Pernickety, two things I know about you.'

'I wonder if I should just give up and go back home.' She bit at the side of her fingernail.

'You will do no such thing; you've always had such a positive outlook on life. Bramblewood seems like a gorgeous place to live. Why not give it three months and if you still feel the same way then yes, go back. But in the meantime, let's look at this as an adventure. I know it's not what you had planned for your life, but plans don't always work out.'

'But what about Ed? He's up there and I'm down here. I think if he could see me then he'd change his mind. I miss him so much.'

'No, you don't and anyway I'm sure Mandy will give him a good taste of his own medicine; she's not known for being faithful. Talking of getting a taste of something, here, let's have a bit of this. It's your favourite and is melted to the perfect temperature for you.' As she spoke, she scooped out huge sloppy portions of Ben and Jerry's Phish Food ice cream, broke a flake in two, stuck one half in each bowl and shook the remaining crumbs from the packet over Poppy's portion.

'You must be feeling sorry for me if you're letting me have the flake crumbs.' Poppy wiped her eyes on her sleeve and allowed the cool chocolatey ice cream to slide down her throat and soothe the pain away from where the huge lump had been earlier.

As she was wiping the ice cream and chocolate from around her mouth with a tissue, she heard a ping on her phone. Her heart leapt as for a minute she thought it might be Ed begging her for forgiveness and wanting her back. But that was probably just wishful thinking.

After rummaging amongst screwed-up tissues, handfuls of receipts and some loose change, she eventually managed to find the phone in her bag. She looked at the sender's name.

'Who on earth is GBF?'

'GBF? I don't know … aah wait, doesn't that stand for Gay Best Friend?' Layla replied. Poppy read the message about her wishes.

'Ah yes of course, Gabe from the other night; he was so lovely and cuddly. Aw, isn't that sweet, I must have told him about my *Sex and the City* obsession and my longing for a gay best friend. I remember telling him that I'd had enough of men and relationships and he said, "Me too." He's obviously volunteered himself for the job.'

Layla giggled, 'Ah yes. Here it is in Urban Dictionary: GBF equals gay best friend. He was great fun if I remember correctly. Why exactly do you want a GBF again?'

'I just think it would be amazing to have a gorgeous man who you get on really well with, who makes you laugh, gives you a cuddle when you need it, but you know he'll never break your heart. It sounds perfect to me.' Poppy cuddled the phone to her chest; this could be just the distraction she needed.

'I must admit that does sound pretty perfect,' Layla replied. 'And he was gorgeous. What did he say?'

'He wants to help grant me my three wishes.'

'What three wishes?' asked Layla.

Poppy felt just as puzzled as Layla looked until a flashback of conversation came to her.

'Oh, of course, he's playing a genie in the pantomime. Wait, he says to check my notes.' She tapped on the notes app on her phone and brought up her wishlist. She giggled.

'What is it?' asked Layla, trying to grab the phone from her hand.

'Wait, hold on.' Poppy read out the wishes including his.

'That's not a bad set of wishes, to be fair, but how's he going to make them come true?'

'I honestly don't know but what better time to find out than now when I've got absolutely nothing to lose?'

'You know what Dr Layla recommends for a broken heart, don't you?' She put her earphones in and held the adapter to Poppy's chest.

'I dread to think,' Poppy laughed, brushing her away.

'Well, as gorgeous Gabe is out of the running, how about some revenge sex with Mr Fancy Man? Now that would be the perfect remedy for heartbreak.'

Poppy rolled her eyes and laughed as Layla made kissy noises. She pressed reply on the phone and typed back.

'Hey GBF
How are you? It's so good to hear from you.
Poppy's Christmas wishes – Bring it on, but only if we can work on yours too!
Love Poppy x'

Chapter 5

The next day was Christmas Eve. Poppy couldn't wait till one o'clock when they would be free from the office for at least a few days; the hours dragged by so slowly. The most exciting idea Burger Breath and Britt had come up with for the last day was a boring quiz, a couple of plates of sausage rolls, mince pies and cheap wine with Johnny Mathis playing quietly on someone's phone. It was depressing. Burger Breath Brian donned a cheap Father Christmas suit for half an hour to dish out the Secret Santa gifts.

Poppy figured there would have been more excitement in a morgue as people opened what looked like recycled unwanted gifts: a really old-fashioned lavender soap set in a crushed box was given to Tania; Britt chuckled as she jiggled about on Santa's knee looking pretend coy with her edible underwear, obviously from Burger Breath Brian judging by the way he was drooling; Poppy smiled as she saw Dan wearing the Christmas tie with flashing lights that she had bought him, knowing he would love it. She wasn't going to bother opening her present, but Britt insisted and called her a spoilsport. In the end she joined in and ripped the paper off, forcing a smile so as not to be seen as a party pooper. However, as soon as she saw what it was, her heart lurched. She dropped it on the floor and ran off to the sound of Britt laughing hysterically and filming the incident.

'Merry Christmas!' she shouted to Poppy's back as she made her exit.

Tania followed her to the toilets and knocked on the cubicle door, calling her name.

'Poppy, are you OK? What's happened?' Poppy blew her nose loudly on some toilet paper.

'I'm OK, thank you. Would you mind getting my bag and coat from my desk so I don't have to go back into the office?'

Tania did as she asked and returned five minutes later. 'I've put some cards and stuff from your desk in a bag. Are you sure you're OK?'

'I'm fine, thanks, Tania, just a bit emotional and Britt is being her usual arsehole self. Nothing a good glass of wine won't resolve.'

'OK, have a lovely Christmas and I'll see you in the New Year.'

'Same to you too, lovely lady.' Poppy gave her a kiss, hugged her and left the building.

Poppy walked home to clear her head. It took an hour and her feet were throbbing. Gabe had texted her about her wishes and they'd decided that Boxing Day was when they would start. In the meantime he had offered her two VIP tickets to that night's performance of *Three Wishes* as one of the cast member's parents couldn't make it. He assured her it would be great fun. She and Layla were looking forward to it.

Once home she threw her bags on the floor as she flumped onto the couch.

'Grrrr, I hate that bitch,' she growled.

Layla came into the living room wrapped in a fluffy pink towel with another one in a turban around her head. She looked like she was frothing at the mouth as she tried to ask her what was wrong whilst in the middle of brushing her teeth.

Poppy emptied her bag onto the coffee table. There was a bottle of red wine from the company, some chocolates, a few Christmas cards and the dreaded present which Poppy had hoped would be smashed.

'Ah did you do your Secret Santa then?' asked Layla, holding out her hand for a closer inspection.

'Oh yes,' Poppy seethed as she dropped the snow globe into her hand.

'Those bastards. Britt the twit and Randy Mandy have obviously been in cahoots over this,' said Layla as she peered into the globe to see the Statue of Liberty inside and the Empire State Building.

'Oh, just bin it, they're idiots,' Poppy shouted.

'No wait,' said Layla, 'you can use this to your advantage because every time you look at it you will be so mad you will be determined to show those bitches of Eastwick just what you are made of. You have always wanted to go to New York so don't let those little gobshites put you off. In fact, when you go back to work you should put this proudly on your desk to prove to them that they're not winning!'

'Do you know what, I think you're right. And I'll damn well make sure that this time next year I will be in New York. Are you in?'

'Yes, I bloody am. Now crack open that bottle of red and let's get ready for our night out at the theatre.'

Chapter 6

The performance of *Three Wishes* at Bramblewood Theatre and Arts Centre, the local playhouse, was a sell-out. Poppy and Layla sat in the best seats in the house, up in the posh balcony with plush seating for six. They introduced themselves to the other occupants, a very shy elderly couple from Scotland who told them they were the parents of Alexia, the leading lady, and two friends of another performer.

'Oh, that's so exciting. We were invited by Gabe, he's playing the genie,' said Layla.

'He's also the writer,' said Poppy.

'Hey look, here it is in the programme,' said Layla. 'So that's what Gabe looks like without his goatee. He's hot.'

Poppy gave an admiring glance. 'He really is.'

The lights dimmed, and the show began.

'This is fantastic,' said Layla in Poppy's ear, ten minutes into the performance.

Poppy nodded. 'The actors are all perfectly cast. I love the way each one seems to have added their own spin on it.'

'Me too, it's hilarious.'

Poppy and Layla shrieked with laughter as Gabe appeared on stage amidst a puff of smoke, with thickly painted surprised-looking eyebrows. He wore baggy, purple silk Baghdad pants and a bright multi-coloured bejewelled waistcoat, he had the most amazing curly-toed slippers on and a silk turban with a huge purple stone in the centre adorned his head.

'Why did he need to shave his head if he was wearing a turban?' laughed Layla.

'Apparently his hair is really thick, and the turban was too tight and wouldn't stay on his head,' Poppy chuckled back.

'Your wish is my command!' Gabe's words echoed around the theatre.

Poppy had a flashback to snuggling with him in the bandstand and recalled the lovely warm feeling she'd had.

'What a lovely funny guy he is, I'm so pleased he's my GBF,' Poppy shouted in Layla's ear so she could be heard over all the clapping and shouting and whooping.

Gabe loved every minute on stage and camped up his role to the max.

At the end of the performance, after many standing ovations and a rendition of happy birthday to Gabe sung by the cast, a huge cake in the shape of a genie covered with candles was wheeled in on a trolley by a lady in a Camilla's Cupcake t-shirt. The audience was encouraged to join in with the singing and the atmosphere was full of fun.

Afterwards Poppy and Layla waited in the packed bar for Gabe to join them. They recognised a few of the people they had shared the bandstand with after the Christmas party and everyone said hello as they passed by. Gabe soon appeared and wrapped his arms around both of them simultaneously, kissing them on both cheeks.

'I'm so glad you could make it,' he gushed, 'What did you think?'

'It was amazing,' Poppy assured him. 'Such a brilliant concept for the others to eventually grant the genie three wishes. We loved it and I actually nearly weed a little with laughter. It was hilarious.'

'Well, I now need to see that on a review poster outside the theatre.' His deep laughter echoed around the room.

'Such a sad but happy ending too,' Layla joined in the conversation. 'I have laughed and cried my mascara off thanks to you, but I loved every second of it. It was genius. You're the best genie ever. Hey, did you see what I did there? Genius and Genie?' she chuckled.

'Aw thanks,' said Gabe who was loving the flattery. 'Now, what can I get you ladies to drink?'

'You put your money away, birthday boy, and we'll get you a drink,' insisted Poppy, heading to the bar.

They sat down at a table and the barmaid brought over a bottle of pinot blush in an ice bucket and some glasses, along with birthday cake on paper plates with plastic forks.

'Is it hard having your birthday on Christmas Eve?' asked Layla through a mouthful of cake.

'Well, not as hard as for my sister who was born ten minutes after me actually on Christmas Day, so at least I still get birthday presents on a different day. She hates having a Christmas birthday, especially when I wind her up and say happy birthmas on Christmas morning. In fact, she doesn't allow us to mention Christmas till mid-day,' he laughed.

'Ah twins, that's so cute but what a nightmare for your parents shopping for Christmas and birthday pressies for two of you. I take it Gabe is short for Gabriel, which is a lovely Christmassy name. So what's your sister called then – Mary?' asked Poppy.

'Ah good guess, my name is Gabriel Joseph and hers is Holly Mary,' Gabe answered. He opened the bottle and filled their glasses as they chatted about the play.

'Poppy swooned a bit when she saw Mr Fancy Man come on stage in his finery; he suits being the baddie.'

'No, I didn't,' Poppy tutted and rolled her eyes at Layla. 'I didn't realise he was American,' she confessed, feeling a wave of heat sweep across her at the memory of seeing him again.

'You bloody did swoon,' shouted Layla. 'My ribs feel black and blue from all the digging into them your elbows were doing every time he came on.'

'He's not American,' clarified Gabe, 'he's Italian but he is good at doing accents, and acting, and dancing, and cooking and getting beautiful women like Poppy here to fall for him. In fact, I'm running out of fingers here on which to count his virtues on.'

'He's so gorgeous though, I can't help it,' Poppy replied, blushing furiously.

'Well he's not my type!' laughed Gabe. 'I don't know what you see in him.'

'Ah,' he continued, 'Just the person I wanted to speak to.' A pretty girl in her twenties waved across the bar to him. 'Meet Pixie, she's our choreographer and she's going to be the first step on the journey to fulfil your Christmas wishes.'

'Happy birthday, Gabe,' Pixie shouted excitedly as she ran over to him and jumped into one of his legendary bear hugs. When he placed Pixie back on the ground, he made the introductions.

'Now Poppy, I know that you don't like the gym and, ahem, neither do I. So I've asked our gorgeous and award-winning choreographer here if she would mind if you joined in with the intensive dance training for their next show that's coming up in March.'

Poppy waved her hands and shook her head; she could see Pixie looking her up and down and felt uncomfortable.

'Dance, me? Err, I don't think so. I mean I can't dance for toffee.'

Gabe's smile disappeared for a couple of seconds.

'What do you mean you can't dance? You were busting some wicked moves on that dance floor last week!'

'Yes, but did you see how much I had to drink to get me there?' she asked nervously.

'Look,' said Pixie, 'you will be fine. Every step and every move is taught in great detail.'

She grabbed Poppy's hand, pulled her to her feet and began to show her the easy back and forth moves to a samba step by standing behind her with her hands on Poppy's hips. Poppy remembered the move from Zumba classes and quite enjoyed it. She tried it on her own then felt Pixie put her hands on her hips again and swivel them more exaggeratedly, which made her laugh, until she looked up and realised Pixie was now standing in front of her and those hands she could feel weren't hers.

Poppy shrieked and spun round to catch sight of Marco disappearing over to the bar, giving her a cheeky wink as he left. Her heart was practically beating out of her chest and she felt dizzy and shot back into her seat.

'Oh, I don't know, I don't want to make a fool of myself,' she said despondently, her voice catching in her dry throat.

'Poppy, my darlin', you have just practically been doing the Lambada with a sexy Italian to some Christmas carols so I hardly think you will have any trouble in dance classes,' Layla piped up.

Poppy laughed but still looked hesitant until Layla looked her square in the eye.

'I have one thing to say to you. SNOW GLOBE!'

'You're on!' Poppy said with determination and took a giant gulp of her wine.

'Wow,' Gabe sounded impressed. 'They seem like magic words, what do they mean?'

'Long story,' chorused Poppy and Layla together then laughed.

The bar closed early that night so everyone said goodbye and Gabe told Poppy he would meet her at his flat at midday on Boxing Day for their first training session. She was surprised it wasn't at the theatre but apparently, she would need to work on her stamina first for a couple of weeks before the dance classes started. He told her to wear comfortable clothes. She felt a buzz of excitement and intrigue with a hint of trepidation about the unknown, but she guessed he wouldn't put her through anything too strenuous.

Chapter 7

Christmas was quieter than usual for Poppy and Layla. They had booked into the local pub, The Flamingo's Leg, for Christmas dinner. It was delightful. The landlord, Ray, welcomed them and handed them the menus. Although the food was good old-fashioned fayre, the interior décor was very modern, with a clean fresh look. Tastefully decorated with burgundy and cream-painted walls, light oak tables and comfortable leather chairs, again in burgundy and cream, furnished the large room.

The place was packed with people wearing gold and silver party hats from expensive crackers. A jazz version of easy-listening Christmas songs played in the background and made a change from the usual tackier songs that everybody knew and loved. Ray's husband Beau brought their food over. Layla's eyes opened wide when she saw the size of the portions of roast turkey for Poppy and roast vegetable Wellington for her, both served with all the trimmings.

'Still makes me chuckle that their names are Ray and Beau,' said Layla. 'I mean how cute is that? They were obviously made for each other.'

'I know, they're so lovely and welcoming, aren't they? I now feel I could come here on my own, which I didn't before, so I'm so glad you came to visit and made me go out and about.'

'Me too,' said Layla as she clinked her champagne glass

with her best friend. 'And thanks for my gorgeous locket, I love it.'

'Well thank you for the beautiful bracelet, but you've already spoilt me with the pamper session.'

'That was a thank you for letting me stay. The bracelet can hold three charms so I thought when you manage each of your wishes, you can find a charm to remember it by.'

'What a lovely idea, thank you. I'm so excited to get started on them and am really looking forward to seeing Gabe again. He's amazing, isn't he?'

'He really is,' replied Layla. 'I feel as though I've known him for ever.'

'Me too, he's just got so much magnetism. Everyone loves him. I really wish I could help him with his wishes; he wants to give up the day job just as much as I do.'

'I imagine he wants to be an actor, doesn't he?' Layla cut into the golden flaky pastry to reveal the roasted vegetables inside.

'Well, it's actually screenwriting that he's passionate about. He said he has lots of scripts he's written, he just needs to get noticed.'

'Well, if there's one thing we're good at, it's getting noticed,' she smiled.

'Now come here, little Mr Piggy, in your blankie,' Poppy replied gratefully as she bit into her sausage wrapped in bacon.

Beau winced as he walked past. 'Ooh I thought you were talking to me then, you cheeky mare.' He gave her a mischievous wink.

Poppy's eyes opened wide.

'See what I mean,' Layla laughed.

'You're right though, I'm going to text him and ask him if I can read one of his scripts.' She picked up her phone and sent him the message. Then smiled as she read his immediate reply wishing her a Merry Christmas and asking for her email address so he could send it to her.

Layla used the excuse to steal the other pig in blanket from Poppy's plate.

'Oi,' said Poppy, 'I love you Layla, but last piggy blankie? I don't think so.'

'Sorry, you know I can't resist,' Layla laughed, her mouth full of non-vegetarian contraband.

'As you've quickly become my favourite customers, I've brought you these for sharing ladies,' said Beau, placing a small bowl of the bacon-wrapped sausages on the table. 'Thank you, Beau,' they said together. Layla blew him a kiss.

'I feel so happy that you have good people around you with Dan and Tania at work, Ray and Beau, and now Gabe and all his gang. It's making me so envious. I want to move here too.'

'I can't think of anything I'd like more. Do hurry up and get the job and my life will be complete,' said Poppy as she clinked her glass of champagne with her best friend.

Chapter 8

Poppy felt pure exhilaration as the wind blew through her tangle of curls as she rode along the towpath of the River Bram. She giggled as she saw Gabe overtaking her again.

'Come on, slowcoach, our lunch awaits in another four miles.'

She'd been intrigued when she arrived at Gabe's place a few weeks earlier to see what he had up his sleeve for the next stage of operation Poppy's Christmas wishes.

Gabe had covered her eyes and led her to the hallway for the big reveal. She laughed when he moved his hands away.

'Da dah, I borrowed it from my sister.'

'Oh wow. I haven't been on a bike since I had my Barbie one, many years ago. I don't even know if I can still do it.'

'Of course, you can, Poppy, it's as easy as, well ... riding a bike,' he chuckled.

He rolled the bike out into the front and held her steady while she threw her leg over it. After an unsteady start with a few wobbles around a small piece of greenery, Poppy finally felt as though the handlebars and wheels were doing what she wanted them to do. Gabe had borrowed Marco's spare bike and off they went along the towpath.

Poppy eventually found that she could concentrate and talk at the same time. 'So how long have you been with BADS?'

'Ooh let me think. Well, I started with them when I was

thirteen, so that's coming up for nineteen years. Wow, that's certainly flown. It used to be held in a damp old portacabin whilst the theatre was being renovated. I was being bullied in school. I mean I was the only black kid there, as well as having spots and being a bit chunky, and kids can be mean. Any slight difference from the norm is homed in on and targeted.'

Poppy's maternal instincts rose to the surface as she imagined a teenage Gabe struggling through this horrible time. 'I'm so sorry you went through all that, it must have been really hard.'

'It was, but lucky for me I had a great teacher at school, Mr Foxwell. He taught history and was one of those teachers who brought the lessons to life. I got an A in my A level thanks to him. Anyway, I confided in him and as he was a regular at BADS, he persuaded me to come along to give it a try. It really helped to bring me out of myself. I was painfully shy. Over the years I gained more and more confidence, and that helped me to study performing arts at uni, which I graduated with honours. I followed that with a masters in a prestigious screenwriter's course.'

'So did you ever think of acting as a career?'

He laughed. 'Oh yes, but after a few years of too many rejections I took the job with Energize because, well, I needed to pay the rent. But one day I hope to go back to my true ambition as a writer. But you know what they say ... don't give up the day job.'

'I'm sure it will happen for you very soon. I mean, *Three Wishes* is amazing. You're a star in the making, Gabe.'

'Oh you, stop it or you'll have me in tears,' he joked.

'I'm serious, Gabe, did you see the reviews in the local paper? They're amazing.'

'Well, I am quite pleased with the reaction so far, I have

to say, and apparently due to popular demand the playhouse has asked if they can extend it for a few more weeks.'

'That's brilliant! I'll have to come and watch it again and that other script you sent me is astonishing, I can't put it down.'

'Ah *Latino*, yes I think that's my favourite out of all the ones I've written so far.'

'I love it, it's so raw, sexy and passionate. You really should send it off somewhere, it's incredible.'

'Ah, I tried a few agents when I first wrote it but I think I made the mistake of sending it too early. Now that I've worked on it, it's improved dramatically but they've already said no and moved on, I guess.'

'You can't give up on it, Gabe, it's too good, and the songs in it are amazing. You're a genie of many talents.'

'Why, thank you, Madame, I'll bear that in mind, but first you and I are going to fulfil my wish of getting fitter.'

They had quickly gone from half-hour bike rides to two-, sometimes three-hour journeys along the towpath and Poppy found them exhilarating even in the pouring rain. Not only was she grateful for the company since Layla had gone home, but having the regular session timetabled into her calendar gave her a sense of purpose. Not to mention the fresh air and exercise giving her mental health a boost. Feeling a bit overconfident she went a little too quickly down the slope by one of the bridges and realised she wasn't going to be able to stop. She shrieked as the front wheel hit a thick branch on the floor. She tumbled to the ground, her hands and elbow scraping along the gravel, whilst the bike slid off in the opposite direction, just missing two lady joggers.

'Are you alright?' asked the blonde lady as she helped

Poppy to her feet and brushed some gravel off her arm and face.

'I think so,' replied Poppy. 'Nothing seriously hurt apart from my pride.' The dark-haired lady picked up the bike and spun the wheels to check they were still working. 'It all looks OK.' She held the handlebars whilst Poppy remounted it. 'I'm Kelsey and this is Sasha.'

'Nice to meet you and thanks. I'm Poppy.'

'You've been cycling along here for a few weeks now, haven't you?' asked Kelsey. 'I just saw your boyfriend up ahead.'

'Oh, he's not my boyfriend, but yes, we are on a fitness drive. He's helping me make my wishes come true.'

'Oh, is he now,' chuckled Sasha. 'He's bloody gorgeous. He can make my wishes come true any time. I mean we could all do with someone like that, couldn't we, Kels?'

'Could all do with someone like what?' Gabe boomed as he appeared from around the corner, his face dropping with concern as he saw the grazes on Poppy's arms.

'Oh no, are you OK? I was talking to you for ages then eventually realised you weren't behind me.' He opened his rucksack, rummaging round until he found some cleansing wipes, antiseptic cream and Batman plasters.

'See, I'm always prepared; I've fallen off this thing so many times. Hey, don't look at me like that, they're for my nephew,' he said as he noticed Poppy laughing at the plasters. While Gabe was cleaning up Poppy's wounds, Sasha and Kelsey explained that they had been running up and down the towpath for about fifteen years.

'This river has known all of our happy, sad and angst-ridden times. It's almost like therapy for us. We just talk the whole way. It's great,' said Sasha. When they saw that Gabe had everything under control, the two ladies continued their jogging and gave them a cheery wave and Poppy a cheeky wink when Gabe wasn't looking. Poppy assured Gabe that she was OK to continue, and they made their way slightly slower to the pub in the next village along.

'I bet they turn a few heads along here. They were gorgeous, weren't they?' said Gabe.

'The most glamorous joggers I've ever seen,' agreed Poppy as they waved to the attractive duo.

Despite being late January, the weather was reasonably warm and the sun shone brightly, but they still relished sitting in front of the open fire in the Cock and Bull, a busy pub along the river. After eating healthily during the week, they had agreed that Sunday was for treats and both chose the roast of the day, which happened to be succulent lamb with an exquisite mint jelly. Gabe had a pint of lager and Poppy had a deliciously warming glass of merlot. They had decided that the ultimate aim of this fitness drive was to be a bit smaller, fitter and more toned. They weren't going to weigh themselves regularly as that could be soul-destroying so they would mark their progress by how clothes felt. Both were chuffed that they were already able to get comfortably into clothes that had been becoming far too tight.

As they enjoyed their Sunday dinner, they chatted about the progress that Poppy was making in Pixie's dance class.

'I love how the whole cast join in with the training. You can see how much they just love to dance.'

'Yes, they do, and it's really helpful because if anyone goes off sick, everyone knows the routine and so can stand in for others.'

'I enjoy the training so much, I feel like I'm in *Fame* or something, it's amazing,' she laughed. 'It feels so liberating to just dance, dance, dance, but especially for me as I don't have to perform at the end of it so there's no pressure. I know

I'm a bit slower than the others, but Pixie congratulated me the other day.'

'Yes, I know, she told me you were a fast learner.'

Poppy glowed as she saw the look of pride on his face.

'How did you get on with your audition for *Dirty Dancing*? I heard Alexia got the lead female role.'

'I haven't heard yet. They narrowed it down to me and Marco for the role of Johnny but I'm not holding out much hope as he's a sex god and well, me ... let's just say I'm not quite as divine.'

'You're both bloody gorgeous.'

'What, even with these?' He poked a finger in his muffin top.

'Especially with those, everyone has love muffins,' she said, trying to grab her own fleshy lumps above the waistband and finding them slightly smaller than before. She nodded impressively whilst still studying them.

'I think you mean muffin tops,' he laughed.

'Why, what did I say?' She looked puzzled.

'You said love muffins, but do you know what, I think I'm going to call them that from now on, they sound so lovable,' he laughed. 'Oh, hold on, who's this?' He pulled his phone out of his pocket, listened to the voicemail, shook his head and shrugged his shoulders.

'Oh well, never mind. I didn't want the part anyway but at least I'm the understudy for Johnny and I do get to be Billy Kosteki.'

'Well, he was always my favourite character anyway.' Poppy felt disappointed for him. The pull in her chest felt stronger as she knew he really wanted the part. He had become her second best friend after Layla and completely embedded in her heart. He looked so different now that his goatee had gone, and as he didn't have to shave his head any more his hair had grown. His features were strong and handsome, his lips full and always ready to smile, especially when he saw Poppy. She'd noticed that his face lit up whenever they met. He was a charmer though and part of his magnetism was down to the way he made people feel, as though they were ten foot tall. Poppy also couldn't fail to notice the admiring glances he received from both women and men.

Gabe looked at Poppy as she ate the last of her roast lamb and felt tenderness for her as she was still smiling despite being covered in grazes from the fall. The waitress came to collect their plates and offered the dessert menu.

'We'll have a look, thank you,' he said. He glanced at the page. 'Oh well, that's my mind made up. Sticky toffee pud for me please, with custard. Also, they have Eton Mess pops, your favourite.'

'Ooh,' said Poppy, 'you know I can't resist that, but will it all go straight to my love muffins,' she giggled, pinching them again.

Gabe laughed too. 'Look it's our official day off and we still have a long ride home, so I say go for it.'

'Oh, go on then, in the words of Oscar Wilde, "I can resist everything except temptation."'

'In the words of Poppy Kale, what about my love muffins?' Gabe joked.

Despite feeling like having a lie down with full tummies and a second alcoholic drink each, they managed to cycle the eight miles back through the beautiful crisp countryside, following the twists and turns of the river. They waved to some of the familiar faces they were getting to know, their breath visible in the frosty air. Plumes of smoke spiralled out of tiny chimneys on the colourful boats moored along the way. They looked cosy and homely. The ride back was a bit slower than on the way there, but Poppy felt content and as though she had really achieved something.

Relief kicked in at the sight of the trees that lined the beer garden of The Flamingo's Leg. It overlooked the river and was a sure sign that they were nearly home. Poppy thought the trees looked sad as the bare winter branches showed little signs of the fruitfulness that Gabe had assured her they displayed in other seasons. He promised her they were cherry blossom trees and in a couple of months would be covered in a blanket of pink flowers, and only a few weeks before she'd arrived were resplendent in autumn coats of burnt orange, red and sienna leaves. But she found that hard to believe.

'You wait and see in spring,' he said.

'I'll very much look forward to that. I love cherry blossoms,' she replied.

'Oh, by the way,' said Gabe. 'My sister said you can keep this bike as her husband has bought her a new one. She said she has some accessories for it that she'll drop in if you want them.'

'Oh wow, that's so lovely of her but I really must give her something for it.'

'No, don't worry she wouldn't accept anything for it, honestly.'

'No, I insist. Even if I just get her some flowers or something because this bike has given me a whole new lease of life. Well, actually, this bike and my GBF.'

Gabe laughed as well, and they raced each other back to Poppy's flat where he made sure she got in safely and stored the bike in the hall under the stairs. She hugged him as he left and thanked him again for a brilliant session.

Poppy closed the front door and went straight to the bathroom to run a steaming hot bath. Even though it was cold outside she still felt sweaty from the ride and her skin was tingling all over. She poured a little luxurious bubble bath under the tap, made herself a cup of green tea with lemon and put her damp clothes in the washing machine. She fetched her Kindle from her bedside table and spent the next hour and a half soaking blissfully in the bath. It was the perfect opportunity to read more of Gabe's fantastic script.

After the bath she sleepily prepared her lunch for the next day. She found she had to take extra in lately as she had been experimenting with lots of healthy options for wraps and sandwiches and her colleagues were becoming more interested in what she was having. According to Dan, it always looked and smelt delicious, so she had started giving out little tasters which were always very well received. Tomorrow's delicacy was a Waldorf salad wrap. She prepared the salad in a lidded bowl and decided to take the wraps in separately and make them up in the tiny kitchen at the back of the office. Before nodding off, she skimmed through her social media accounts and saw a very interesting tweet which caused her eyes to ping wide open again. Because she was supposed to be going to New York, she'd followed and signed up to theatre news and what's on accounts. This could be just the thing, she thought, as she followed the directions and copied the email address down. Wide awake now, she sent off the email along with some screenshots from the local online newspaper. Satisfied at a job well done, she lay down and slept with a huge smile on her face.

Chapter 9

Poppy still wasn't enjoying her job that much. It was boring. Britt or Britt the twit as Dan called her – which was much more polite than Layla's nickname for her – had digs at her whenever she could. Nothing serious enough for her to complain about, it was just something that chipped away at her. She wouldn't retaliate because she knew if they brought up New York again or mentioned Ed and Mandy then that would upset her too much, and she couldn't trust herself not to cry. Sometimes she would hear her on the phone to Mandy and her stomach would clench every time she laughed a bit too loudly. Britt would invariably look over at her just in case she hadn't quite realised she was the target of their mirth. At least Poppy knew that Layla would be proud of her because the dreaded snow globe had pride of place on her desk as she attempted to hold her head high.

Poppy checked her emails and scrolled through all of the boring ones until she saw one from Layla and one from HR. The HR one was marked urgent to all staff and spoke about the cutbacks that needed to be made to the company due to the current financial climate. Apparently in order to try and save jobs they had decided they would have to close down the subsidised staff canteen as of next week. It was in need of refurbishment and new equipment was essential, but they could no longer look at that as an option. Many of the staff used the canteen and some of the other companies in the building used it too, although they weren't subsidised. There were coffee shops around the high street, but they were often packed and it just took too long to be served as they only had an hour for lunch at the most. Dan must have read the email at the same time as Poppy and shouted across to her, 'Well, Poppy, it looks like you are going to have to look after me now as my mum will worry if I don't eat so you will have to bring my lunch in too. Just remember I like huge portions,' he joked. Tania stopped typing and joined in the conversation, pushing her glasses down to the tip of her nose and looking over the top of them so she could see them properly.

'Oh yes please, Poppy, can you do mine too?'

Suddenly she felt a sharp snap to her back and heard Burger Breath Brian behind her.

'Ooh yes, me too, Poppy. I could do with a couple of your large portions.' She jumped up in disbelief.

'What the hell do you think you're doing?' she shouted, the skin on her back still stinging from the twang on her bra strap.

Brian snorted a laugh as he made his way back to his office, calling out to Tania, 'Miss Moneypenny, come and take some dic please!'

Tania grabbed the Dictaphone and followed him into the office, trying to appease Poppy on the way, 'Oh, just ignore him, you know what he's like. He's an idiot. At least you haven't got to sit in his stuffy office listening to him drone on about a load of crap.'

'But he's just twanged my bra strap again!' said Poppy angrily. 'I'm so fed up with this place.'

Britt walked past and gave Poppy such a filthy look, Poppy could see she was seething with jealousy. Everyone knew she had been sleeping with Brian since Christmas and she obviously thought he was a bit of a catch as she seemed very insecure whenever he ventured near Poppy.

'What's all the noise for?' she stopped to ask.

'Oh, you know, just up to his old bra-twanging tricks again,' Poppy replied.

'Are you sure you weren't flirting? You are a bit of a tease, you know. Brian is a red-blooded man and, I mean, look at you. That blouse is so see-through, no wonder he twanged it if it's on offer like that.' Her face twisted in disgust.

Poppy couldn't believe what she was hearing.

'Are you serious? My blouse is not in the least bit see-through, especially at the front, and even if it was, that is still not an invitation for a man to twang my bra strap.' She gestured with her head and hands to the front of the blouse, which was patterned with bright coloured flowers. 'And anyway, what would possess anyone to flirt with him? He's not in the least bit fanciable. Ew yuk, give me a break please.' Poppy shuddered outwardly at the thought of anyone flirting with Burger Breath.

Britt sloped off, but not before tossing another insult over her shoulder. 'Just because you couldn't keep your man doesn't mean you can get your claws into someone else's.'

Poppy gasped and felt as though she'd had a blow to her stomach. By the time she thought of something to say in retaliation, she'd gone.

She opened Layla's email and thoughts of Bitchy Britt dissolved as she read that Layla's interview was on Friday, and she wanted to know if she could stay over for one night only. She had to get back as she'd offered to babysit for the friend she had been staying with. Poppy was desperate to see her but also a little worried about her as she still didn't know why she had left home. She had fallen out with her mum and dad just before Christmas and it still didn't seem anywhere nearer to being resolved. Poppy felt it was a shame as she quite liked Layla's mum and dad. Although they were very old-fashioned and strict, Layla respected their wishes and knew they didn't like drinking, so she had always stayed at Poppy's or another friend's house if she was having a heavy night. Maybe Layla would tell her on Friday.

At lunchtime Tania joined Dan and Poppy in the canteen and they shared out the wraps and Waldorf salad. As Tania bit into it, she gasped at the delicious burst of flavour in her mouth.

'Oh wow, what have you treated us to this time?'

Poppy blushed with pleasure as she explained she had added honey and lemon zest to the mayonnaise mixture.

'Mmmm it's gorgeous,' gushed Dan. 'Do you have any more?' The girls had one and a half each and Dan had three all to himself.

'I'm serious Poppy. You said you needed to earn a bit more money and I would pay you a lot to make my lunches for me.'

'I'm serious too,' added Tania as she licked a little sauce from her thumb. 'The canteen is nothing special. In fact, the food there is as grey as this office, but your food is fresh and healthy and as good as any deli. I'd rather give you my money too.'

'I'll definitely think about it, I promise, and you're both so right, I do need the money as I hadn't expected to be living in the flat by myself.' She thought it might work as a distraction to keep her mind off Ed. She was done with grieving for him and now she was downright angry.

That evening was dance class and Poppy cycled to the theatre as it was only round the corner. She had been prac-tising her steps in the flat nearly every day and had to admit she wasn't doing too badly. She had tripped over her own feet once, which resulted in Mr Ives coming up to check she was OK.

This week they were putting the whole routine together for the chorus dancers and she clapped her hands at the end after managing it with only a couple of slight hiccups. She danced at the back as the rest of the ensemble dancers were practising in order to perform whereas she was just keeping fit. At the end of the session Poppy spoke to Pixie about a couple of the steps she was having trouble with, and Pixie worked through them with her. Once it clicked, Poppy felt elated and repeated the move over and over.

'That's it, you've got it,' said Pixie, clapping. 'Are you sure you don't want to be in the show as you know it so well now and I've had someone drop out? It would really help me out if you could do it.' Poppy felt a mixture of excitement and sheer terror soar around her body. In her imagination sometimes she could see herself up on the stage performing to a bunch of strangers and bowing to the rapturous applause, but the reality was that she would most likely trip over and land on her arse to the sound of hysterical laughter. But then, she'd been practising with everybody else and had enjoyed the camaraderie. Surely, she would feel a little left out when they went on to celebrate the show? She had sometimes wished that she had the confidence to perform and here was her chance to do something different. No, she thought, she couldn't do it, but when her mouth opened, she surprised herself at her answer.

'OK, I'd love to,' she said. Pixie jumped up and down and hugged her.

'Are you serious? Thank you. That's brilliant. Come on, let's go and get you a drink.' Pixie linked her arm through Poppy's, and they went through to the bar. Pixie got them some drinks and they sat down.

Pixie's face lit up when she saw Gabe enter the room. Poppy waved to him, and he began to head over to their table. It took him a while to reach them as everyone stopped him to say hi as he made his way through the crowd. He winked at her and she suddenly felt her cheeks burn as she realised who he was with.

Eventually he and Marco arrived at the table. Both guys kissed Pixie on the cheek and Gabe kissed Poppy too, placed his drink and a plate with a sandwich wrapped in cling film on the table before formally introducing her to his flatmate. Marco leaned across to kiss her on both cheeks.

'Ah, the lovely Poppy I have heard so much about, we meet at last. This man here will never come out for a drink with me anymore because he is always doing something with you.' Poppy was positively beetroot at this point, especially as it was the first time she had heard him speak with his tantalising Italian accent.

'It's lovely to meet you properly too,' she croaked gruffly as her throat had dried with nerves. She coughed a little and managed to sound a little more feminine as she asked him how his rehearsals were going.

'Yes, all good, all good so far,' he replied, his eyes darting around the room as if searching for someone.

'So how long have you two been flatmates then?' she asked.

'Ooh, let me see, it must be nearly four years now, right Gabe? Since Chris left you. Gabe couldn't pay the mortgage by himself and I needed an excuse to escape from the family business in Italy.'

Poppy looked puzzled and also a bit taken aback at Marco's bluntness.

'OK, thank you, Marco. We don't need to dwell on that

now it's all water under the bridge and if I never see Chris again it'll still be a day too soon,' said Gabe.

'He still doesn't like to talk about it as it hit him pretty hard, but he was about to lose his flat.'

Gabe flushed with embarrassment and crunched the ice in his diet Coke. He looked into his glass as he spoke, clearly uncomfortable with the situation.

'Shall I just parade up and down here naked too, Marco, or are you content with my soul being laid bare for all to see?'

Marco carried on.

'Ignore him, Poppy. Sometimes he feels sorry for himself.'

Poppy looked at Gabe and he winked at her, allowing her to release the breath she hadn't realised she was holding as she worried about him.

'Now where was I up to? Gabe got dumped, nearly lost his home, oh yes but his mum had the perfect solution. My mum told his mum that I was desperate to come and spend some time in England and so it was all arranged. My dad gave me time off from the restaurant and Gabe managed to get me a couple of jobs teaching dance over here. So our mothers arranged the whole thing. They are sisters – twin sisters actually.'

Poppy looked from one to the other. Gabe hadn't mentioned this before. She felt her toes curl in embarrassment as she did tend to go on about Marco a lot when they were on their bike rides, but she never would have done had she known they were cousins. But now she thought about it there was a definite likeness between them. The only differences were that Marco had brown eyes and Gabe's were the brightest blue, Marco's complexion was more olive whereas Gabe's was golden-coloured. Gabe was stockier than Marco, which made him cuddlier. Her eyes were drawn to Marco,

73

but her heart belonged to Gabe. He was her GBF and he was hurting.

Finally, Marco's eyes, like ballistic missiles, homed in on their target as Alexia walked into the room talking to Jean-Paul, the director of the show. He bid a hasty farewell to the others, and kissed Poppy on the hand.

'You must come to the flat one evening and we will cook for you,' he said hurriedly. He blew a kiss to Pixie and went over to Alexia, who didn't look particularly pleased to see him but kissed him nonetheless. Then with a flick of her shampoo-advert-worthy, curly red hair she turned her attention back to Jean-Paul, who seemed happy to include Marco in the conversation.

'Well, that was fleeting,' commented Gabe, laughing as he saw Poppy fanning herself with the tatty menu, entitled Cath's Caff.

'Oh yes, our Marco does have that effect on the ladies, although it does wear off as quickly as it appears. Not like with our gorgeous Gabe. When you fall in love with him you love him for ever,' said Pixie.

Poppy could feel the flush creeping up her neck to her face and hoped no one would notice it.

Gabe fidgeted with his glass and appeared to be fascinated with it. He unwrapped the cling film from his sandwich.

'Anyway, Gabe,' said Pixie, 'I have the most exciting news! We have found our replacement chorus dancer.'

'Oh, that's brilliant.' His face lit up. 'Is it anyone I know?'

'Ta dah,' said Poppy, doing jazz hands.

'It's you!' He threw his arms open, and she dived into them. 'Oh well done, Poppy. I'm loving all this newfound confidence you've got.'

'It's all down to you,' said Poppy, 'you introduced me to all this.'

'No, it's down to you Poppy, you're starting to believe in yourself and now you can make anything happen.'

'Oh, I don't know about that … but yes, I thought I could fight my nerves and give it a go.'

'You're going to smash it, I'm telling you. Congratulations.' He picked up one of his sandwiches and took a bite.

'Thanks, Gabe.'

'He's right, you are.' Pixie looked at her watch. 'Oh wow, is that the time? I need to go. Bye and thanks again, Poppy, you're a lifesaver.'

'Thank you for being a great teacher.'

Pixie blew a kiss to each of them and hurried off.

'So, how was work today?' Gabe asked between bites.

'Boring as usual except for a little bit of excitement. The canteen is closing down and Dan and Tania have asked me to make their lunches for them. They've offered to pay me.'

'Well, that's good, isn't it? You were saying you could do with extra money.'

'Yes, I really could, and I do enjoy preparing food for other people and experimenting with different flavours.'

'I think that's a great idea and sounds like it could develop into wish number two. With a few more customers you could be the new Heston Blumenthal with, I don't know, lasagne-flavoured ice cream or snail vol au vents. People could come from all over the world to try out your cuisine. In fact,' he said, lifting the lid on a very dreary-looking sandwich, 'we could do with someone like you here. I don't think poor Cath has ever experimented with a flavour in her life, if I'm honest. Actually that's a lie, she does make delicious cakes. Maybe you should ask her for a part-time job.' He looked at Poppy expectantly.

Poppy looked at the menu and then around the room.

'Well, it's a bit tired-looking and the menu is uninspiring, and I do need the money. I'll think about it.' Poppy made a mental note to find Cath next time she was in and have a chat with her. The more she kept herself occupied, the less time she had for moping about Ed.

Chapter 10

The next evening was bike ride day and not as pleasant as usual what with raindrops bouncing a couple of inches from the ground. Their waterproofs at least kept them dry but had huge mud splats up the back when they returned. At least they had managed five miles, which they felt good about. On the way back they could smell fresh scones being baked and so stopped at Serendipity, the café boat on the river. It was always busy, but they were lucky that two people were just leaving, so a table became free.

Rosie, the owner whose cheeks lived up to her name, smiled in welcome, scrubbed the table clean and put fresh cutlery and napkins down for them. The atmosphere was warm and ambient, a huge contrast to the awful weather outside. Several conversations mingled with the sound of a radio station as the customers enjoyed their food. Rosie pulled her notepad out from her red-and-white checked pinny, which matched the tablecloths and curtains, and fluttered her eyelashes at Gabe as she spoke.

'Hi, how are you? Do I need my pad or are you two having the usual?'

'Definitely the usual please, Rosie, darling.' He looked at Poppy and she nodded in agreement. Rosie blushed beetroot. Poppy guessed she was carrying a torch for Gabe, or should that be a scone, she laughed to herself. Rosie popped the pad back in the pocket of her pinny, smiled and went back behind the counter.

'Two cream teas it is then or should I say cream hot chocolates?' Rosie giggled at her own joke and soon came back to the table carrying two large hot chocolates and two gigantic cranberry and raisin scones with cream and a selection of mini jam jars. This had become a weekly treat and they both really looked forward to it. Rosie had taken a little while to warm to Poppy but when she realised that she was living in the flat above her parents' shop she now treated her like an old friend. A couple of men in work boots stood up to leave a table. One of them slapped Gabe on the back in greeting. Gabe turned round and smiled his broadest grin.

'Finn, how are you? Hey thanks for sorting out the theatre for us, you are a real lifesaver.'

'No problem, mate, the show must go on as they say.' He smiled and nodded a hello at Poppy. Her stomach fluttered; there were a lot of handsome men in this town.

After they'd finished, Gabe paid the bill, pretended to catch Rosie's kiss that she blew at him and as they collected their bikes, he explained to Poppy that Finn had saved the show due to the hoist not working on opening night. 'He's an engineer but can turn his hands to most building work.'

The rain had eased off a bit when they got back so Gabe asked if they could pop to his as he wanted to pass on the accessories that his sister Holly had dropped in to give to Poppy.

'You will laugh when you see what it is,' he told her. He opened the door to the flat and she saw it straight away; it was a beautiful, white woven-lidded basket to clip to the front of the bike, but it also had two fold-down handles so that it could be used independently as well.

'It's a basket,' she laughed. 'Well I never expected that, how posh.'

'I don't think the word basket does it justice so if you want to be posh, how about calling it its correct name of pannier? That's what Holly always called it.' He laughed. 'She said she has cleaned it a bit, but it could probably do with another going over; it's probably a bit dusty but has hardly ever been used.'

Gabe fetched his toolbox and began to attach the pannier to Poppy's bike, continuing to chat whilst tightening the screws. 'How did you get on with your friends' lunches today? Did they enjoy them?'

'Yes, they did actually, very much, and a few other people have asked me to make theirs too.'

'That's fantastic, your empire is growing slowly but surely. I just know you're on your way to leaving Brian and his burger breath far behind.'

She laughed. 'Now that is wishful thinking.'

'There you go, that's not going to budge,' he said, after attempting to move the fitting for the basket from side to side. 'In fact, it's so sturdy that I'm sure you could carry loads of lunches in it, possibly even a banquet or two.'

'It's funny you should say that because that's exactly what I thought when I first saw it. Cycling into work would also save me the bus fare and I need every penny I can lay my hands on at the moment. I was thinking I should make up some simple leaflets with all of my lovely healthy wraps and stuff I've been making, put an order form on the back and get my colleagues to choose what they want for the week in advance.'

'It's a great idea, Pops, maybe start with a quick questionnaire to see how much interest you get. Then you can eventually start cycling to other places as well with your little basket, ahem, I mean posh pannier of goodies.'

Tears sprang unexpectedly to Poppy's eyes as a wave of

emotions washed over her. This guy really believed in her. Ed had never looked at her with that much encouragement. Gabe's voice was as smooth as melted chocolate. She could listen to him talking all day and actually felt disappointed when he stopped.

'Please thank your sister for me, it's brilliant. And thank you too,' was all she could manage.

'There's no need to thank me, I'm just the messenger,' he said, showing her how to unclick the pannier for when she wanted to remove it.

'No, you're not, you're much more than that.' She squeezed his arm and was taken aback at the response her body had to his strong hard muscle. She wondered if Gabe felt it too as he caught his breath and his eyes met hers. She smiled and looked away before she blushed again.

Gabe helped her back to her flat as the pannier took some getting used to and threw Poppy off balance a bit. Once home she ran upstairs quickly and brought a package down to him.

'Can you please pass these on for me?' She handed over a pretty pink gift bag. 'It's just a bottle of wine and some of my triple chocolate brownies.'

'Oh, I told you she didn't want anything for the bike but thanks anyway.'

'I know, but it means a lot to me and I'm sure that gel seat she has given me will make my journeys far more comfortable.'

For the next couple of days Poppy kept herself busy during her lunch hours designing a leaflet advertising her new selection of healthy wraps and flatbreads, and experimented at home with some new recipes. She had heard about a recipe for chocolate brownies made with sweet potatoes and had been dying to try it. Also, she was always buying bananas and never getting round to eating them, so she decided to try a healthy banana bread recipe too. When she had baked them, she cut them up into squares, wrapped them in cling film and brought them into work to hand out as little free samples with the leaflets.

She put the samples on a tray in the canteen, took some around to the other offices and put some next to the kettle in their little kitchen. She was buzzing with excitement about this venture and even if it didn't come to anything, it would keep her busy and happy. She was always happy when cooking and baking but couldn't really be bothered doing it just for herself.

After some consideration she had decided on the perfect name for her new venture: 'Poppy's Posh Pannier'. Her leaflets were simple. Along with the name she'd added a little cartoon logo of a pretty bike with a basket laden with French baguettes and festooned with flowers. Gabe would laugh so much when she told him the name. She loved having the ability to make him laugh, they were always on the same wavelength. She smiled at the thought of him and ran her eye over the leaflet just to make sure she'd included everything. Her stomach rumbled as she read the list of fruity fillings such as prawns with mango in a marie-rose sauce; tuna with sweetcorn and grapes in a sweet chilli mayonnaise; chicken, avocado and bacon in a light lemon dressing; and her newest flavour, which was inspired by her delicious roast on Sunday, lamb with yogurt and mint. She had more traditional fillings on the list such as ham and cheese with salad, and also included a line for people to request what they would like, within reason.

She had included her phone number and an order form on the back with the days of the week, a price list and room for the person to write their name on it. She had also printed out a few A4-size copies which she dotted around the place.

She soon had people coming over to praise the brownies and banana bread. They couldn't believe how chocolatey it tasted and asked if it was really sweet potato in there. Soon, only crumbs remained. As it was Friday Poppy knew she would soon see Layla after her interview had finished, and she really couldn't wait.

At a quarter past two she came into the office and they hugged each other tightly, Layla looking so sharp in her designer skirt suit, her silky blonde hair up in a tight chignon. She certainly looked smarter than most of the other candidates they'd seen. She sat on Poppy's desk with her legs crossed, swinging them as she told her how it went.

'You know how it is. They seemed impressed, but you never can tell. I've been disappointed at interviews before when I had been so confident of getting the job, so I don't want to get my hopes up. Likewise, I've come away from an interview thinking I'd done badly and then was offered the job. So, who knows.' She undid her hair clamp and allowed her hair to swish around her shoulders. 'Can you come for lunch now as I'm starving? I couldn't eat on the way down as my nerves were gone. I really hate interviews.'

'Sorry sweetie, I can't, but I'm finishing at four so not too long to wait. Here, I saved you some of this.' She opened her drawer and handed over a piece of each of the cakes she had made. Layla unwrapped them and happily munched on them whilst waiting for Poppy to finish. Tania was going to a meeting so insisted that Layla use her desk to check up on her emails. Dan, who had been mesmerised by Layla, went on a coffee run, bringing her a cappuccino with a cocoa powder love heart dusted on the top.

'I could get used to being spoilt like this,' she said, giving Dan a cheeky wink.

Just before four, Poppy was called into her boss Andrew's office. He was usually a sheepish person, but his lips were pressed tightly together, and his eyes looked troubled.

'Hi Poppy, I'm afraid HR have asked me to have a word with you,' he said in his usual monotonous, nasal voice.

Poppy's heart sank.

'Apparently it has been reported to them that you have been printing lots of personal stuff in office time and also that you have another job that you haven't declared. Now is this true?'

As she answered, she happened to look out of the window into the main office and could see Britt hanging round the photocopier giggling and smirking at her. Calmly, she explained to Andrew that she had gone through the proper channels and spoken to the lady in the print room who had printed the work for her at a cost. This service was available for all members of staff and as for the other job, she could only think it was the sandwich round that she was planning on starting.

'Right, well, I must apologise to you, Poppy. I'm getting a bit sick of certain people trying to drop other people in it, it's just wasting my time and is obviously a completely unfounded allegation. Not being funny, but I would watch my back if I were you as it sounds like you may have an enemy in this office, and I for one do not like underhanded people. Anyway, as far as I'm concerned, as long as the new enterprise doesn't interfere with the day job then I'm perfectly happy. Could you drop a leaflet in for me please?'

She thanked him and left the office, went to her drawer and got the last remaining piece of brownie and a leaflet and took them back into him. Ten minutes later his voice reverberated across the office just as Poppy was leaving.

'Wait! Poppy, you can't go yet.'

Britt stopped pretending to work, her face twisted in glee at the thought of Poppy being in even more trouble. But the smile was soon wiped off her face as Andrew continued speaking.

'I haven't given you my lunch order for next week yet. And by the way, that brownie was amazing.' He handed her the leaflet and turned to Tania.

'Tania, can you please discuss corporate catering needs with Poppy on Monday for our client meetings in future. We thought we were going to have to have the headache of going externally with the closure of the canteen but that was before Poppy's Posh Pannier came along.'

'What a wonderful idea,' Tania smiled.

Poppy waved cheerily to everyone as she left arm in arm with Layla.

'Have a lovely weekend, peeps, see you Monday.'

Chapter 11

Monday morning came far too soon. Poppy was astonished to have had ten orders for the first week and went shopping on Sunday before her bike ride with Gabe to buy all of the ingredients she would need. She also baked a fresh batch of sweet potato brownies and decided to throw some leftover blueberries into the banana bread mix. It provided amazing bursts of colour and flavour in the final product and looked splendid; she couldn't resist pressing her fingers to her mouth in a chef's kiss after she'd tasted it. She made up all the wraps and flatbreads she had on order and a couple of extras of each flavour in case some people hadn't had a chance to see the leaflet.

She packed all of her goodies into the pannier and at the last minute decided to empty the contents of her fruit bowl into it too: five Pink Lady apples, three satsumas and two bananas. As it was raining, she had to wrap the pannier in something waterproof so she ripped the clear covers off her dry cleaning and used that. It should be OK, she thought, as it wasn't in direct contact with the food.

As she cycled in with her work shoes safely stored in her backpack, her stomach was doing flips. 'A new enterprise' Andrew had called it. How exciting. It took about twenty minutes to cycle, which she was more than capable of after all the practice she had been having. But the heavier basket on the front unbalanced her and she stumbled off just as she approached the building. Britt turned up just in time to witness the accident and was openly laughing. By now Poppy had mastered the art of falling off the bike and could do it quite graciously; she didn't hurt herself this time but did ladder the knees of her tights.

'Shit, shit, shit,' she swore as she realised some of the sandwiches were a bit crushed. She hadn't wrapped the covering round tight enough to keep the basket closed, but nobody complained about them, and all the extras were snapped up immediately. She realised that she had forgotten to do her own sandwich but luckily, she found a banana in her desk drawer so she had that. Everybody loved the sandwiches and cakes and there were five new orders on her desk by the time she left that day.

She met with Tania regarding the corporate catering and gasped when they worked out how lucrative that could work out to be in the long term. She felt herself stand that little bit taller and imagined her grandparents' faces glowing with pride.

'OK, so that's the monthly director's meetings which are held on the evening of the first Thursday of every month, not to mention all the client meetings, workshops and training courses that we hold regularly throughout the year,' said Tania.

Poppy was having palpitations at the thought. 'Oh my God, Tania, this could potentially be massive, but it's only little old me. I hope that Layla gets the job down here so she can help me out.'

'You'll be fine,' said Tania, squeezing her hand.

Poppy thought back to Layla's visit, which had gone far too quickly. On the Friday night they had been invited around to Gabe and Marco's for dinner. Poppy's stomach had flipped when an extremely attractive woman answered the door, who she assumed was Marco's girlfriend.

'Hi and welcome, I'm Holly, Gabe's much younger sister. Come in, it's so nice to meet you.'

'Ah I can really see a likeness between you both,' said Layla as they followed her down the hall.

'Everybody says that,' replied Holly. 'The funniest thing is that I told a woman I worked with that I had a twin brother and she asked if we were identical twins.' She chuckled, shrugged her hands out and shook her head. 'I mean how do you answer that one? I couldn't stop laughing.'

'That's hilarious,' said Layla. 'And very worrying,' added Poppy. 'I'm Poppy and this is Layla, it's lovely to meet you too.'

Poppy took to Holly immediately. She was beautiful, with the same colouring as Gabe, slender but curvy in all the right places. She had light hazel eyes with darker brown specks almost as if her irises had freckles. She wore a patterned wraparound dress in swirls of orange, black and white, which fitted her perfectly, showing off her hourglass figure. Her hair was a mix of dark and light brown glossy curls that fell loosely around her shoulders, framing her face beautifully. She reminded Poppy of Leona Lewis.

'You do look alike but you are far prettier than Gabe,' Poppy smiled. 'Oh, and thank you so much for the bike. It's been a life-changer for me.'

'Ah, that's OK, I'm so glad you could make use of it and thank you for the treats, but you really didn't need to.'

'Oh no problem, I wanted to. The bike's been brilliant and not just for keeping fit. I've started to use it for work too so that will save me money on bus fares.'

'That's great and Gabe is loving the bike rides. It's lovely to see him out and about again.' She led them down the hall. 'Gabe, your guests are here,' she shouted as they walked into the kitchen.

87

'Ah, you're here.' He kissed each of them on both cheeks and with his arm round their shoulders he took them into the dining room, introduced them to his brother-in-law Franco and gestured for them to sit. Holly joined them and Poppy blushed as Marco entered the room with a bottle of red in one hand and white in the other. He filled their glasses.

'Your hair looks good, sis, have you done something differently?' asked Gabe.

'Ah, thanks, I was in the salon for ever. I had a Brazilian done.'

Gabe nearly choked on his red wine.

'Oh my, too much information for the dinner table, methinks, sis.' As he wiped his mouth and chin with a napkin, she looked at the other two girls and tutted, laughing.

'Not that!! It's similar to a relaxer for my hair, you fool.'

'Oh, thank God for that,' Gabe laughed with relief.

'I really should try that too,' said Poppy. 'My curls sometimes go crazy and I can't do a thing with them.'

'It's great for taking out the frizz but it doesn't make your hair go poker straight, like everyone imagines. It's great for humidity and holidays though,' Holly replied.

'Isn't it funny,' Layla joined in, 'how none of us are happy with the hair we are given? I mean mine is poker straight and I'm always trying to curl it but the curls disappear after about half an hour.'

'Well, I think you should all just be happy with how nature intended you to be. Here's to three very beautiful women.' Marco toasted as he raised his glass. 'Now please let's eat.'

They clinked glasses and Poppy blushed as Marco looked straight into her eyes and winked at her. She picked her water glass up and glugged profusely to cool herself down.

She saw Gabe roll his eyes and tut before calling Marco out to help him carry the food in.

'Excuse me while I just go and get Luca from Gabe's bedroom, he's playing on his Xbox,' said Holly, before returning a minute later with a young boy with dark hair like his dad and hazel eyes like his mum. Holly introduced him to Poppy and Layla, and he shook hands with them shyly.

'Can I sit next to Uncle Gabe *and* Uncle Marco please?'

'Of course you can, little man, you come and sit round here.' As Gabe spoke, he picked up a napkin and tucked it in the top of Luca's shirt. 'Right, just be grateful that we're not having spaghetti, everyone, because this little Luca is a pasta monster. Last time he sucked up the spaghetti, it was flailing about the room like Mr Tickle arms and the sauce was splashing everywhere. Me and Marco had to put umbrellas up so we didn't drown in all that sauce.'

Luca giggled as Gabe tickled him.

'OK, so for starters we have a selection of hot and spicy chilli prawns and a cooling tricolore salad, followed by a colourful bowl of rainbow salad.' He pointed to a large, well-used casserole dish in the middle of the table. 'This one is bang-bang chicken, which you will find is made of tender chicken portions in a mouth-watering peanut sauce and this is Marco's traditional lasagne.' Poppy gazed in wonder at the dish, which was bubbling under the slightly browned cheese topping.

'Oh, and Layla, here's your veggie option: Gorgonzola gnocchi.'

'I have to hand it to you, Gabe and Marco, you guys can really cook, this food is delicious,' said Layla as she tucked into both veggie and non-veggie dishes.

'Yes, Gabe definitely inherited the cooking gene out of him and Holly,' Franco laughed.

89

'Oi cheeky,' Holly elbowed him in the ribs then turned to the others. 'Actually I can't deny it, I could burn a boiled egg.'

Poppy and Layla laughed.

'She's telling the truth. I swear to God she was boiling the eggs one minute and then bang bang bang, I thought it was fireworks. These eggs exploded everywhere, there were yellow circles on the ceiling and the walls, it was amazing really, like a science experiment.'

'Well, I may not be the world's best cook but I'm good at other things and don't forget, Franco, I married you for *your* cooking skills so that I wouldn't need to.'

Franco put his arm around her and kissed her. 'And I wouldn't have it any other way. Beautiful and intelligent, what more could I want. I agree though, let's have a toast to Marco and Gabe for this top-quality cooking.'

He raised his glass, and everybody joined in with the toast. Poppy couldn't help wishing that she had a relationship like Holly and Franco did. They seemed made for each other. For the first time she realised that whatever she had with Ed was nothing like that. She began to wonder if she'd ever made eye contact with Ed as she couldn't remember him ever looking at her the way Franco looked at Holly. He made Ed seem like a cold wet fish. In fact, even Gabe looked at her with more warmth in his eyes than Ed ever did, and they were just friends. She had been going to marry Ed.

'Thank you, everyone,' said Gabe, 'we just wanted to cook our own favourite meals that we grew up with. Our mums were originally from the Caribbean and moved to England when they were small.'

Holly explained, 'Our mums are twins. Mine and Gabe's mum, Rosa, married an Englishman and they recently took early retirement and moved to a lovely beach house in

Mum's hometown that they bought about five years ago. They're enjoying travelling too at the moment.'

Marco continued, 'My mother married an Italian man and they still live there in a small village, in the same house that my father was born in. Along with Franco's parents they had three very successful restaurants, simply called Abruzzo's, where both sets of families worked. Franco is my best friend as well as my cousin, but he abandoned me in Italy many years ago to drink elderflower wine with the love of his life and then I finally escaped.'

'Yes, and you never let me forget,' said Franco. 'We love it there but neither Marco nor I are interested in the restaurant business. I came to England to study law and Holly had offered to show me around. We became inseparable and now we're both solicitors and we have a smallholding where Holly makes elderflower wine and flavoured water. My parents couldn't be more proud of us. We visit regularly with Luca as he loves it there.'

'It sounds amazing,' said Poppy.

'I'll take you there some time,' said Gabe. 'Both of you, I mean.' He pointed his knife to her and Layla. He winked at Poppy, and she smiled back at him.

'Wait,' said Layla, a thoughtful expression on her face. 'If you two are cousins,' she pointed to Holly and Marco, 'and Marco and Franco are cousins. Then doesn't that mean ...?'

Holly burst out laughing. 'I can see why you'd think that but it's really not as incestuous as it sounds. Marco and Franco's dads are brothers so we're absolutely no relation whatsoever.'

'It's perfectly legal in this country to marry your cousin so I don't know what all the fuss is about. Come here, Marco.' Gabe grabbed Marco and planted a kiss firmly on his forehead, much to the amusement of Luca.

'Get off.' Marco pushed him off and made a point of wiping it off.

'I have to say that I'm so impressed with your cooking skills, gentlemen, the different flavours worked so well together, and my lips are tingling from the lovely spices,' said Poppy.

'Me too,' said Luca, 'I love having dinner here.'

Gabe ruffled the young boy's hair. 'Our little Luca just can't resist his uncles' food, can you, Luca?' The boy shook his head.

'Go on, who's the best cook?' teased Marco. 'You know it's me, don't you?'

'Sorry, Uncle Marco,' he replied.

Gabe clapped his hands together. 'Yes, thanks, Luca. I'm the cooking champion.'

'No, you're not either,' said Luca. 'It's Mummy, silly.'

'Oh, thank you, Luca.' Holly kissed his head as Gabe and Marco pretended to sulk.

Poppy's heart melted as she saw Gabe in the heart of his family, obviously so good with children. Gabe was like a magnet, surrounded by love and admiration wherever he went. Her heart warmed as she felt part of his world. She was filled with gratitude that their chance meeting had led to this extraordinary friendship and that this extraordinary man had opened up his life to her and welcomed her into it. She'd felt that gravitational pull towards him too; it was as though someone up above was controlling them, pulling their strings like marionettes and bringing them together. Maybe he really was an angel like his namesake. Her heartbreak didn't seem nearly as bad after he'd picked her up and dusted her off, even if the plasters did have Batman on them.

She knew he'd been hurt but they'd decided at the beginning of their friendship not to delve into each other's past relationships as it would only bring them down. She was pleased about this but was beginning to feel more and more interested in why he split up with Chris and why he didn't seem likely to open up his heart to someone else.

After dinner, they enjoyed a delicious tropical fruit salad, drizzled with rum for the adults, with homemade coconut ice cream. Holly and Franco started gathering their things together as Luca was getting tired. They hugged everyone at the door and said they hoped to meet Poppy and Layla again soon.

After many more drinks Marco, Gabe, Layla and Poppy had exhausted most of the songs on Singstar. They'd performed an impressive Abba routine which had them falling over each other with laughter. Especially as, for some reason, Gabe was able to produce authentic Abba wigs and someone had thought it would be a good idea to video the whole show. Poppy laughed until her stomach hurt. Gabe and Marco were like a double act and she could see another side to Marco as he loosened up and didn't seem as concerned about how he looked. As the music slowed, Marco pulled Poppy into his arms and they swayed to the sound of Chris Isaak's throaty tones. She wondered if he could feel her heart racing. He tilted his head towards her and she saw his mouth approach hers when they heard banging on the ceiling.

'Whoops, better turn the music off, it's two a.m.,' said Gabe.

'Oh, is that the time?' said Poppy. 'I must help you with the dishes,' she slurred and made her way into the kitchen, precariously balancing some plates and bowls. Gabe got up to help her, but Marco gestured with his hand for Gabe to stay where he was. He followed Poppy into the kitchen and slid his arms around her waist. She shrieked in fright, almost dropping the dishes as she hadn't heard him come in. He nuzzled into her neck as he took the dishes from her hand and clunked them into the sink, then turned her around to face him. She looked into his dark brown sexy eyes as he pressed her back against the wall. She giggled with anticipation as his hands reached for her face to tilt it up to him. He held her with his fingers entwined in her hair, sending shivers down her spine. His beautiful lips pressed against hers but instead of the passion she had imagined, she felt nothing. It was as though her lips were not attached to the rest of her body. Her arms were round his back and she could feel his taut muscular body beneath her fingers, but she realised he wasn't who she wanted. Where was the electricity? Or the adrenaline running through her body? She had really thought that this was what she wanted. Her desire at one point had been so much stronger than her misgivings of sleeping with someone who could break her heart. The red wine and rum clouded her judgement and her head started to spin. She tried to pull away, but he was pushing himself against her passionately. She gently touched his beautiful olive-skinned face with her hand, feeling the stubble that would no doubt have given her a rash on her face.

'I'm sorry,' she whispered. 'This isn't what I want.' He jumped away from her with his hands in the air.

Gabe entered the room. 'Ahem! Oops sorry, Poppy darling, your taxi is here.'

Her face burned that Gabe had caught her like this. She raced out of the door, shouted a thank you over her shoulder and joined Layla in the taxi.

Layla quizzed her all the way back, desperate for details.

'So, what happened?'

'Well,' said Poppy sleepily, 'I suppose you could say I got my Mr Fancy Man at last. The trouble is, the only words going round my head now are, be careful what you wish for.'

'Oh, isn't he a good kisser?'

'No, I mean yes he was, but it didn't feel right, I just feel ...' she hesitated whilst trying to find the right word. 'Empty, I suppose is the best way to describe it.' The rush of excitement from lust and wine had gone and been replaced by feelings of shame. She thought back to Marco's lips on hers. 'There was nothing there, no feelings at all, just a hollowness where my heart used to be. Thank God I didn't sleep with him or I would have been filled with so much regret right now.' Her mind flicked back to Gabe's face when he'd walked in; she had been trying to understand what his expression had shown, and it suddenly came to her. He had looked hurt. She cringed inwardly and held her head in her hands. She really cared about what Gabe thought of her.

By the time they got up the next morning, they didn't have time to speak much as Layla had to catch her train back to Liverpool. They hugged each other goodbye and Layla assured her that it hopefully wouldn't be long before she could move down to Bramblewood too. Poppy smiled and promised she would contact the landlord as she knew he had been advertising for another person to share the flat. She hadn't relished the thought of sharing with a stranger, but it was too hard paying all the rent on her own. Poppy emailed the landlord straight away to tell him that she had hopefully found someone to share with, though she didn't hear back from him.

Chapter 12

'You'll never guess what?' said Layla as soon as the Facetime app connected.

'What?' replied Poppy, smiling at the obvious delight on her friend's face.

'I didn't get the job,' she pouted.

Poppy's heart plunged through her stomach; she was so looking forward to Layla moving down to Bramblewood so they could have fun and adventures together. Her shoulders slumped and the corners of her mouth turned down. Then she realised how selfish she was being. She couldn't let Layla see how disappointed she was as she must be really fed up.

'Oh no, is it because of the cutbacks as the staff morale at our branch is getting quite low?' she asked.

'Yes, it is,' Layla giggled.

'Wait a minute, why are you giggling? Are you winding me up? Oh, please tell me you are because I can't bear the thought of staying here if you can't come; I'll have to apply for another job back up there.'

'No, I really haven't got it, but—' she lifted a cocktail and took a sip of it. 'I told them here that they can stick their job up their arse.'

'You didn't?' Poppy's mouth gaped open. She hadn't realised that Layla was quite so kickass.

'No, of course I didn't,' she laughed, 'I got made redundant so I'm still going to move in with you and I'll look for another job down there. The payoff will keep me going for a few months. Hey, what are you doing?'

Poppy had kicked off her shoes and was now jumping up and down on the couch.

'Oi, don't you be going all Tom Cruise on me,' she chuckled. 'Go and get a drink so we can celebrate together from afar.'

Back at work the next day, Poppy was feeling a little less lonely and a little more at home. Due to her sandwich round, she was bonding with so many more people in the building and they were recommending her to their friends. However, there had been an announcement in her branch that there were opportunities coming up for more voluntary redundancies and she was sorely tempted to go for it and maybe move back home to Liverpool. After all, that's where Ed was and she still couldn't shake her feelings for him away, but then she remembered how excited Layla had been to move in with her and she was just excited to see where the adventure would take them.

An image of Gabe's face flashed in her mind, his head thrown back mid-laugh, and she couldn't help smiling. He was the one she would miss the most if she did leave. He was the one who had kept her going when she felt a bit wobbly from time to time. With him she felt safe. Especially when tucked into one of his amazing bear hugs. So, she decided to hang on until she could support herself with her new business. Her boss Andy had decided to take up the redundancy offer, which meant that she was now going to be working for Burger Breath Brian. The mere thought made her shudder.

Most of the people in the company had welcomed Poppy's Posh Pannier with open mouths but Brian, Britt and another

97

of Britt's friends had refused to have anything to do with it and made derogatory comments, such as moaning about the smell if there was something unusually spicy on offer that day. If anyone ever mentioned feeling unwell then these two would be quick to try and point the finger of blame on Poppy's sandwiches. She, however, tried to just let it go over her head.

The specials on offer that day were a delicious homemade sausage and roasted vegetable plait and a scrumptious coffee and walnut cake. Poppy could see Britt almost drooling down her wobbly chin at the sight of it. She laughed inwardly at the spiteful woman cutting her nose off to spite her face as she munched on the huge greasy pork pie she had brought in. Poppy had indigestion just looking at it. She ignored the miserable looks and thought about how happy she was that Layla would soon be moving in with her.

Chapter 13

Since the snogging incident, Poppy had only seen Marco in passing at the theatre as he and Alexia practised in a different room from the others. She blushed when she did see him, but he simply smiled and winked. Once she had sobered up, she realised on reflection that it had taken her back to her youth when snogging a teenage boy ended up in a wrestling match with an octopus. The sting of embarrassment flushed across her neck and cheeks. What had she been thinking getting into that situation? Her hand covered her mouth as she recalled Marco's hands wandering around her body which thankfully, she had put an immediate stop to. There was just no spark between them at all. A shiver ran through her as if trying to shake off the memory. It was the look on Gabe's face that haunted her more than anything. He looked so hurt, shocked, disappointed in her even, and angry at Marco. But whatever it was she was glad she hadn't done anything to regret. Gabe's friendship was far too important to her to risk over a stupid fling with an albeit sexy but shallow Italian love god.

She hadn't been single since she was a young girl as she had always gone straight from one relationship to another. To her surprise, she found that she actually enjoyed being on her own. She had taken charge of her own life, working full time, starting a new business whilst finding time to look after herself too. She was an independent woman for the first time in her life and that felt good. She couldn't deny missing the love interest in her life though and Ed did darken her thoughts occasionally. However, not so much since Layla moved in, which had been the best day of Poppy's life. She didn't have much with her apart from a suitcase and a cat carrier with her beloved Misty inside. Layla still hadn't said anything about her mum and dad and Poppy really didn't want to pry as she knew that if Layla wanted her to know then she would tell her. After a few days of settling in, Poppy was trying on dresses and asking what she should wear tonight as they were meeting Gabe and Marco at The Flamingo's Leg for dinner and drinks. She loved having her bestie back with her again, she felt almost complete.

Gabe and Marco were already standing at the bar when the girls walked in. They kissed their hellos and Ray showed them to their table near the window. Poppy had turned a lovely shade of beetroot after she had seen Marco's appreciative glance up and down her body. She was wearing a black fitted dress with see-through chiffon sleeves and sequins around the neckline and cuffs, opaque black tights and black heels. She carried herself with more confidence and if people looked at her, she no longer worried that it was because they thought she was fat. The exercise had given her a healthy glow, which Layla said shone through her skin. Her body had taken on a new toned look and feel. She had neither the time nor the inclination to eat junk food at home as she was so busy with her new business venture, especially as she was making such delicious healthy food for her customers. She also couldn't remember the last time she had moped around about Ed.

Ray brought the menus over.

'I thought my luck was in then, seeing two handsome dudes hanging around the bar and then my hopes were dashed on seeing you two sexy stunners snap them up.' They all laughed, and Poppy looked across the table and realised how alike the two cousins were. Both were undeniably gorgeous. Marco was handsome in a bad boy kind of way with dark brooding eyes framed with thick lashes. Toned to within an inch of his life, he had a strong athletic, dancer's body. Gabe was broader and slightly taller. The softness he had carried around his middle was long gone, and he was hunky. His black curly hair was kept short and his new beard trimmed tidily into a sexy stubble. His bright blue eyes were sparkly, full of mischief and laughter, which complemented the smile that danced on his lips whenever he saw her. He and Layla were laughing about something that Poppy hadn't heard and she remembered Layla at the Christmas do suggesting that Gabe would be a better match than Marco. She could see why now; Layla had seen through Gabe's dodgy goatee to the man behind it. But how shallow must she be to have overlooked him for Marco. She and Layla had discussed the men on the way over.

'So, do you still have the hots for Marco?' Layla had asked.

'No way,' replied Poppy. 'I mean he's gorgeous, there's no doubt about that, but that's it. He treats women like pieces of meat. I thought I'd enjoy a sneaky snog with him but no. Never again …' 'Whereas with Gabe his gorgeous personality is completely on a par with his devastatingly handsome attributes.' Her face broke into a smile at just the thought of him and she had flutters in her stomach.

'Ah you love him, don't you? I can see it from your face.'

'I really do, and do you know why? Apart from him being the loveliest person I know. Except for you of, course.' She laughed when Layla pulled her face into a fake sulk. 'Because I feel safe and secure when I'm with him as though he's wrapped me in layers and layers of giant bubble wrap.

And even if Ed were to roll me down a hill, then Gabe's protective force field would shield me from all the hurt. I know he's never going to break my heart because we'll never be in a relationship. He gives the best bear hugs ever and he always makes me laugh until I almost wet myself. He's literally the male version of you, Layla, maybe that's why I love him so much.'

'He's a lovable guy,' replied Layla, 'and I mean Marco is quite funny sometimes but completely not boyfriend material. I'm really glad you had Gabe here to look after you, he really has been your guardian angel, or should I say guardian genie,' she giggled.

'A toast to our beautiful Layla,' said Gabe, after getting the drinks in. 'Welcome to Bramblewood, you lovely Liverpool lady.'

'To Layla,' the others chorused, their glasses raised.

'Thanks to all of you for a lovely welcome, I'm sure I'll be very happy here,' said a smiley Layla.

'Well, we love having you here,' said Gabe.

Marco had been pressing his leg against Poppy's under the table for the last five minutes, but she had been too busy inside her own head to notice. She eventually realised that Ray was waiting for her order as the others had already made their choices. She decided on the salmon risotto. The two guys were having steaks and Layla had chosen beetroot and butternut squash lasagne. 'Ray, I have to say you deserve tons of praise for your vast choice of vegetarian options.'

'Why thank you, dear Layla, that's because Beau is a veggie who was fed up with only being offered a nutloaf or stuffed peppers whenever we went out to eat. So we decided to use his imagination and experiment with more interesting dishes. Can you imagine how his poor mother must have felt; not only was he gay but a bloody veggie as well.' He laughed. 'My mum would have been horrified if I didn't like my meat and two veg.' He pecked Beau on the cheek lovingly as he arrived to pour the wines, chuckling at the tail end of the conversation.

They sat companionably chatting and listening to the live jazz band playing that night. Marco as usual had wolfed his food down. He expended energy quicker than he ate it so was now helping Poppy and Layla with their leftovers.

Gabe's phone rang and Poppy noted a look of confusion on his face as he looked at the screen. 'That's weird. Looks like a New York number,' he said before speaking into the phone. 'Hello? Yes, this is Gabe. I'm sorry I don't understand. Could you just hold please?' He stood and gestured to the others that he was going outside. Poppy's heart was beating almost out of her chest. She hoped that the call was what she thought it was.

Ten minutes later Gabe practically moonwalked back into the bar to join them, He grabbed each of them one by one and planted a big kiss on each of their foreheads, including Marco. He then picked Poppy up and swung her around.

'What's happened?' she giggled in response to his infectious smile. She hadn't realised the full depth of the dimples in his cheeks, but then she'd never seen him this genuinely happy before.

'I take it this is good news then?' said Marco, pulling out Gabe's chair for him to sit.

'Yes, come on, Gabe, spill. You can't leave us hanging,' said Layla.

'What's happened?' asked Poppy again, revelling in the obvious delight that shone in his eyes.

'I'll tell you what's happened, Little Miss Innocence over there.'

'That was a call from a lady called Berry from Midnight Moon Productions in New York. Hold on.' He stopped to take a swig of his beer. 'Apparently I sent her a couple of my scripts and some reviews for *Three Wishes*.'

'What do you mean apparently? Surely you know if you sent those things,' said Marco, looking confused.

'That's because I didn't send them, but I did send them to my dear friend Poppy here to read ages ago.'

Poppy's face burned as the secret was obviously out.

'I'm sorry, I should have asked but when I saw the call out on social media for final submissions, I didn't have time to ask you and I thought you might have said no.'

Gabe rolled his eyes affectionately. 'And you would have been right because I've come to realise that I'm more afraid of success than failure.'

'What do you mean?' asked Poppy.

'Well, failure keeps me in my little comfort zone, which is where I feel safe and my writing is just mine, but success is a whole other story. Success opens you up to the world, highlights your insecurities, you have to allow other people access to your work. Success is scary.'

'But Gabe, you're the most talented person I know, and your work deserves to be seen by the world,' said Poppy. 'Also, I'd much rather ask for forgiveness than permission. Anyway, stop keeping us in suspense, what did they say?'

Gabe's face glowed as he couldn't contain his news any longer. 'She wants to meet me. She's coming over to the UK soon and, get this.' He nudged Marco with his elbow. 'She wants to show it in her independent theatre, which is very near Broadway, at Christmas.'

The girls shrieked and jumped up and down clapping,

causing other customers to look over and smile at their obvious joy. Marco grabbed Gabe in a bear hug and rubbed the top of his head with his knuckles. 'You'll smash that, cuz, well done.'

Gabe took a deep breath and pretended to smooth his hair again as though Marco had messed it up. 'Hold on, that's not all. Let's sit down and I'll tell you what I know so far.' When they were seated, he began. 'This lovely lady Berry said that normally they don't take more than one submission and the callout had been for contemporary takes on fairy tales, so *Three Wishes* fit the bill perfectly.'

'Just as I'd hoped,' said Poppy, thrilled with herself.

'She said that a producer friend of hers was looking for a brand new musical, something raw and passionate and sexy. She said when she saw the other attachment from me,' he made inverted comma signs with his fingers as he said the word 'me', 'she said she was intrigued. She opened it and didn't put it down again until she had finished. She wants my permission to pass *Latino* on to this other guy.'

'Oh my God, Gabe, that is amazing.' Poppy left her seat to hug him.

Marco slapped him on the back and Layla blew him a kiss. 'That's for our famous writer, Gabe,' she said, 'I'm so proud of you.'

'So come on, what's this *Latino* all about, it sounds right up my strada,' said Marco.

'It's about a young Italian man called Salvatore who comes to America to find his father, who had got his mother pregnant during the war. The only clues he has are a name, a photo and an engraved gold signet ring. He has no money and ends up eventually making a name for himself as a dancer.' Poppy had never seen Gabe so animated; he spoke with his hands, and his voice rose and fell with such passion as he portrayed the emotions. He was almost in character as he continued. Layla and Marco were listening in awe.

'However, he upsets some fellow migrants who helped him when he first arrived in America, and they feel that he doesn't deserve the fame and fortune he has earned and so are eager to put a spanner in the works for him.'

'I think you mean hammer but that's not important, this sounds amazing and perfect for me,' said Marco.

'No, Marco, it's only you that says *hammer* in the works,' Gabe laughed.

'Well, hammer, spanner, whatever, I'm guessing it involves a lot of hot Latin American dancing and some fight scenes as well so whoever plays Salvatore will need to be really fit,' he said as he flexed his own muscles.

'Don't worry, I'll be sure to mention you if anything comes of it,' teased Gabe. 'Now come on, let's dance, we've got a lot of celebrating to do.'

Marco grabbed Poppy's hand and led her to the floor to join some of the other customers who had started dancing. He expertly twirled her around with ease and she laughed light-headedly, enjoying the moment. Thankfully their illicit kiss had chased away every last scrap of the crush she'd had on him, and she was relieved about that. She could treat him like a normal person now and not fawn after him like he was some love god. As she spun around again, she noticed that Layla and Gabe were up dancing too, a little more sedately than they were but they looked lovely together. She felt a flutter of something but didn't quite know what. She smiled at them as they started joking around, Layla twirling Gabe as they both giggled. Then Marco and Gabe started dancing together and Poppy and Layla partnered up. They noticed Ray and Beau were also joining in along with lots of the other customers. At the end of the song 'The Boy from

Ipanema', the singer announced that she was going to slow it down a little. Gabe stood in front of Poppy and opened his arms wide. She stepped into his embrace and relished the warmth he surrounded her with. The singer crooned the haunting melody of 'The First Time Ever I Saw Your Face.'

'Oh, I love this one,' said Gabe and proceeded to sing it in his Barry White voice. As he did so he looked deep into Poppy's eyes and stopped.

'Are you OK, Poppy?'

'I'm fine,' she sniffed, her eyes felt watery and blurred her vision a little. 'This used to be my grandad's favourite song. I remember him singing it to me and we would dance together. I was only small so I'd stand on his feet and he'd twirl me round. It was like nothing in the world could ever hurt me when I was with my grandad. He and my nana taught me everything about how to be a good person and have a good work ethic. They also showed me what the perfect relationship could be like.'

'What did he do, workwise? Your grandad, I mean.' Gabe reached and smoothed her hair out of her eyes. The softness of his touch stayed with her long after he moved his hand away. 'He was an insurance man and my nana worked in a car factory making car seats. She used to make funny little hats out of the leftover materials. They were tartan, and they called them "ecky thump hats".' She smiled as she recalled her memories. 'She was a brilliant seamstress. Once she made me the most gorgeous Little Red Riding Hood outfit for a fancy dress party I was going to. It was beautiful, made from red leather and red velvet; I can still remember the silky softness of it as I stroked my cheek with it. The best thing was I won the competition.'

'Congratulations,' said Gabe. 'Do you still have it?'

She laughed. 'I wish I did but I wore it so much that there

wasn't much left of it in the end. Oh Gabe, my grandparents would have loved you, I can just imagine you and Grandad playing golf and laughing. He loved to laugh, just like you.' She met his gaze and continued, 'Anyway, enough of this sad talk. Come on, genie boy, cheer me up. Tell me something nice.'

'Ooh let me think, something nice. OK, well, I have something nice about the words to this song.'

'Yes, that sounds good.'

'I remember exactly every little thing about the first time I saw your face.'

Poppy found herself getting lost in his sapphire blue gaze. Her heart expanded and she sighed. 'Really?' she asked before realising that she could also remember the first time she saw those eyes and the warm smile that melted her and pulled her towards him.

'Yes, of course. You looked so beautiful but so, so sad, as though the stuffing had been kicked right out of you.'

'Well it had; I'd just been dumped in a town I didn't know by the man I thought I loved.'

'So, you don't love him anymore then?' he asked, squeezing her hand gently as they swayed to the music.

'No, well, yes. I mean I don't actually know anymore. I feel confused, but I don't want to talk about him. I want to talk about you and the first time I saw your face.'

'Go on then, tell me.'

'Well, first of all, it was your laugh. It echoed round the room and was just so full of fun. Me and Layla laughed our heads off, it was so contagious. The goatee was … let's just say unique, and made you look a little like a James Bond baddie.'

They both laughed and she continued, 'But the eyes, so blue and twinkling with magic, were mesmerising and that goddamn smile of yours, so genuine, it really touched me.'

'Oh stop, you'll have me weeping in a minute.' He pretended to wipe a tear from his eye. She slapped him gently on the arm as they swayed in time to the music. 'So, do you remember anything else about me then?'

'Mmmm, let me think.' He put his finger to his lips. 'Ah yes, you were wearing a cobalt blue shimmery dress with killer heels and an angel halo, I remember your black hair was so glossy in an elegant bun, it framed your beautiful face perfectly. You looked like you'd just stepped off the front cover of a magazine.' She blinked up at him, eating up his compliments like a box of chocolates.

'And those bright green eyes of yours were bewitching. There's just something magical about them, especially with the contrast of such dark hair. I know it might sound corny, but your eyes are like little galaxies. Seriously, I've never seen anything like them.' She gave a happy sigh. She wished straight men could talk like that.

'You know what, Gabe? Some day you are going to make someone a wonderful husband.' She wasn't sure if she imagined it but she thought his sparkle dulled a little at that comment. He was obviously still very hung up over his ex. As the song came to an end, he squeezed her and they walked over to join the others, his arm still around her.

The guys walked the girls home. Layla gave both a peck on the cheek and went into the flat, Marco pecked Poppy on the cheek and walked a few steps away.

'Come here, you,' said Gabe, his voice full of affection. He picked her up and swung her round. 'Thank you, Pops, I can't properly explain how thankful I am to you for what you did because I've had too much beer but I really, really am.'

'Congratulations Gabe, you deserve the best of everything,'

she said, giving him a squeeze. 'I can't believe you're going to have a show on almost Broadway.'

He put her down. 'Almost Broadway, it's got a certain kind of ring to it, hasn't it?'

'It sure has,' she replied.

He winked and followed Marco home. She smiled as she heard them singing 'Volare' in deep baritone voices as they crossed Market Square.

Chapter 14

As Poppy turned the key in the door, she heard the sound of Layla screaming and Misty wailing. Her heart almost beat out of her chest as she ran into Layla's bedroom to see what was going on. She tried to turn the light on, but the bulb must have popped, and she could just about make out two people struggling on the bed shouting at each other.

'Call the police, Poppy, there's an intruder,' screeched Layla.

'Get off of me,' shouted the other voice. 'I live here.'

'WHAT?' shouted Poppy and Layla together, confused.

By this time Poppy had managed to turn the torch on her phone on and shone the beam of light onto the intruder's face.

'Arrgh, my eyes,' said the girl.

'Who are you?' asked Poppy.

'I'm Cassie,' she replied in an Australian accent, breathless from the shock of being rudely awakened by a crazy woman jumping on her as she slept. 'Jake, the landlord, is my brother. He told me you were looking for a flatmate to share with so I thought it would be OK. He said he had sorted it.'

Poppy and Layla looked at each other blankly and back to the girl again.

'Ah wait, he hasn't passed on the message, has he? That's just typical of him. He's probably having too much of a good time back in Australia. He popped home for a friend's wedding during his round-the-world trip.'

'I'm so sorry,' said Layla as she tried to smooth Cassie's

hair down where she had grabbed it when trying to apprehend the intruder. Cassie ran her own hands through her pale pink choppy haircut and laughed. 'It's OK, no worries.'

Poppy put the kettle on, while Layla got the cups ready for a much-needed strong cup of coffee, giving Cassie a chance to make herself half decent. Layla's cat Misty was frantically rubbing herself against Layla's legs, meowing loudly as she had been frightened too. Cassie soon joined them in the kitchen, wrapped up in a purple silk kimono with large pink and white flowers on it, cuddling a little black and white cat with a black moustache. They all giggled, and the two cats meowed loudly at each other.

Cassie Hoxton was extremely pretty with dainty features. Her pink hair was swept over to the side in a trendy choppy cut which gave her a slightly boyish look that she really suited. Her eyes were so blue they were almost violet. She was about five six tall and twenty-five years old. She had a delicate pink gemstone piercing at the side of her nose and a tattoo on the inside of her left wrist which apparently was a Thai symbol for love and femininity. As they all dipped bourbon biscuits into their coffees, she told them how she came to end up in Layla's bed.

'Basically, in a nutshell I was travelling with my girlfriend; we'd been to visit my family in Australia then round Thailand and Europe on the way home. We were meant to be gone for another couple of months. But little did I know that she was cheating on me left right and centre and her final choice of lowlife ended up stealing all of our money, including bank cards which she used to empty our accounts. So, the holiday and the relationship were both cut dramatically short, and we've basically both come home with our tails between our legs. I got back late last night, and picked this little one up from her mum who'd been looking after her.'

As she spoke, she gently kissed the cat she was cuddling on the top of her head. 'Jake had told me that you were looking for someone to share with so I thought it would be a perfect solution until I decide what to do next. I still had a key from when I stayed here before but don't worry, if you just let me kip on the couch tonight, I'll be out of your hair tomorrow.'

Poppy and Layla looked at each other and agreed with their eyes what they should do next. Layla spoke first.

'The living-room couch is a sofa bed so you and I could take turns on it if you like and we'll just muddle through somehow.'

Cassie looked exhausted but excited and very grateful.

'Thank you so much. Don't worry about taking turns, the sofa bed will be fine for me. I'm so sorry, if I'd known you had already found a flatmate, I would never have dreamed of turning up like this.' Tash jumped out of Cassie's arms and spent the next twenty minutes with Misty running up and down the curtains and round the flat like crazy, whilst the girls set up the sofa bed for Cassie.

Poppy explained that she hadn't heard from Jake, the landlord, although she had told him about Layla joining her. Cassie admitted that she hadn't heard from him either and thought he was probably in an area with a bad signal. She'd just assumed it would be OK, not realising that Layla had moved in quite so quickly.

Layla still felt terrible for attacking Cassie, but they all managed to laugh it off and in fact had nicknamed Cassie 'Pinkielocks' by the end of the night. Layla joked that she didn't want to be responsible for making her porridge in the morning as it was bound to be too salty or too sweet.

It was really late now and so they all bade each other goodnight and exhaustedly fell into their respective beds.

Misty and Tash had gotten over their differences and, after licking each other noisily for quite some time, were now curled up together in Misty's snuggly bed in the living room.

Cassie was a breath of fresh air about the place. She loved life and her energy was almost tangible. She enjoyed a drink and was soon preparing exotic cocktails for the girls and cooking delicious Thai dishes. She had quickly picked up a job in a local cocktail bar where she used to work as a mixologist and she was keen to help with Poppy's Posh Pannier as much as possible, including suggesting new recipes such as a Thai chicken wrap with spicy peanut sauce. She was also brilliant at cleaning the flat, which she insisted on doing in lieu of keep until she started bringing some money in, so the place was spotless.

Jake had eventually got in touch when he realised there was a conflict of flatmates and was relieved to find that the girls had sorted it out amongst themselves.

Poppy felt like a huge weight had been lifted off her shoulders as before it was just her doing all of the shopping, preparing and delivering of the PPP products. Now she had the luxury of not one, but two helpers and it was fantastic. The catering for the monthly executive meetings was going really well and Tania had also commissioned her to take on some client meetings too, which she was able to do with the extra help. Business was booming and the only problem was that their little kitchen in the flat just wasn't big enough. She remembered the conversation she'd had with Gabe about Cath in the café needing help and wondered if they could come to a mutually beneficial arrangement. She picked up her phone and called the theatre to speak to her. After an interesting conversation she arranged to meet up with an exhausted-sounding Cath.

Chapter 15

Poppy arrived at the theatre with both Layla and Cassie.

'OMG, has anyone seen Charlie? I've just found his angels,' said Gabe, swooning at the beauties in front of him. The girls laughed.

'I'm serious,' he replied, 'that entrance was like the opening credits of *Charlie's Angels*, all sassy walks and bouncy hair. You're not even aware of how many heads you've turned just now, are you? What a formidable trio.' He kissed them all one by one and gave Poppy an extra bear hug.

'It's so nice to have a fan club even if it is just one person between three of us,' Poppy smiled and hugged him back with as much enthusiasm as he gave her.

'What are you doing here?'

Poppy was about to answer when an old lady came through and shooed him out the way.

'They've come to see me.'

'Oh, I see, so that's who you've baked your delicious lemon drizzle cake for, is it?'

'Yes, it is and if you don't get back to rehearsals then I won't be saving you a piece.'

'OK see you later.' He winked at Poppy.

'Hi Cath, it's lovely to meet you. This is Layla and Cassie and we're all working together on Poppy's Posh Pannier.' They shook hands. Cassie scanned the room. 'Nice to meet you, Cath, this place looks perfect with lots of space to work.'

'Thank you dear,' said Cath. 'It's a nice place and the customers are lovely, but I just get so tired now.'

'Thank you so much for meeting with us, Cath, I know you're not looking at taking anyone on, but I was wondering whether we could actually rent the space from you when you're not using it as our place is far too small to cope with the demands we have now. We could also supply the café if you're interested.'

Cath cut the cake and plated it up, handing each of them a hefty slice. 'Here, take this and help yourselves to tea.'

'Oh, thank you,' said Layla, picking up the heavy teapot and pouring it out. 'We could help you out too if you get stuck.'

'Thank you so much, darling. You won't understand how much this mean to me; I'm exhausted now, and I really think it's time for me to put my feet up. The lease expires in a couple of months,' Cath explained, 'and I'd like to spend whatever time I have left with my husband.'

'That's fine, Cath. Would you be happy for us to maybe take over the lease and that way we can see how it goes with a view to maybe taking it over permanently?'

'I would be so relieved, honestly. My heart is really not in it anymore and you are all bursting with enthusiasm. I did have an offer from a junk food business, but I think yours sounds far more wholesome and I love the name, Poppy's Posh Pannier. I'm happy for you to start working from here with immediate effect.'

'Well, the rent you've mentioned when we chatted on the phone sounds good; I just have one more request before we shake hands on it.'

'Of course, dear, what is it?' Cath twiddled with the chain around her neck.

'Would you mind every now and then baking this delicious cake for us as it's absolutely scrumptious?' said Poppy as she took another forkful of the citrusy delight. She thought Cath would burst with pride.

Poppy noticed Gabe walk past and he nodded and smiled at her. She could tell he understood that she was making Cath still feel useful and relevant and a part of all these exciting new changes that were about to take place.

'Hey, you should taste her Cherry Bakewell too, Pops, it's out of this world,' he suggested, winking at the older lady.

Cath blushed joyfully. 'It would be my pleasure, darlin',' she replied. 'Here's to new adventures,' she added, as she clinked teacups with everyone.

Once they'd finished their tea and forms had been signed, Cath left the others to it. Gabe brought over a bottle of Prosecco, which he popped and poured into three glasses. Poppy hugged him.

'Well done, ladies,' said Gabe. 'This seems like the perfect solution for everyone. This place really could do with being brought back to life and I think you are just the angels to do it.'

'Thanks, Gabe, and the good thing is we can now take on even more work. Especially with Layla's investment,' said Poppy.

'Oh well done, Layla,' he said. 'A sound investment, I'm sure.'

'Well, my redundancy money was just lying around doing nothing and I really believe in this venture. It's so exciting and will keep me busy at the same time. I can't wait to get started,' she said, clapping her hands.

'And now we have Cassie and her marketing skills on

board, we have a full house. Welcome to the team everybody,' said Poppy as she raised her glass.

'Delighted to be part of it. Cheers,' said Cassie.

'To Poppy's Posh Pannier,' said Layla.

'To Poppy's Posh Pannier,' chorused the others, before Gabe left them to it.

'Right first things first, we need to do an inventory of everything that's already in the kitchen cupboards and storage areas to see what we have and what we need to buy.' She shuffled some papers around. 'Here's the list from Cath of everything that should be here so let's divide that up and make a start.'

Chapter 16

Poppy had been so wrapped up in work that she hadn't been able to make a couple of Sunday bike rides with Gabe and he'd also been pretty busy lately with rehearsals for the upcoming show. But both were determined not to miss another. Exhilaration swept through Poppy as she sped along the towpath behind him.

'I've really missed this, the great outdoors,' she shouted to Gabe's back.

'Me too, it's so good to see you again, even though I can't actually see you right now,' he laughed.

As it was a glorious day, they took a picnic in the pannier and found a small clearing quite far up the river where there was an RSPB sanctuary and a large lake where they sometimes spotted otters. Gabe had made a new tongue twister up.

'I'm a spotted otter spotter and my otter's name is Spot. He's always in the water except for when he's not. I'm not an otter spotter, I'm an otter spotter's son, I'm only spotting otters cos the otter spotter's gone.' They made each other laugh trying to say it quicker and quicker. When they laughed together, they often had tears rolling down their cheeks and sometimes they had to move away from each other so they couldn't physically see the other person because just one look could set them off again. Poppy often had rib ache when she got back.

★

Their favourite place was by a patch of wildflowers, including some beautiful poppies, which was only a step away from the edge of the lake where lily pads formed resting places for tiny frogs. Gabe took a picture of Poppy sitting amongst the flowers making a daisy chain out of some really giant daisies they had found. She looked beautiful. He had caught her just as she was looking up at him and laughing, so he had captured the Poppy he knew and loved. He also took a selfie of both of them sticking their tongues out to the camera; she looked tiny in his big protective hug. After they'd enjoyed their picnic, a little black Labrador puppy came bounding over and greedily devoured the leftovers on their picnic blanket. Gabe grabbed him and held him as the little bundle of energy licked his face excitedly.

'Hey, little guy. Where did you come from?' he asked.

Poppy was delighted with him and took him from Gabe for a cuddle. She felt electric shocks through her body as their arms touched during the handover. She looked at him, realising he had felt it too, and their eyes locked. Poppy's heart was beating so fast that she felt a little dizzy. As the puppy struggled in her arms and licked her face, she reluctantly broke eye contact and giggled at her little furry chum. Gabe held his hand out to her to help her up.

'We need to find out who this puppy belongs to,' he said.

They followed in the direction he had come from and came across a crumbling brick wall, which surrounded the garden of a magnificent thatched cottage with a sign outside saying Angel Cottage. The back gate was open, revealing the most impressive flower garden containing a circular area covered in a blanket of poppies with a small bench in the middle of it and stepping stones leading to the bench from the patio area.

'Hello,' boomed Gabe as he knocked on the splintery wooden gate. He heard voices shouting, 'Cindy, where are you?' then an elderly lady with her son and two grand-daughters came running to the gate, sheer relief showing on their faces.

'Oh, thank you so much,' said the man as he gratefully took the puppy from Poppy. 'The girls must have left the gate open.'

'That's OK,' said Gabe. 'What a beautiful garden this is and such a charming cottage.'

'Thanks,' replied the man. 'My mum is poppy mad.'

'So am I,' said Gabe, winking cheekily at Poppy, who felt her cheeks burning. They said goodbye and were chuffed with their new discovery.

'Wouldn't you just love to live in that cottage?' Poppy asked wistfully.

'Well, it certainly beats my flat, that's for sure.'

One of their favourite things to do on their bike rides was to lie on the picnic blanket and look for shapes in the clouds. He always managed to find rude ones and she would find really bizarre ones like the Taj Mahal or the Houses of Parliament, or the Liver Building.

They really talked to each other and never ran out of things to say. As it was a particularly hot day, Gabe took off his t-shirt to sunbathe and fell asleep lying on his front with his face to the side resting on his muscly arms. Poppy had also nodded off for a little while but woke up and leaned against a tree reading. She tried so hard to concentrate on what the book was about but found herself a little distracted by the sight of him lying there. His skin was a deep golden brown, his back broad and muscular with a trim waist, his hair jet black and very short. She took a sneaky picture of him and wondered whether he would notice if she touched him. She crept up nearer to him, her hand hovering over the contours of his shoulder blades. She slowly and gently lowered her hand until she touched that soft smooth skin. She shrieked and jumped out of her skin when he jumped up suddenly.

'Gotcha,' he boomed, grabbed her hands and rolled her onto her back. She giggled and shouted, 'There was a fly on you; I was just batting it away, I promise.'

'I don't believe you,' he said, 'I think you were pretending to be a fly to scare me awake.'

'No,' she shrieked, giggling as he started to tickle her around the waist. He pinned her arms behind her head, and their giggling subsided as his mouth hovered over her lips so close that she could feel the heat of his breath on her. He looked deep into her emerald, green eyes, and she dared to stare straight back into his. The meeting of their eyes caused an electric response in his body and he could tell she felt it too, though both had to pretend it wasn't happening.

'Come on, let's get back,' he said, kissing her cheek softly, completely unaware of the jolt that shot through her body. He then jumped up, offered her his hand and they raced back home.

Arriving back from the six-mile cycle, they stopped at Serendipity, the boat café, for a bite to eat. Rosie welcomed them and sat them at a table by the window, and a young boy came to take their order.

'Hi Jackson,' said Gabe, ruffling the young boy's hair. 'I didn't know you worked here.'

'Auntie Rosie is letting me earn some pocket money, so what would you like?' He held his pen poised over the pad.

'I'd love a juicy fat scone please and a hot chocolate.'

Gabe winked at Poppy as Jackson wrote down every word he'd said.

Poppy waited until he'd finished writing and looked at her.

'I'll have the same please.'

'The same,' he said out loud while he wrote. 'Are you Gabe's girlfriend?' he asked.

Poppy blushed. 'Erm ...'

'Well, to be fair, you are a girl, and you are my friend.' Gabe shrugged his shoulders. Poppy laughed and nodded. 'To be fair you're not wrong.'

'Gabe's got a girlfriend,' Jackson sang as he went to the counter.

'Oh hi, I didn't notice you there. Your son is tormenting me,' Gabe joked to a couple at another table who were just leaving.

'Hi Gabe, how's it going?' They came over to his table and the man shook his hand and said hi to Poppy.

'Poppy, this is my friend Dom and his wife Lucy, Jackson's mum and dad. Dom works with my brother-in-law Franco, and Lucy owns the Signal Box Café. This is my friend Poppy, owner of Poppy's Posh Pannier.'

'Hi,' said Poppy, 'it's lovely to meet you.'

'You too,' said Lucy. 'So, you're the mysterious Poppy we've been hearing so much about. The one who's put the sparkle back in Gabe's eye apparently, according to Franco and Holly. You'll both have to come round for dinner some time.'

'I'd love that,' said Poppy.

'I don't go on about her all the time, do I?' said Gabe.

'Maybe just a smidge,' said Lucy, holding her finger and thumb a couple of millimetres apart. 'But we love that.' She kissed Gabe on the cheek.

'Bye then. OK Jackson, we're going now.'

Jackson chased after them, fist-bumping Gabe on the way.

'Bye Gabe, bye Gabe's girlfriend.'

'Her name is Poppy,' said Gabe.

'You know everybody,' Poppy laughed.

'Yes, I think I probably do. But then I have lived here all my life.'

Poppy could see the attraction as she gazed out of the window to see swans and geese gliding by on the still waters of the River Bram. A few hundred yards away she could see the picturesque bridge across the river which formed part of the high street. It was certainly a town that pulled you in and held you tight to its heart. Gabe was Bramblewood in human form; he had pulled her in, and she felt quite sure that at this moment she didn't want to leave either of them. They made her feel secure and as though she belonged.

Rosie brought over the raisin and cranberry scones and drinks they'd ordered and placed them on the table. Poppy undid the cloth which held the scones.

'Thanks Rosie,' she said with a smile. 'Ooh they're still warm,' she exclaimed.

'You're welcome and yes, they're fresh out of the oven. Enjoy,' she beamed and made her way back to the counter, collecting dirty dishes as she went.

'So now we finally have a chance to talk, how's things?' Poppy put a scone on each of their plates and Gabe began cutting his and spreading the cream and jam.

'Well, you know I said I might have something to tell you,' he said, taking a huge bite from the scone.

'Yes,' she said, licking her finger after spreading her toppings a little more delicately than he had.

'Well, Berry Bright from Midnight Moon productions has been in touch.'

'Oh yes, what did she say?'

'She gave me a couple of suggestions about *Three Wishes* which were really quite good, so I've been tweaking the script and she definitely wants to put on the show for Christmas.'

'That's amazing,' she spluttered, spraying most of the table with scone crumbs. 'Oh sorry,' she said, wiping them away with her napkin.

'I know, I can't quite believe it's happening to me, to be honest. She told me a bit more about the small theatre she now owns that used to belong to her dad, a famous producer called Bernard Bright. If you google all the famous actors, a lot of them started out at this tiny place. It's a lesser known theatre but hey, it's still freakin' New York.' He chomped on the rest of his scone.

'Almost Broadway.'

'Indeed, it's literally a few doors away.'

'That's not even the best bit,' he grinned, his dimples on show.

'How can you top that?' she laughed, losing herself in the sparkle of his eyes. Giant butterflies fluttered inside her, and she sensed her cheeks were burning. What on earth is wrong with me? she asked herself.

'They want me to play the genie and they want our cast to play for the first month or so. It means everyone will have to register in lieu of equity cards, but they'll help with all the details. I suggest you put one in too as you never know, you might get to be in the ensemble.'

'Well, I suppose I could, but I'd be terrified up there in front of all those people.'

'But you're performing in our show here?'

'I know, but this is Bramblewood; you're talking Broadway, that's scarier.'

'Almost Broadway,' he corrected, 'and I'm not gonna lie, I agree with you. It's terrifying.'

She nodded thoughtfully.

'But you'll be amazing, Gabe, it really is your time to shine,' said Poppy, her cheek bulging with scone. 'I'm so proud of you, you're an incredible person.' She grabbed his hand and squeezed it. He squeezed back and stroked her hand with his thumb.

'Thanks, it really is a dream come true.' His eyes looked deeply into hers. 'There's more. You know Berry said she wanted to show her producer friend my other script? Well, his name is Nathan and we met on Zoom.'

Gabe looked like he would explode if he didn't get this news out and Poppy felt her eyes widening in anticipation. 'Here's the best bit. He only wants to put *Latino* on to run simultaneously with *Three Wishes*.' Poppy clapped and hugged him across the table.

Rosie came over. 'Sounds like you've had some good news.'

'He's had some unbelievably good news, Rosie – do you have any champagne? We need to celebrate right now. Our gorgeous Gabe here has got not one but two shows going to almost Broadway.'

'What, in New York, you mean?' asked Rosie, her voice raised a pitch or two.

Gabe nodded.

'Well, congratulations, Gabe,' said Rosie. 'I haven't got a licence to sell champagne but I do have a bottle chilling in my fridge so we can have a private celebration.'

'Oh no, thanks, Rosie, but you don't have to go to any trouble,' said Gabe.

'It's no trouble for one of my oldest friends who is on his way to New York with two fantastic shows. Hold on a minute.' She hurried off to the back of the boat and returned with the bottle of bubbly and three glasses. She popped the bottle, keeping the cork safe in a tea towel and filled the glasses. 'Poppy, can you do the toast as you know more about it than me.'

Poppy raised her glass. 'Our gorgeous Gabe, what can I say? I'm so proud of you for getting this far. Not only are you a fantastic performer but you are an amazing writer too. Congratulations on your fantastic shows being picked up by New York and not only that, but you will be starring in one of them as well. To Gabe and almost Broadway.'

'To Gabe and almost Broadway,' repeated Rosie. She took a sip of her drink, pulled a chair up to the table and joined them. 'So Gabe, tell me all about it.'

Gabe explained as Rosie listened, her eyes wide with amazement.

'Sounds like we need to toast Poppy too for sending them in,' said Rosie.

'To Poppy,' said Gabe, raising his glass. 'I'm so glad you did.' He winked at Poppy and continued. 'Midnight Moon and this particular theatre are renowned for a fast delivery. They wouldn't normally have taken *Latino* off the back of another submission but apparently Berry was bored on a long flight and so gave it a go. She read it in one sitting and sent it to her producer friend Nathan O'Brien. I met with him on Zoom and he loves it. He asked if I had anyone in mind to play Salvatore, so I told him who I'd based the character on and he wants him to audition.'

'Oh really, who is it?' asked Poppy.

'Marco,' he said. 'He's the best dancer I've ever seen.'

'He is fantastic,' agreed Poppy.

'He's a dreamboat,' said Rosie. 'Anyway, congratulations again, Gabe, you've made my day with your good news.'

She stood up as a customer came in. 'Enjoy the rest of your champers.'

'Thanks, darling,' said Gabe, before turning back to Poppy. 'They're arranging the auditions as we speak.'

'That's so exciting. I'm so happy for you. Have you been doing any more writing?' Poppy asked.

'Yes, my crime thriller series that I could never quite pluck up the courage to write is now two episodes in and going really well. I'd love to see that as a TV show, so I've been working every spare minute on it. Thank you for the nudge though, it's just what I needed. Ever since I heard from Berry, it's like a creative tap has been turned on.'

'That's OK, I just knew you couldn't let that talent go to waste,' she beamed.

'I love how much you believe in me, thank you.'

'You're welcome and of course I believe in you though not everyone believes in genies, I must warn you.'

'I've got to say ...' He paused and studied her face.

'What?' she said self-consciously.

'Do you know, Poppy, you have undoubtedly come on leaps and bounds from when I first met you. You carry yourself with a certain confidence and are just smashing through your hopes and dreams or should I say wishes.' He laughed. 'I remember you hugging me so tightly and falling asleep on me. I mean it's not the best compliment I've ever had, but the way you've picked yourself up after such a crappy time and just got on with it and thrown yourself into everything has really shown me what it was that I needed to do.'

'I'm happy to help,' she said.

'If this almost Broadway show comes off then maybe I can begin to get over my ex and just maybe think about falling in love again one day.'

'Well, wouldn't that just be the perfect, happy ever after,' she replied.

'I'm serious, Pops, helping you to achieve your goals, sorry I mean making your wishes come true, has really helped me to focus on what was important to me. It has helped me to get back on track in fulfilling my ambitions— I mean wishes.'

'That's fine, I don't mind taking the credit for a breath-taking Broadway show or two,' she teased.

'Actually, it's Marco I have to thank for giving me the initial push for my *Three Wishes* script.' He drank the rest of his drink and continued, 'I hadn't written for ages, not since I was living with Chris years ago and first wrote it. I hadn't been that confident about my writing and after the split I kind of gave up for a while; I thought it was rubbish although Chris had always liked it and tried to encourage me to send it somewhere. Anyhow when Marco moved in, he found it stuffed down the back of the wardrobe in the spare room, crumpled and covered in dust. He was intrigued by it and started to read it in bed.' Gabe looked downward, shook his head and a small laugh escaped his mouth.

'I would hear him laughing in the middle of the night and would bang on the wall like a neighbour from hell telling him to shut the hell up. Anyway, you know what he's like, being a passionate Italian, he also cried at the sad parts.'

Poppy blushed at the thought that she did know he was a passionate Italian but not because of his crying.

'The next day he took it to a producer friend who was also a member of BADS, and he loved it and encouraged me to go for it, despite my reluctance. Now three years later we have managed to put it on for Christmas for the second year running. It seems that people are not getting bored with it at all, instead they're bringing their friends and loved ones to see it. It seems Chris was right, and audiences did fall in love with it.'

'Well, I certainly fell in love with it when I saw it, I thought it was an absolute hoot. Here's to New York.'

'New York,' he echoed and clinked his champagne glass against hers.

Chapter 17

Gabe's parents were visiting from their travels. Rosa and Stanley Sellers had decided to pop in and see their children before they went to their holiday home in the Caribbean. They were staying at Holly's house, but Gabe had invited them round to his for a little party and to meet his friends.

Holly and Franco struggled with a heavy pan as they walked up the path behind Luca, who was in his element with a grandparent on each hand swinging him along happily. Gabe greeted them all lovingly.

'Where's my handsome nephew?' asked Rosa.

'He sends his apologies, Mum, he had an audition so decided to pop home and see the family afterwards,' said Gabe.

'Oh, was it in Italy?' she replied.

'No, it was in Nice so only a couple of train stops to Ventimiglia. He was looking forward to it.'

'Ah, that's lovely, I'm sure my sis will be delighted to see her gorgeous boy again. Ah, was this the audition for your show?'

'Yes, it was, Mum. I popped over to watch them and I have to say he was by far the best but there were so many other brilliant dancers too.'

'Oh, I am just so proud of you, my boy,' she said, pinching his cheek before hugging him.

'Thanks Mum. I'm kind of proud of myself too.'

Poppy, Layla and Cassie arrived shortly after, armed with

chocolates and wine for their lovely host. The kitchen was chaotic as Holly and Rosa helped Gabe with the food preparation. He had kept it simple with a huge pan of chilli con carne with rice and peas in a separate serving dish. A whole tray of jacket potatoes, another of garlic bread and the pan from Holly's house, which was full to the brim with Rosa's own spicy chicken recipe, left little room on the worktops.

'We had bang bang chicken last time, but this is firework chicken, just how my mother used to make it. It'll blow your socks off,' she said to the girls with a smile that revealed beautiful deep dimples just like Gabe's.

'Ah I can really see where Gabe gets his smile from just by looking at you,' observed Poppy.

'Ah yes and Holly has my eyes. Gabe has his father's beautiful deep blue eyes,' she replied. Stanley walked in and indeed he did have the same eyes as Gabe's except his were a little more tired-looking with more crinkles down the sides.

Stanley and Rosa made quite a striking couple and they fitted Gabe's description of them perfectly. He was a very smartly dressed skinny white man with the sort of tan that showed he had spent lot of time in hot countries and indeed he had as he had travelled with the Navy in his younger years. Rosa was a beautiful voluptuous black woman with clear glowing skin. Her lips were coated with her favourite pink lipstick which, as she showed the girls, was also called Rosa.

Although in her sixties, her skin was completely wrinkle free, which she credited to Nivea. She wasn't overweight but was softly rounded. She wore a black dress with bright pink flowers on it which really matched her cheery disposition and her lipstick. Around her neck an oval locket hung from a long chain.

'Oh, I love your locket,' said Poppy. 'It's like one that my nana had with two lovebirds embossed on the front but hers was silver, not gold.'

'Oh, thank you, it was a present from my beautiful babies when they were born. Well, what I mean is Stanley bought it for me when the babies were born. Here, look inside.' She pulled the locket apart with her nails and showed Poppy somewhat faded pictures of an adorable baby in each side, one with a blue blanket and one with a pink one. She then turned the locket over to reveal the engraving which said,' 'To our Mummy, Love Always Gabriel and Holly xx'.

'Oh, that's so sweet,' said Poppy. 'I feel terrible about my nana's one though. My grandad had it specially made with the lovebirds on it and engraved on the back with the words "To Peggy, my love, my heart, my life, always and for ever, your Danny Boy x".' As she spoke she held her hands to her heart.

'And there was a picture of them on their wedding day in it and one of me and my mum just when I was born. She had a chance to hold me for a few minutes before she was rushed off into the operating theatre and died.'

'Oh, I'm so sorry, my dear, that is so sad,' said Rosa kindly. Gabe had heard what Poppy had said as he had been pouring them drinks at the other end of the kitchen and gave Poppy a hug as he passed the drinks to her and his mum. Poppy rested her head on his chest, noticed how firm it was and didn't want to move. Gabe was her safe haven.

'So, what happened to the locket, poppet?' Rosa asked.

'Well, that's what I feel so awful about because when I was a teenager, my nana and grandad went away for the weekend and I stupidly had a party, which we all got completely drunk at. There was one older boy there who we didn't know but who everyone had assumed was someone else's friend. He was seen wandering around upstairs and although we managed to clean the whole place up before my nan and grandad came back, a couple of weeks later my nana noticed that the necklace was missing, and she was heartbroken. She thought she must have lost it, but I think that this horrible person had stolen it and I never wanted to confess because I didn't want to get into trouble. I have tormented myself with guilt this whole time.'

'Oh you poor thing, you must forgive yourself. You were so young and we all make mistakes. If I could tell you half of the things that Gabriel and Holly used to get up to when they were younger. One time they were playing rounders indoors and smashed a beautiful round glass bowl that my dad had had specially made for my mother on their wedding day, which they had passed down to me. I was broken-hearted but kids will be kids, we all do stupid things,' Rosa said as she gave her a squeeze. 'Now talking of stupid things, did Gabriel ever tell you about the time he took his goldfish to bed one night because he wanted to keep it warm and I had the joy of finding it in the sheets the next day?'

'Oh, Mum, don't remind me of poor little Jaws. I loved him with all my little five-year-old heart,' Gabe laughed.

'What about the time when you must have been dreaming that you were swimming around in a goldfish bowl and wee weed in the bed,' Rosa teased, laughing heartily.

'Right, I think that's enough wine for you, Mother,' Gabe mock scolded.

Poppy laughed along with them, feeling a little better after Rosa's advice. A few more guests had turned up by the time Poppy left the kitchen. She recognised a few of the guys from BADs and amongst them was Pixie. Rosa and Stanley greeted her very warmly with big hugs. They must have met before, thought Poppy. When Pixie had finished talking to Gabe's parents, Poppy joined her to say hello and to introduce her to Cassie, who was busy playing dinosaurs with Luca. Pixie kissed her hello and accepted the glass of Prosecco and a kiss on the cheek from Gabe. Pixie chatted a bit about *Dirty Dancing*, which was on the next week, the excitement in the air almost tangible at the very mention of the show. Pixie said she was a little worried that Alexia wasn't around to finalise her dance moves.

'Oh, isn't she well?' asked Poppy.

'Oh yes, she's fine, she's off gallivanting in Italy with Marco as they had auditions in Nice. At least Marco had booked his time off in advance.'

Poppy blushed slightly at this revelation although she didn't know why. She tried to shake off the memory of his kiss and shuddered involuntarily.

A look of panic flashed across Pixie's face.

'Oops I'm so sorry, I forgot you had a thing for Marco. Oh but you do know about him and Alexia, don't you? They have a can't live with them, can't live without them sort of thing going on.'

Poppy quickly composed herself, relieved that no one else knew about her kiss with Marco. 'Oh yes of course; no, there was never anything between us. I did initially think he was quite hot but we are friends now so it's more like a brother and sister relationship. He is good fun, but he does love himself.'

'Yes, he does,' agreed Pixie, 'and he does get a little jealous of his cousin too. He always wants what Gabe has.' As she said it, her eyes followed Gabe around the room woefully.

Poppy hated the fact that people knew she'd fancied Marco, it seemed so last year to her. She wondered if she should make a point of letting Gabe know that her crush was very firmly in the past, extinguished, kaput. As she contemplated, her phone pinged with a text. When she saw who it was from, her heart nearly pounded out of her chest and she read it quickly, at least a couple of times to make sure it said what she thought it did. She couldn't wait to tell Gabe and was relieved to find him in the living room setting up his keyboard. The gentle collaborations of Simon and Garfunkel had been playing when they arrived and according to Gabe it was now time for a singalong. Cassie had picked up Gabe's ukulele and was teaching Luca how to play it. He stared at her wide-eyed and laughed as she pulled funny faces when she hit a wrong note.

Poppy helped Gabe unravel the cable while he set up the stand and so she broached the subject with him. 'Guess what?'

'What is it, my little Poppydom?' he asked while looking distractedly at the stand to fix the keyboard to it.

'I think you have managed to make my wish come true.'

'Oh yeah, that's great, tell me more,' he said, whilst checking the sound as he pressed a couple of keys.

'Well, first of all, I'm fitter than I've ever been in my life after all the exercise you've put me through. Then after all these months of not hearing from Ed, he's literally just sent me a text actually apologising for what he's done and asking to see me.'

He looked up so quickly his elbow bashed against the keyboard, making an awful noise as the volume was turned right up.

'Erm, I've just realised that your first wish was technically two wishes, but aside from that, how do you feel about that? I thought you had gotten over him and moved on.'

'Well yes, I did get over him, but my wish was to get him back, so this is a good start surely. He did sound very sorry.'

'Oh well, that's OK then if he's sorry,' he said, his voice dripping with sarcasm. 'I still happen to think he's a shit for treating you like that, Poppy, you deserve so much better.'

'Well, yes, but I think I should still see what he has to say,' she muttered sulkily; this was not the reaction she had expected, and she felt nauseous.

'I thought your wish was for a decent, loving, loyal man, wasn't it? And to have the sort of relationship that your nana and grandad had.' Gabe spoke through gritted teeth. 'Well unless your grandad was a liar and a cheat then it looks like you got your wish, and after all it was my command, so congratulations, Poppy,' he said, failing to hide his annoyance. After all, what did her love life have to do with him? Apart from the fact that she was all he could think about lately, he had hoped that she wouldn't get serious with Marco as he knew she would only get hurt. He wished this Ed guy would just piss off, but then it didn't matter really because she would never be interested in Gabe anyway, not in that way. She had completely friendzoned him on the night they met and although he loved being her genie bear friend or GBF as she called him, he couldn't stop his pupils dilating like a junkie or his heart beating faster whenever he saw her or his mind going blank when she spoke to him. She occupied most of his thoughts, but he had to accept that although their friendship was like nothing he'd ever known before, her heart belonged to someone else.

Poppy's mouth was downturned, and she looked close to tears. He went to cuddle her, but she turned away from him.

'Why are you being so horrible?' she asked. 'Isn't everyone entitled to make a mistake?' He hadn't wanted to hurt her but couldn't hold back on his thoughts of that jerk.

'Look, you're right, I'm sorry, I just couldn't stand the thought of you getting hurt again.'

'I won't, I promise. He's only asking if he can meet with me to talk about everything. I can look after myself,' she sniffed. 'Please don't hate me, Gabe, I couldn't stand that;

you and Layla are my best friends, and I couldn't stand to lose you. But at the end of the day, Gabe, I need answers.'

'I completely understand, you've got unfinished business. Of course, I don't hate you. Quite the opposite in fact.'

'What, you love me?' she laughed.

'Well yes, I do as a matter of fact. I know you think I helped you when you were at a low ebb, but you've actually helped me too and I'm starting to feel that I might be ready to get out there again. Maybe I can find my one true love.'

'Oh, I really hope you do, Gabe, you deserve someone really special. And I love you too.' Her eyes met his and his emotions played a little tune on his heart. She turned to her phone and typed a reply to Ed.

Feeling the need to lighten the mood, Gabe did what he did best: hid his emotions with humour, this time behind a huge pair of joke glasses. He launched into a rendition of 'Crocodile Rock' by Elton John, accompanying himself far too loudly on the keyboard. It wasn't long before everyone was up dancing and singing along. After a few more Elton numbers, some of the other guys, Damon and Raf from BADS, took over the keyboard and ukulele. Layla and Pixie were the backing singers and hammered out the Beatles, Rod Stewart and Abba, real fun timeless party songs. Gabe swirled Poppy around and managed to get her to smile again by mouthing 'Are we OK?' to her. 'Always,' she said in reply. Franco and Holly danced with Luca and Cassie, Stanley and Rosa were jiving energetically, and everyone was having a blast.

'Right,' shouted Gabe loudly to be heard over the noise, 'who's ready to have the time of their life?'

'Me!' they all shouted.

'I can't hear you,' he shouted again even louder. 'Who's ready to have the time of their life?'

'We are!' everyone shouted as loudly as they could in unison.

'Well come on then, Damon, Raf, let's take it away. Pixie, you come to the front and show everyone the moves.' He beckoned Pixie over and she delightedly joined him as the boys started to play the fantastic song from *Dirty Dancing*.

'Hey, nobody puts Pixie in the corner,' he boomed, much to the amusement of everyone. The whole gang ended up in fits of giggles as they tried to emulate the steps that Pixie showed them. At the end everyone cheered as Gabe lifted Pixie, who was as light as a feather, into the famous lift from the show. The music finished and he gently put her back down.

'And it's a wrap!' he announced, the theatre folk laughing again.

By the end of a brilliant evening, Holly was finishing tidying up the kitchen with her mum, and Franco carried a sleeping Luca into the car. Poppy came to say goodbye and mentioned to Holly what a great night it had been and how good Pixie was at dancing.

'She's a lovely girl,' said Rosa, 'I just don't understand why they broke up; they seemed like such a lovely couple.'

'Oh, I didn't realise she had been seeing someone. Who did she break up with?' Poppy asked, puzzled.

'Why my Gabriel, of course, I really thought she was going to be the one to mend his broken heart, but it obviously wasn't to be. Although I'm sure I saw some sparks between them today. Anyway, it was lovely to meet you, Poppy, I do hope to see you again one day soon.' Rosa kissed Poppy on the cheek and went to say goodbye to the others.

Poppy felt bewildered and spoke to Holly, who was now putting her coat on.

'But Gabe is gay!'

Holly laughed. 'I'm sorry, what? What on earth would make you think that?'

Poppy felt foolish.

'Well when we met, I said I had given up men and he said so had he. He would never discuss his disastrous relationship with Chris, who I assume was a man, then he saved his name in my phone as GBF.'

Holly apologised for laughing.

'I'm so sorry for laughing but the truth is that Gabe was such a man whore when he was younger. He had so many girlfriends that he made Marco look like a monk. When he met Chris, he fell hook, line and sinker, but to cut a long story short, she broke his heart. After a little while he got closer to Pixie, but then *he* broke *her* heart as he just wasn't ready for another relationship. Then Pixie did something really stupid to console herself. Gabe felt so bad that he wanted to give her another chance until he found out what she did, and he couldn't forgive her.'

Poppy's imagination was running riot, trying to think firstly what Chris had done to Gabe, then what on earth Pixie had done to upset him further.

'But anyway, that's all water under the bridge,' Holly continued. 'But I'm now intrigued so do tell, what on earth is GBF?'

As she asked the last question, Gabe walked in behind Poppy and they both answered at the same time.

'Gay Best Friend,' said Poppy.

'Genie Bear Friend,' said Gabe.

'What?' they said simultaneously as they turned to face each other before erupting into giggles.

They were still laughing at this little misunderstanding after Holly had gone and they explained to Layla.

'Oh, Gabe, I'm so sorry. I feel terrible, because I was the

one who looked up GBF in the urban dictionary and it said Gay Best Friend. It was me who told Poppy what it was,' said Layla.

'I probably did joke about giving up men too, but the truth is I have given up on relationships full stop. I'm going to be honest as well: you are not the first person to be mistaken so I obviously give off a gay vibe,' he joked.

'I'm so sorry,' said Poppy truthfully.

'Don't be, I do camp it up a little in my genie role so I'm sure that doesn't help,' he laughed. 'And I can admire the beauty of a handsome man.'

'But ever since I used to watch *Sex in the City*, I've wanted a gay best friend,' Poppy joked.

'Hey, I'll be whatever you want me to be,' he laughed.

Poppy felt as though she'd been hit by a thunderbolt, her heart was pounding, and she couldn't figure out why. She'd always hoped that Gabe would meet someone and live happily ever after but now that his happy ever after would be a woman, she felt something she couldn't quite put her finger on. Would it affect their friendship? She felt confused. She'd kind of got used to being Gabe's number one woman but now that could be in jeopardy. A feeling of shame washed over her, and she scolded herself for being so goddamn selfish. Poor Gabe deserved happiness more than most people she knew, including herself, and she had no right whatsoever to be jealous.

Cassie joined them and asked Poppy if she was alright. Poppy nodded and forced a smile before they all said their goodbyes. Poppy felt a twinge in her stomach as she saw Pixie snuggled up to Gabe and laughing at whatever he was saying. She'd always believed that she didn't have a jealous bone in her body, but she was wrong.

Chapter 18

As soon as Poppy took over the theatre café, it became apparent that it needed a damn good clean, so she took a couple of days off from her day job and joined Layla for the endeavour. They wore old jeans and t-shirts and hired an industrial steam cleaner to do a thorough job. It took a whole day to go through everything and sort out the cupboards but at the end of the day they felt a huge sense of achievement. Cassie joined them in the afternoon as she had spent the morning preparing and delivering the sandwich round, which meant that Poppy didn't have to go into work on her day off.

Wandering round the kitchen admiring their handywork, Poppy noticed some screws in a wall panel, one of which was coming loose. Ever inquisitive, she grabbed a screwdriver and began unscrewing them.

'Wow, look what I've found over here.' Cassie and Layla joined her and helped to remove the panel. 'It's a window that looks like it's been boarded up for years.'

'Fascinating,' said Layla. 'Look, the wooden panels have been placed over the outside too, which is no doubt why it's gone unnoticed.'

'If we removed these then we could turn this window here into a serving hatch for takeaways as this leads out onto the high street. That would increase our customer base dramatically as people wouldn't have to traipse through the theatre just for a sandwich.'

Layla and Cassie surveyed the wooden window and nodded in agreement.

'That's a great idea. We would probably have to check with the council for permission but yes, I love it. It'll be fab.' Cassie brought the tea over and heated up a batch of Thai green curry she had cooked that morning.

'Oi, don't splash on my nice clean hob,' laughed Layla, who could barely keep her eyes open. Every muscle in Poppy's body ached but the kitchen was done and tomorrow they could deep-clean the seating area, which would hopefully be a little easier. Poppy should have been going to the dance rehearsal tonight but like the others, she needed a good night's sleep.

She decided to sneak off before anyone saw her and tried to drag her into the rehearsal room. They locked up the café area with the keys that Cath had seemed very relieved to hand over. There was still a separate bar area that was open but it belonged to the theatre and so wasn't part of their remit.

Poppy slept well that night and the next day they felt quite refreshed and eager to get the job finished. The tables and chairs were a bit tired-looking but they would do until the new ones arrived and they had to throw out the reusable sauce bottles as they weren't allowed in catering establishments anymore, but otherwise things were looking good.

In just one day they could start preparing food in their new headquarters. Layla had stayed to sort the sandwich round out and joined them for lunch. She gave each of them a sandwich bag filled with delicious duck wraps with plum sauce, shredded spring onion, cucumber and carrot.

'Oh, this is delish,' Poppy gushed. 'Food always tastes so

much better when someone else has prepared it, don't you think? This has definitely got to be added to the menu.' Cassie and Layla nodded their agreement, their mouths too full to utter anything audible.

When they had finished eating, they had their first official business meeting. Poppy started the proceeding by making a small announcement.

'Now, ladies, it's nothing huge but I just wanted to let you know that I am changing the name of Poppy's Posh Pannier to The Posh Pannier.'

'But why?' asked Layla.

'Because I couldn't have done this without you two guys and so it's only fair to make it a little less personal to me. I can live without a little narcissism, I think.'

'But you did this by yourself, Poppy, you deserve some recognition,' said Layla, ever supportive of her bestie.

'No really, I think I prefer not to have my name as I think it sounds more professional and contemporary.'

'I actually think it's a great idea from a marketing perspective,' agreed Cassie. 'It's clean, classy, fresh and very leading edge. I love it and the timing is perfect as I've managed to convince my lovely brother to create a web page for us. I've emailed him one of your current leaflets so he can work on the logo and stuff and then we can update the content ourselves.' She picked up her phone and began tapping in a message. 'I'll just email him the name change before I forget.'

'That's amazing, thank you,' said Poppy, 'How much will that cost?'

'Do you honestly think he would dream of charging his little sister?' she laughed. 'He owes me big time for all the scrapes I've managed to get him out of with the ladies over the years. And he's really grateful for the way you two helped me out when you really didn't need to, so thank you from him and from me as well.'

'Ah, it's been our pleasure and you have been worth more than all of our weight put together in gold, sweetie. You're adorable and we love you,' said Poppy, blowing her a big kiss, an action quickly repeated by Layla.

'Ah thank you honey, mwah mwah.'

'Anyway, I've been thinking of some promotional strategies that we can action. First and foremost, we have to let people know we are here and available for takeaways too and obviously deliveries within a certain radius.' She pulled a notebook out of her bag and opened it on a page stuffed with all sorts of pictures, cuttings and business cards. 'One of my brother's uni friends is a signwriter so he can paint us a new sign as soon as we have the OK to open the hatch outside.'

'I'm onto that, just waiting for the council to get back to me,' said Layla.

Cassie continued, 'OK, so Poppy managed to buy these gorgeous pink and white picnic baskets from the shop below the flat. They've got handles and guess what? The pink ones are heart-shaped. These would be great because the one on the bike is a lovely size, but we need more. Oh, and by the way, I decorated it with flowers, and it looks really good.'

'That's amazing,' said Poppy. 'I also propose we get some t-shirts and leaflets printed and go out on the high street giving out tasters. We could tie it in with events that are going on in the theatre too. We would also need some aprons, which shouldn't cost that much. Mr Ives from Odds'n'Sods is brilliant; he has a contact that can get us all the personalised things for a great price.'

'Fantastic,' said Cassie as she ticked off the items from her list and continued, 'I have started writing press releases that

I can send off to the local paper when we're ready. This will just be a soft launch and then by the time we take over the lease, we will have had to make a reasonable-sized investment and we can go hard. I've done a SWOT analysis to check out competition etc; if all goes well, I estimate that we'll be looking to take on some extra staff by then as well. Poppy's— I mean The Posh Pannier has proved really popular already in that one building so once we start hitting the others, this could be massive.' Cassie stopped to draw a breath.

'Wow, you've been working so hard, Cassie, you're like a little rocket. They are brilliant ideas, well done,' said Poppy. 'Oh, just one other thing,' she pulled out three copies of a table she had devised for the weekly order form and handed one each to Cassie and Layla, 'we have too much variety all the time, which is not proving to be efficient in the long term and is too fiddly for us to make all of the fillings every day. So, I've narrowed the choices down to just three or four per week, but the whole selection is available over the month. This will ensure that people don't get too overwhelmed with choices or that they don't get bored with the same things on offer every day, it just shakes things up a bit. Then we can buy in bulk, which will be more cost-effective. I also suggest accurate recipe cards to show exactly what and how much of each ingredient goes into each wrap or flatbread; these would also have photos of the finished products to show precisely how they are to be presented. That way when we need to hire extra help, we can be assured that the quality of our goods is never compromised. This goes for the cake selection too.'

Layla was impressed and showed her appreciation by clapping her hands excitedly. 'This is all looking brilliant. The BADS lot are all really excited at the thought of having healthy food here too. I've agreed to provide a selection of goodies on practice nights and there's a show on next week with real customers, so we should get some flatbreads in for that.'

As Poppy added to her notes, her phone pinged, which distracted her. Her heart pounded as she saw a message from Ed. Desperate to know what it said but not wanting to alert the girls as to who it was from, she turned it off, and hoped that the others hadn't noticed her blushing. She got back to her conversation, speaking a little more animatedly than before.

'Oh yes, come over here so I can show you something brilliant.' She led them into the kitchen and held her arms out to the new equipment. 'Ta dah! I've managed to source a second-hand panini maker and a traditional jacket potato oven. Gabe dropped them off earlier. They were so cheap. I got them from work as they were just getting rid of everything due to the canteen shutting down.'

'Oh, I love the glass panel around it so you can see the potatoes baking. Well done, Poppy, they're amazing,' said Cassie.

Poppy threw her arms around her friends' shoulders. 'It's all going to be amazing and maybe one day soon I can give up my crappy day job and work here full time. One thing's for sure though, I couldn't have done it without my angels. Thank you both.' She kissed each of them on the cheek.

'It's going to be a blast,' said Cassie.

Chapter 19

Upon Marco's return from his audition in Nice and a few days with his family in Italy, he stood on the stage and held everyone captive as he told the cast and Poppy about his adventure.

His eyes sparked as he recalled what had happened.

'Auditioning for the role of Salvatore in *Latino* has been the highlight of my entire life so far. It was the hardest thing I've ever had to prepare for; the dancing was fast and intense, the acting passionate and exciting. I needed to let the directors know that I was made for this role. I was Salvatore, and Salvatore was me. I could see the light go on in their eyes as they realised I was a new discovery, and my arrogance is what they need. When I got to the final dance— well, here, you can see for yourselves as they videoed it.' He held his phone out and everyone gathered round closer.

Poppy watched as he spun around as if in slow motion, his jet black hair flicking sweat out at every angle. He had given this audition everything he had. His passion came alive when he danced and was almost tangible as though it were a character in itself. She was proud of him, as were the rest of the cast, and joined in with the applause.

'I fought off some very tough competition and when I found myself down to the last three, I dropped to my knees and blessed myself with the sign of the cross. I shook hands with some of the best dancers in the world and there's no doubt they will play the bad guys in the film. That is if I get the part.'

'When will you find out if you've got it?' asked Poppy.

'In a couple of days,' he replied.

'I'm really proud of you, cuz, and if it was just up to me you could have the role straight away, so we'll have to see what the others think. But now you need to get your head back out of the clouds because *Dirty Dancing* is about to start in half an hour. Come on everybody, let's go.'

The show received a standing ovation; they couldn't have asked for a better performance. Poppy's nerves were frayed beforehand, but as she joined in with the dancing, they soon disappeared, adrenaline coursing through her body as she felt the throb of the music in her chest. She felt alive. Her feet went the wrong way a couple of times, but she had missed a couple of practices, so she forgave herself for that. Once her bit was over, she sneaked round to the back of the theatre to watch the show and couldn't resist dancing.

Gabe was on stage and could see some movement at the back of the audience. When he saw her, his heart did a little flip. She glowed with happiness. Her confidence had come on dramatically since he had first met her. He just hoped she didn't give this Ed a chance to bring her down again but only time would tell.

At the end of the show the applause brought the house down and as the curtains opened for the third time, Marco's agent appeared at the front of the stage and asked for everybody's attention, calling Marco over to him.

'Ladies and gentlemen, it gives me great pleasure to announce that our beloved Johnny here, AKA Marco Abruzzo, has been chosen to play the lead role of Salvatore in a brilliant production of the brand new musical called *Latino*.

Which, as many of you will know, was written by his amazingly talented cousin Gabe Sellers and will be performed in the Big Apple.' The audience and cast erupted. Marco held his hands to his head with a look of complete disbelief on his face. The cast were rushing to congratulate him. Gabe was so proud of his cousin and grabbed him in one of his legendary bear hugs, squeezing him tight. Marco returned the hug and kissed him on both cheeks.

'Thank you, Gabe, this is all down to you. Maybe Poppy is right: you are a real genie as you have helped make my wish come true too.'

Gabe punched him playfully on the arm as they were getting a bit soppy.

'I think it helped that you dance like the devil incarnate but if you want me to, I will take all the credit for it all,' he laughed. 'Although don't forget you were the one who encouraged me to put *Three Wishes* out there.'

The curtain had closed, so Gabe gathered up the troops.

'Come on everyone, it's a wrap, now let's go and party and celebrate my boy's tremendous news. To the pub!' he shouted, his arm outstretched and finger pointing in the direction of the exit.

Changing as quickly as possible, they all met up at the trendy wine bar, The Grape Escape, a couple of doors away.

Marco hugged Poppy and she congratulated him sincerely. They had a mutual understanding that there was nothing between them but friendship, which they both valued deeply. They'd had some great times with Gabe and Layla. Marco had to leave in a week's time and sort out accommodation in New York; she would miss him and Gabe would *really* miss him.

Layla and Cassie joined in the fun at the wine bar after

Poppy had texted the news to them. They, too, were really excited and Poppy had a brainwave.

'Layla, remember our pact that we were both going to be in New York next Christmas. Why don't we do it? Let's book our holiday now and then we can see Marco and Gabe in their shows. Cassie, what do you think?'

'Oh, I love that you invited me, girls,' Cassie replied, 'but I really am skint and besides, you'll need someone to take care of The Posh Pannier if you're both going to go.'

'She's right,' said Layla. 'Although nearer the time we might have someone else working there so why don't you play it by ear, Cass? We know you hate to commit to stuff anyway because you're such a free spirit so we could leave it that if you change your mind, you can join us.'

'You know me so well, ladies, but that's a brilliant plan. I know I'll be jealous if you're both gone and I'm stuck here.'

'Well, I'm in,' said Layla, clapping excitedly. 'Gabe, what do you think?'

'Are you kidding me? I think it's a brilliant idea. I would love you to come and see the shows. We can all spend Christmas together.'

'That would be amazing,' said Poppy. 'You've certainly managed to sprinkle Marco with that Big Apple magic dust. The trouble is they might think that you're too good and keep you there for ever.'

He nudged Poppy.

'Hey Poppy, do you remember how much you had the hots for him when you first saw him?' She squirmed with embarrassment and giggled. 'Yes, and you used to call him Mr Fancy Man,' he teased, laughing at her pink cheeks.

'Nooooo, stop, I was getting over a heartbreak; Marco was like a little plaster to cover it up for a while. But you were the one who put me back together again, Gabe, and it was your soul I fell in love with that night. You are the loveliest person I've ever met. I don't sleep with everyone on a first date you know.' Gabe laughed but deep inside, his heart fluttered. Pixie and Marco overheard the latter part of the conversation and almost choked on their drinks.

'What?' they yelled in unison. 'No, I don't mean that,' laughed Poppy. 'I was so drunk that I fell asleep on him in a bandstand singing Christmas carols.'

'Yes, and you thought I was your gay best friend,' he added chuckling.

'Well, you are my gay best friend, you just happen to be straight and hate shopping. We can't all be perfect,' she laughed. 'Anyway, I think I prefer you as my Genie Bear Friend; now that makes a lot more sense.'

'So that's decided then,' said Layla, getting back to the previous subject. 'We are going to New York for Christmas. Yay. Let's book it this weekend and Poppy, then you can shove that snow globe right up Britt the twit's arse.'

Poppy cheered. Gabe looked at Cassie and shook his head.

'Do you know what, Cassie, sometimes I think that these two lovelies talk in their very own language.'

152

Chapter 20

Poppy hated leaving home in the morning knowing that Cassie and Layla were able to sleep in for a bit longer. But, she reasoned, at least she didn't have to spend most of the night on her own making sandwiches anymore, thanks to all the help they were providing. As well as the sandwich rounds, The Posh Pannier was also catering for the finance meeting that afternoon.

Poppy's stomach had been flipping ever since she'd had a message from Ed asking her out in the evening as he was coming down from Liverpool for two days of meetings. He'd said he wanted to explain himself. She had taken extra care of her appearance today and wore a smart fitted dress patterned with swirls of turquoise, black and white. She always received compliments in this dress and felt fantastic in it. She wore opaque black tights and knee length leather boots, which she knew Ed had a thing for. Her hair was tied up in a neat ponytail, but she would shake it loose later when they went out.

She had a touch of glitter eyeshadow on just for the added bit of sparkle, and her eyeliner was sleek and black giving her a feline quality. Her full lips had a slick of nude gloss on them. She oozed confidence.

As she walked along the sterile corridor leading to the office, she heard footsteps behind her accompanied by a long, slow wolf whistle. She decided to ignore it but found it did make her swing her hips a touch sexier; she wanted Ed to see exactly what he had been missing. Her fingers began to shake with the anticipation of seeing him again after so long that she dropped her pen and bent down to pick it up. The footsteps quickened to catch up with her; she straightened herself up, smoothed down her dress and took a deep breath to prepare herself to face him. All of a sudden, she felt the familiar pull at her back as her bra strap was twanged painfully against her skin.

The bra she was wearing had an unusual fastening which immediately snapped open, freeing her boobs. Embarrassed she crossed her arms over her chest and spun round to come face to face with Burger Breath Brian.

'What the hell do you think you're doing?' she screeched in disgust.

'Oh, come on Poppy, you know you love it. Now how do you fancy coming into my office to take some dic?'

'You're disgusting,' she fired at him.

'Oh, come on, can't you take a joke? You know full well its short for dictation. Everyone else finds it funny except for Posh Poppy the sarnie girl. You need to get a sense of humour. And if you don't want people looking at those puppies then put them away for God's sake, you tease.'

Feeling upset and offended, Poppy knew there was no sense in arguing with him, so she stomped off and headed to the toilets. She had to literally strip off completely in order to refasten her bra strap only to discover that the bloody thing was completely broken and now totally useless. She stuffed it into her bag and hoped no one would notice. Then she had a brainwave: she could text Layla and Cassie and ask them to bring another bra when they brought the food up later.

When she was back at her desk, her phone pinged and she checked it to see a text from Gabe.

'*I'm not sure that one of mine will fit you??*' followed by a puzzled face emoji.

Poppy laughed out loud.

'*OMG! Sorry, that wasn't meant for you. U won't believe this, but Burger Breath Brian has buggered my bra, the bastard!*' she added an angry face emoji.

'*Well, that's a tongue twister if ever I heard one, I'll have to practise saying that but seriously Popsy, you might be better reporting that to HR. That's just not on.*'

'*He's just an idiot. I'll be fine, GBF, speak soon.*' She added emojis of a genie and a bear followed by one blowing a love heart kiss.

Poppy sent the text to the correct person this time and received a reply from Cassie saying no problem. When Tania brought some tea round later, she asked Poppy if she was alright. Poppy realised she felt quite violated and that she was a little shaken by it all. She explained what had happened, annoyed with her bottom lip for quivering involuntarily and her eyes for leaking somewhat.

'He is nothing short of a prick, that sorry excuse for a man. Poppy, if you want me to then I will go to HR with you so you can report this,' Tania said in support.

'Oh, I just don't know if I can be bothered with the hassle of it all. I mean he's a director isn't he, so he'll be protected. It's not worth it.'

'OK,' said Tania, 'but what I do think you should do is give me a written account of the whole incident and I will keep a record of it. We can take a picture of the damage to the bra as well. Then if he does or says anything like this again, we can note it down with the exact date and time. I could have a list as long as your arm with all of the offensive things he has said to me. So, do you promise me that you will do that?'

'I will, but only if you begin logging incidents too, Tania, you shouldn't have to put up with this.'

'You're absolutely right, Poppy, and I will. From now on I'll take no crap, just like you.'

She showed Tania the bra so she could photograph it and jotted down what had happened. Poppy laughed.

'Oh my God, people would think we are a right pair of weirdos taking a picture of a broken bra. Good job no one can see us.'

'At least it's all documented now,' replied Tania as she read through Poppy's account of what had happened. She tutted her disgust and added her opinion about how she found Poppy to be quite upset and shaken. They both dated and signed it and Tania filed it away.

Poppy finally managed to get on with some work and was distracted by various emails and tasks that she had to sort out and before she knew it, it was lunchtime. She popped to the kitchen to make a cup of tea and as she put the kettle on, her phone rang and Cassie's name appeared on the screen.

'Oh, thank God, Cassie, are you here? I can't let the girls hang free for much longer,' she laughed.

'Hi Poppy, I came in and out of the back stairs in order to lay out the lunch, but I just realised on my way out that I've left your bra in a bag at the bottom of the pannier. I was about to go back into the room but heard the managers coming in, I'm so sorry.'

'Don't worry, Cassie, thanks for bringing it. I'll go and sneak in and get it. See you later, bye.'

'Bye and good luck.'

As Poppy approached the meeting room, she could hear the murmur of lots of voices as the managers made their way back in for the lunch. Luckily, they hadn't sat down yet. Maybe she could run in and whip the pannier back out again before anyone could see what was inside.

She rushed over, excusing herself as she meandered through the crowd of about thirty managers who were milling about and talking about key issues and strategies and other business jargon. She saw the pannier across the room; it was one of the large new white ones. She made her way over to it discreetly and grabbed the handle. She immediately looked inside but could only see some folded napkins. She scrabbled them about a bit in the hope that the M&S bag that Cassie had said she'd put it in would miraculously appear.

She jumped as a familiar voice whispered in her ear, 'Is this what you are looking for?' She looked up straight into Ed's face, his twinkling grey eyes full of mischief. He held the M&S bag in one hand and her pretty racy, lacy, turquoise bra dangling from the other. She turned puce.

He laughed.

'Thank you,' she squeaked in a high-pitched voice and she snatched the offending article and ran back out to her desk. Tania had to laugh as she listened to what had happened.

'It could have been worse, it could have been one of your old beaten-up grey ones, now that would have been embarrassing,' she laughed.

Poor Poppy was mortified for the rest of the day but at least she wasn't jiggling all over the place now and had brought some order to her chest area by putting the bra on.

Just before five, her phone pinged in her bag and she rummaged through the contents to locate it. She swore that one of these days she would be like other more sensible women and have a beautifully organised bag with everything in its rightful place but until then she would have to constantly scrabble about amongst old bus and train tickets, wage slips, tissues and receipts. As soon as she found the phone, she realised it was a message from Ed.

'*You are looking so hot, baby. Can't wait to see you tonight. Btw I prefer the braless look.*' He ended it with a winking emoji.

She flushed again. He had some nerve sending that, but despite herself she couldn't help feeling a little excited and pleased. This is what she had wanted, wasn't it? Her wish was coming true. She was getting her Ed back. Obviously he had a lot of making up to do to her and he would have to prove himself over time but now he really wanted her.

She wished she could share the news with Gabe and Layla, but she knew they would disapprove and whilst that hurt, she couldn't just switch off her feelings for Ed.

After work, Poppy was in the ladies trying to control her hair, which was now loose around her shoulders. She added a little more make-up, a more sparkly lipstick, heavier mascara and a spritz of a sultrier perfume, then took a deep breath and headed for the door before realising she needed another nervous wee. As she hovered over the loo, she heard another text come in. She finished up, washed her hands with the cheap company soap and checked her phone. It was Ed again.

'*Can you meet me at the Ruthkin Hotel in ten minutes, as I had to go on ahead with one of the bores from the meeting.*'

Oh, damn! Poppy had hoped to walk out with him in front of the Britch.

She arrived at the hotel and saw Ed sitting at the bar waiting eagerly for her, her heart fluttering just as it had when she first met him. He approached her and kissed her cheek softly, his slight stubble scraping her skin a little.

'You look so beautiful,' he whispered.

Despite enjoying the familiarity of his hot breath tickling her ear, she pulled herself away from him and put her hands up on his chest as he looked like he was about to zoom in on her again.

'Look, Ed,' she warned, 'I said that I would meet you but that doesn't mean that we are back together. You really hurt me. I don't know if I can ever trust you again, or anyone for that matter.'

'Please come and sit down,' he said, leading her to some comfortable chairs in the lounge area. He ordered a bottle of Sancerre to be brought over. It was his favourite and a little too heavy for Poppy, but she had some anyway.

'Poppy, I can never ever let you know how truly sorry I am for all the hurt I've caused you. I guess I just panicked. You had moved all that way to start a new life with me but when the other offer came up, I couldn't refuse. A director-ship is what I've been working all my life for, you know that. I felt horrible for what I did to you. I did try and arrange for your job to move back but it was all too late. I'm so sorry. I would do anything to make it up to you.' He spoke quickly and finished with a loud sigh.

'What about Randy Mandy?' she asked, tears springing to her eyes at the thought of Ed sleeping with her.

'Poppy, I really want to be very honest with you. I've been a total idiot for the way I've handled this whole thing, but I don't want to upset you anymore. Are you sure you want me to tell you everything?'

Poppy sniffed and sat taller in her chair. 'Yes, I need to know the truth.'

He took a large gulp of his wine. 'OK, as long as you're sure. The thing is I found her crying in the office one night after I'd been working late. She was heartbroken and I felt sorry for her. Her boyfriend had finished with her, and she was devastated. I offered to get her a coffee, meaning from the vending machine, but she misunderstood and grabbed her coat, thinking I was taking her out for a coffee.' He tried to touch Poppy's fingers on the table, but she pulled away sharply so he didn't get any ideas. He continued; his brow furrowed. 'We went out and I soon realised that she had no intention of drinking coffee and was soon ordering champagne. I ended up telling her about you and how bad I felt about getting the new job and leaving you there on your own. I honestly felt like a total shit after what I'd done to you. She asked about what I was doing with the New York tickets, and I said I was wondering whether to ask you if you still wanted to go and then she told me that that was a terrible idea because you'd been seeing some guy. I'm not going to lie, and I know I deserved it, but it broke my heart, Poppy. I—'

Poppy gasped, 'Wait,' she interrupted, 'what guy? I haven't been seeing anyone. What's she talking about?'

'Poppy look, that doesn't matter anymore, it's all in the past. You don't have to make any excuses.' He averted his eyes.

'I'm not making excuses, Ed. I haven't been seeing anyone.'

'Well, she showed me photos of you and this guy dancing all romantic in one of those,' he gestured loosely with his hands, 'bandstand things and it looked like you were kissing.'

'You must be talking about the Christmas do and that would be Gabe, my friend, and we were certainly not kissing. We were dancing to keep warm actually.'

'Here, look, I've got the photo.' He showed her his phone and she could tell it had been taken from a car, probably a taxi, by one of the guests. It didn't take much for her to figure out which one. She had to admit it did look like they were kissing.

'Look, not that it should matter because I had every right to kiss someone else seeing as you'd dumped me. But we weren't kissing.'

'But you are seeing him?'

'No, I'm not. Well not in that way anyway, we're just friends.'

Ed's face broke into a beaming smile.

'Look, Poppy, I know it's none of my business what you get up to and with whom, but I am so happy to hear you say that because, well, she said she was told on good authority that you were seeing someone.'

'So, what happened next with you and her?'

'Are you sure you want to know? I mean it might be best if we draw a line under all that.'

Nausea shifted from Poppy's stomach to her throat.

'I need to know.'

'We kept on drinking, and she basically fed me a load of flannel. Told me I was gorgeous and that she'd be honoured to go to New York with me and well, it went on from there really.' She shot him a look that she hoped showed him exactly what she thought of him at that moment.

He bowed his head. 'I know what you're thinking but honestly I swear to God, I didn't mean for it to happen, and I know that's no excuse.'

'It did happen though, didn't it, Ed?'

He shifted uncomfortably in his seat. 'Yes, it did and there's nothing I regret more, especially now that you've told me you hadn't been seeing someone. I need you to forgive me, Poppy, I just want us to start again.'

She took a sip of her drink.

'It's important to me that you know I didn't cheat on you.

We weren't together when this happened and then going out with her became a habit really.'

'Did you know her friend Britt kindly got me a snow globe when she found out I was supposed to be going to New York with you and that you actually took Mandy?' she said matter-of-factly.

He looked forlorn.

'Oh Poppy, I'm so sorry for what I put you through, I can't believe I did that. The person that I was then seems so alien to me now. I think I hate him. I promise I am going to make up for it.'

Poppy tutted and rolled her eyes.

He pulled at his collar and swigged his wine, emptying the glass. The waiter came over to refill it. He waited until he'd gone again. 'I honestly tried to get you your job back, but it was too late, and I felt terrible. I couldn't tell you because I knew how upset you'd be. I couldn't see a way of the long distance working when I had to give everything to the job. I was going to ask you to wait for me and then I thought well that's just not fair. The point of me getting the directorship was to work for our future, mine and yours, that is. A life with you is all I ever wanted.' His eyes looked pleadingly into hers.

'But why didn't you tell me any of this? I could have got a different job and stayed up there, we could have been happy.'

'The reason why I didn't— couldn't tell you was because I'm a coward and I couldn't bear to see this look on your face when you found out. I thought it would be better to let you start a new life in Bramblewood. Especially as you'd got the job and the lovely flat, it would have been unfair to leave you jobless back up in Liverpool.'

'More like you wanted me out the way so you could get randy with Mandy.'

'It really wasn't that at all.' He closed his eyes and rubbed his face with his hands. 'I screwed up badly and got caught up in a situation that I wanted out of. I realise now that you are worth far more to me than any job and I really want and need you back. I knew I had broken your heart and I didn't know how to fix everything.' He looked into her eyes as he continued. 'Poppy, I love you and I've never stopped loving you. I just want to make you happy.'

'But what about her?' asked Poppy, determined not to let him off the hook.

'It's over with her, there was never anything substantial there anyway. I've been spending all my time working; I cracked a fantastic deal and now I'm reaping the rewards. I can afford for you to pack your job in if you want.'

He reached for her hand across the table and Poppy's heart picked itself up off the floor and soared through the ceiling.

She realised he'd carried on talking whilst she tried to process her thoughts.

'I'm sorry, what did you just say?'

'It didn't work out with her because I couldn't stop thinking of you. And when I thought of you and him, I was jealous, Poppy.'

Poppy's mind was a whirr of emotions blurred with the effects of drinking wine on an empty stomach.

'Poppy, the deal I'm working on will be career changing, life changing even. I just need a little more time. But I need you to give me another chance. This all means nothing without you.'

'My friends can't stand you.'

'I can't stand me either, Poppy, but this is the new me and you won't regret it, I promise. Now, can we order as I'm starving.'

She patted his hand and gave it a little squeeze. His body

language changed, his shoulders dropped with relief and a smile appeared on his face, chasing the frown away.

She couldn't help it, the love for him was still there along with her body's natural responses to his handsome face, his touch and his smell. All those feelings couldn't just be erased in a manner of minutes.

'You really hurt me, Ed, and although they're invisible to you, the pain you caused me left me with scars. But guess what, I've bounced back stronger, I've learned to live two hundred miles from home where I knew no one, and I've set up my own business, which I really don't think would have happened if we had stuck to the original plan. So, I can promise you that I'm not the same Poppy that you left behind and if you ever let me down again, it will be you that comes off worse. Just to be clear, we are not back together but I'm willing to talk and see how it goes.'

'I will make it up to you. I promise. I love you, Poppy.' He reached into his pocket and handed her an envelope. 'Open it,' he urged.

She opened it slowly as though something were about to jump out of it. Her hand flew to her mouth. 'Two tickets to Paris!'

'For tonight, what do you say?'

Chapter 21

Poppy's trip to Paris with Ed seemed a distant memory now. It was somewhere she'd always wanted to visit. They'd seen the sights and spent the evening outside a café drinking champagne and watching the Eiffel Tower light up with sparkles every hour. They'd agreed to put the past behind them as much as possible and whilst it was romantic and she couldn't quite believe he was by her side again, she felt there was something important missing. She had told him she wasn't ready to sleep with him yet and he'd accepted that one grand gesture wouldn't be enough to mend her heart, but he was trying and that was a start. They still had a long-distance relationship to deal with so Poppy's cure for that was to throw herself into work.

Cath's little run-down café was no more; the council had approved the hatch window out of the front, and Finn, Gabe's hot builder friend, had knocked it through for them. It now let in so much light. They had the signwriter come and paint the words 'The Posh Pannier', with a logo outline of a breadbasket with two French sticks, on the outside of the window. It was very tastefully done in gold lettering. The girls had all worked extremely hard and the marketing had been a great success.

Cassie had sent a press release to the local paper with a picture of the three girls wearing their new The Posh Pannier aprons, burgundy with gold embroidered letters and logo. Gabe had taken the picture of them as they posed outside the window, which they had decorated with a couple of pretty hanging baskets. Poppy stood holding the bike with all sorts of tasty goodies poking out of the pannier. Layla and Cassie were either side holding the pink and white baskets, also overflowing with goodies.

They had advertised a taster day, which was coming up soon, and were holding a competition to win a picnic pannier complete with everything a family of four would need to eat al fresco. The website was up and running, thanks to Jake, and Cassie was maintaining the content and managing all of the social media accounts she had set up. The orders were flooding in, so it was brilliant to have the theatre kitchen to work in. Their offer for the lease had been accepted so Layla and Poppy had invested cash into it. They were now bona fide businesswomen.

'You know, I think we need a separate name for the indoor part of the cafe as The Posh Pannier works for the takeaway and delivery service, but I don't think it's quite right for the theatre café, so we need to get our heads together for that,' said Poppy, leaning on her mop.

'Ooh yes, I see what you mean. I'll have a think. It's looking fab in here now, what a huge difference it's made by replacing that tatty old furniture with these bright citrus colours, it gives the whole place a clean fresh look. We did good,' said Cassie.

'We certainly did and our first lot of guinea pigs, AKA the cast, seem to love our new menu ideas. The jacket potatoes were extremely popular as was the chilli and Thai green chicken curry, but the most popular dish of all were the wraps. The choice of fillings we can offer is endless, from all-day breakfast wraps to Mexican chicken and rice wraps to

Chinese duck in plum sauce with shredded spring vegetables. Maybe we could call it Wrapper's Delight. Do you get it?'

Cassie laughed. 'Yes, that's a good one. What about something like Wrap 'n' Roll, you know like Rock 'n' Roll? Actually, don't worry, that's rubbish.'

'It's quite good actually.' Poppy dipped the mop in the bucket and twisted it.

Gabe had been filming for a school in the rehearsal room, which was opposite the café, and as some of the kids burst through the door, they heard Gabe's familiar booming voice shout out the words that he had become synonymous with, 'And it's a wrap. Well done, everybody.'

Poppy stopped mopping and shouted to the others.

'That's it, it's perfect!'

Layla saw Poppy looking animated so took her earphones out and shouted, 'What?'

'If I asked you to do an impression of Gabe then what would you say?' asked Poppy.

'Well that's easy, I'd say "Aaaand, it's a wrap..."' she boomed in as deep a voice as she could.

'Exactly,' said Poppy. 'It's the perfect name for this place.' They both cheered and clapped; Cassie loved it too. Gabe came walking past and Poppy threw her arms around him, desperate for one of his bear hugs. He squeezed her tightly.

'OK my little chicken pop, to what do I owe the pleasure?'

'You've only gone and done it again, you bloody genie genius, you've come up with the perfect new name for this place.'

'Erm, I have?' he queried, looking blankly at them.

'Yes, we are going to call it It's a Wrap. How perfect is that?'

'Do you know what,' he said, 'you're right, I am a bloody genie genius in generous jeans. There's another tongue twister for you.' As he said it, he pulled the waistband of his jeans out to show how loose they were. Poppy caught a glimpse of the smooth golden skin on his stomach as he did so. She had a sudden urge to touch it, then mentally slapped her hand and told herself off for having such impure thoughts.

Chapter 22

Layla and Poppy were snuggling down on the couch having a girls' night in whilst Cassie was out working. Poppy had been looking forward to it for ages as they'd been so busy lately. She'd stocked up on popcorn, sweets and hot chocolate. They'd each chosen a feel-good movie to watch. Poppy had chosen *Walking on Sunshine*, which always made her happy, and Layla chose *Sunshine on Leith*. Both sang along at the top of their voices, in Scottish accents for the latter.

'This just reminds me of our girlie nights in Liverpool,' said Layla affectionately between songs.

'Me too,' agreed Poppy, 'it makes my heart happy.'

'Ooh can you pause it, I just need a quick wee,' said Layla, untangling herself from her blankie.

'Oh, have one for me will you,' said Poppy. 'Actually I'll put the kettle on for more hot chocs.' As she rinsed out the cups, she heard Layla's phone ping on the worktop and automatically glanced at the message.

Hi L, I can't stop thinking about you, I'm going crazy here.

She couldn't see any more as it was on lock screen.

'You've got a message, Layla. Have you been breaking hearts again as someone is going crazy over you.'

'What?' said Layla, having changed into pink and white pyjamas, her blonde hair flopping from a ponytail on top of her head. She snatched her phone up from the counter and clutched it to her chest.

'Oh my God,' Poppy teased, 'you're really blushing now. 'Who is it?'

'No one you know, just someone I met before I came here. It ended before it began really.'

'Well, it must have been good because I've never seen your eyes light up like that before,' she laughed.

Layla picked up the mugs and gently bumped the side of her hip into Poppy's. 'You know me,' she said. 'One night with Layla just isn't enough.'

'Well, you've certainly left a trail of broken hearts behind in the past, that's for sure.' She looked down at the drinks. 'Hey, we've forgotten something.' She opened the fridge, took out the can of squirty cream and swirled a generous portion on each mug. She laughed when Layla stood there, mouth wide open and obliged with another squirt which caused Layla's cheeks to bulge comically.

They laughed and headed back to the couch to continue with their film, but Poppy wasn't fooled. She had known Layla long enough to sense that she was definitely interested in the sender of that message. She figured that Layla must have had her reasons for not telling her who it was.

Chapter 23

Poppy's heart fluttered when she saw the text from Gabe: 'Tonight we celebrate, Flamingo's Leg at 8.xx'. She had seen a missed call from him but when she rang back, she just got his answerphone message.

She missed her one on one time with Gabe. She saw him occasionally when she popped into Pixie's dance class when It's a Wrap wasn't too busy, and they still did their bike rides every Sunday but for the last few weeks Pixie had been joining them and it just didn't feel the same. Although she really liked Pixie, she considered saying she couldn't make it next time but realised that might come across as childish. There had been a bit of a wedge between her and Gabe anyway since she had told him about wanting to give Ed another try and he hadn't asked how her meeting with him had gone.

She appreciated his concern for her, but she was a grown woman and capable of looking after herself.

Poppy wasn't sure what the situation was with Gabe and Pixie, but she guessed they were seeing each other since the night of his party. She was definitely feeling some vibes from her, which made her feel a bit uncomfortable. Especially if Gabe joked with her or hugged her, but everyone knew that Gabe was a touchy feely person. He was lovely and whenever Poppy thought about him, she felt a comforting warm glow. He had a heart of gold and an amazing soul that shone through, like a bright light warming up the very cockles of her heart, whatever they were. It was a term her nana used a lot. There was certainly no hug in the world like a Gabe hug.

Ray and Beau were running around like rats in a maze trying to cope with this last minute table of twenty. Gabe had texted everyone from BADS to meet up as it was the first chance they'd had to meet up together to celebrate his fantastic news, what with various shows being on. One of the directors of BADS, Mr Foxwell, Gabe's old teacher, was also invited, and Gabe knew he would be immensely proud when he heard about the New York news. The invitation was extended to the It's a Wrap staff too. Cath was also there as she was still supplying her delicious cakes, along with finally enjoying some retirement time with her husband. She looked delighted to be involved. They were a team.

Pixie was the last one to arrive and looked gorgeous. She wore a short sequinned black dress, high heels and lots more make-up than usual; she looked stunning. Poppy noticed her eyes scan the room for Gabe when she walked in and her face lit up when she saw him about to open a bottle of champagne.

The cheers were deafening when Gabe finally managed to tell everyone his amazing news.

'So, first of all, I just wanted to gather you all here to say a huge thank you to each and every one of you for helping me get to the extraordinary situation I find myself in now. As some of you already know, Midnight Moon Productions have made me an offer and have commissioned *Three Wishes* for a three-month stint at the Random Theater on "almost" Broadway, it's unbelievable. I'll be working with Dean Moretz to tweak the screenplay slightly in order to suit an American audience, but I still maintain full control over it.' He put his hands up to silence the applause.

'And the best bit is they want me to play the genie so they can get a feel of how it's done. Everyone else is welcome to audition and Pixie, can you stand up please?' Pixie looked puzzled and a little self-conscious. Gabe played a drumroll by banging his hands on the table. 'Pixie, my darling, they want you to be fully involved in the choreography.' Pixie burst out crying, overwhelmed with excitement and joy. Gabe rushed over to her and squeezed her tightly.

Poppy felt a tug at her heart. She looked away and took a large swig of her wine.

'Poppy, Layla, I would just like to say that this Berry lady was also very impressed with It's a Wrap. She loved the concept, especially the bit about the locally sourced products, and said they could do with something like that so I'm going to work on her as soon as I can get my ass across that ocean. She loved Holly's elderflower water and even took a couple of bottles back with her as a gift.' The two girls smiled delightedly.

'So, what happens next with *Three Wishes*?' asked Poppy.

'Well, the lovely lady is going have a contract drawn up, which her lawyer will send to my lawyer. Ooh look at me with "my lawyer".' He laughed. 'What I mean is my brother-in-law Franco will look at it for me. The contract will run from the beginning of November to the end of January with a few weeks' rehearsal time at the beginning. This means that I can finally give up my day job, hurray! But don't worry, I won't give it up until my contract is signed, sealed and delivered.' He then burst into the signature song he wrote for *Three Wishes* and everybody joined in, including some of the other customers who had obviously seen the show.

Mr Foxwell was glowing with pride and as he left, he shook Gabe's hand.

'I'm proud of you, son, and I have a favour to ask of

you before you go gallivanting off across the pond. You see, my daughter is fostering a young lad who has not had the greatest start so I was wondering if you could maybe mentor him if I bring him along to BADS some time.'

'Of course, I'd love that. It'd be great to give something back, even if it is over Zoom from New York.'

'Thanks, Gabe, bye for now then.'

'Bye, Mr Foxwell.' No matter how many times Graeme Foxwell had asked Gabe to call him by his first name, Gabe just couldn't do it. Having had him as his history teacher for seven years, he could only ever call him Mr Foxwell. He liked showing respect to the older man.

The drinks flowed all night till 2 a.m. Gabe was legless, so Pixie ordered a taxi to get him home.

'He could kip at ours,' said Poppy, feeling protective of him. 'We're only round the corner.'

'Yes, I'm going to kip at Poppy's because she's my BFG. No, hold on, wait, she's my BFG, beautiful girl friend. No wait, I'm her GBF, Genie Bear Friend. Yes, yes, that's it,' he rambled.

'No, don't worry,' said Pixie. 'The taxi will be here in a minute.'

Cassie and Poppy kissed them and Ray and Beau goodbye and linked arms as they made their way around the corner. Layla had gone home earlier saying she was tired.

Poppy had ignored a couple of texts from Ed, she really wasn't in the mood. She couldn't stop thinking about Gabe and how much she would miss him when he was in New York. Why couldn't she have been a choreographer so that it would be her that got to go with him? She felt nauseous thinking of him and Pixie together but then what business was it of hers?

Chapter 24

Poppy had missed Layla and greeted her excitedly at the door. 'I swear if I was a dog, I'd be wagging my tail and bringing my favourite toy to see you,' she said, hugging her tightly after she'd put her bag down.

'I've only been gone a few days, but I did miss you too. Which is why ...' She rummaged in her bag. 'I got you a prezzie.'

Layla handed Poppy a little purple gift bag, decorated with a silver ribbon. 'You too, Cassie,' she said. Cassie was half asleep on the couch watching *Tipping Point* but her ears pricked up when she heard the word prezzie.

'You know you Liverpudlians are as bad as us Aussies for shortening words, aren't you?' she laughed, her face lighting up when Layla handed her an identical gift bag.

'And there's one for me too.' As if by magic, she produced a third identical bag.

'Layla, you didn't have to buy prezzies – you've only been gone a few nights ... even though it did feel like weeks. Anyway, how was it?' asked Poppy, tearing off the silver tissue paper which was wrapped around the gift.

'Oh, it was lovely, I feel thoroughly relaxed and spoilt,' she said. 'There was an amazing little gift shop nearby and as soon as I saw these, I knew we had to have them to celebrate our new standing as business women and what I believe is the completion of your second wish, Miss Poppy Kale.'

'Ah wow, it's lovely, thank you so much,' Poppy said, hugging Layla as she saw the exquisite little silver charm of a bicycle with a pannier on the front with a couple of tiny baguettes sticking out. 'This is amazing. Now all I need to do is work out how to leave the boring day job.'

Cassie hugged Layla too and immediately threaded her charm onto the chain she wore around her neck where it settled in nicely with the kangaroo charm from her best friend back home.

Layla fixed Poppy's one to the charm bracelet she had bought her for Christmas and asked Poppy to do the same for her as she had one her parents had bought many years before.

'One wish down; and two to go hey, Poppy?' she smiled.

'Well,' said Poppy. 'Technically it's almost two down if you count Ed wanting us to get back together.'

'Early days I suppose,' said Layla. 'Let's see how it all pans out. I mean I thought your wish was for a loyal wonderful man to love you.'

'It was, I mean it *is*. But you know how it is; I can't just switch off my feelings as much as I want to. He's been sending me texts and Spotify playlists of special songs from our time together.'

'Is that who they're from?' Layla asked, gesturing to a massive bouquet on the sideboard.

Poppy nodded. 'Aren't they gorgeous? I got these as well.' She reached for a large box of luxurious chocolates on the coffee table and offered them to Layla.

'They are pretty but still don't make up for what he's done to you,' Layla said whilst popping one in her mouth.

'I know and I'm trying to stay strong, but he said he was confused about me at the time and let's face it, Randy

Mandy is sex on legs. I think even I'd be swayed by her if she came on to me,' she laughed.

'Look, you're my best friend and I love you, so I'll support whatever decision you make.'

'Thank you, lovely, and thanks again for this. It's just the loveliest.'

Poppy held up her arm and jiggled her little Posh Pannier charm with delight.

Later, when Poppy was on the phone to Ed, she told him all about the charm bracelet, the three wishes and the new present from Layla. 'That sounds great,' he said. 'Anyway, I have found the perfect job for you. Remember the company who I'm doing the huge deal with?'

'Yeees,' she said, drawing the word out, surprised as to what he seemed to be suggesting.

'They're looking for an accounts assistant. I've put a good word in for you so they should be in touch soon. It's all I want, Poppy, for us to get back together again properly, and you to move back here.' Poppy was taken aback. It hadn't occurred to her that she would move back. Although she did love the place with all of her heart, she had made a home down here now in Bramblewood. She had been so busy with the business she supposed maybe that's why she hadn't given it any thought.

'Oh, I hadn't thought about moving back,' she admitted.

'Well of course you'll move back, Poppy, this is where my job is and you can set up your little sandwich round anywhere. That's the beauty of it, it's mobile. You do want a family one day, don't you?'

'Well yes of course, but I just hadn't thought about it. Let me have some time to ponder it.'

'You take all the time in the world as long as it's soon,' he joked.

Chapter 25

'Are you OK?' asked a concerned Layla.

Poppy awoke, tangled in the bedsheet, covered in a hot sweat and panting out of breath, and was startled to see Layla standing in the doorway of her room.

'Oh yes,' she answered. 'It was just a nightmare.'

'Thank God for that,' said Layla. 'I thought you were being attacked in here, you were screaming and shouting quite loudly. I'll go and make you a nice cup of tea. You've still got an hour before you need to get ready for work.'

Poppy threw herself back down into her comfy pillows. That was no nightmare; she had just had the most amazing mind-blowing, energetic, multi-orgasmic sex that she had ever had in her life. She was blushing just thinking about it. She'd been dressed like the genie out the programme 'I Dream of Jeanie', which was being rerun on the telly and the person that she had been dallying around with left, right and centre was the gorgeous Gabe. He had also been dressed in his genie costume. Her heart was racing, and she felt quite breathless; it had been so real and so unbelievably fantastic. 'Phew,' she thought. 'That was insane.'

Work was boring again; she would have to give her notice in soon as she couldn't stand it. Dan was leaving and moving on to a much better job so she was happy for him, but she would miss him as he and Tania were the only people making it bearable there. She decided to sneak off and have a chat with her bestie. He was fresh in her mind after the dream she'd had.

'Hello, Gabe's phone,' said Pixie. Poppy's heart sank.

'Oh, hi Pixie, is he there?' Poppy managed to squeak trying to keep her voice normal. 'Oh, I'm sorry, Poppy, he's in the shower, I'm just about to join him. Shall I get him to call you back?'

'Yes please,' she said resignedly.

'Will do, see you soon. Bye.' She hung up.

She didn't hear back from Gabe, but he was obviously too busy having sex to ring her back, she thought sadly.

Chapter 26

Next morning Poppy heard the doorbell ring and a few minutes later heard a kerfuffle coming from the lounge area.

'Hey Poppy!' Ed shouted, 'there are two hot girls in here stroking their pussies!'

'Oh, piss off, Ed, you idiot,' Layla shouted at him, throwing a well-aimed cushion at his head whilst simultaneously trying to stop Misty escaping from her arms.

Cassie's cat was afraid of nothing and sat purring on her lap.

Poppy joined them wearing her PJs and fluffy slippers.

'I'm sorry about him, please just ignore him, he's being stupid.' She gestured for him to shush by holding her finger to her lips. He winked at her.

'It's good to see you, Poppy,' he said, planting a kiss on her cheek.

'What are you doing here today? You said you were coming tomorrow.'

'Well, that's no way to greet me, Poppy. I travelled early because I couldn't wait to see you.' His voice was uncharacteristically flat. She realised she'd knocked the wind out of his sails. 'I'm sorry.' She gave him a gentle peck on his cheek, inhaling his aftershave, the smell of which took her back to happier times. 'It's just that it's Layla's birthday and we've got plans.'

'Oh, I see, I'm sorry. I'll get out of your hair but it's too early to check into the hotel. Do you mind if I have a quick kip and a shower? I left at four this morning.'

'Go on then,' said Poppy.

She got him some towels from the airing cupboard and had a quick tidy round her bedroom.

'I need to show you something.' He sat on the bed and pulled her towards him, so she was sitting on his knee. 'I've missed you so much, Poppy.' The dreamy look in his eyes and the warmth from his body sent shivers through her. He kissed her gently on the lips and she was taken aback by the strength of the tingling effect it had on her body. She kissed him back, softly at first, but the passion built gradually until she was lost in him, floating away. It took all of her strength to pull away from him. She'd dreamt of this moment for so long and it would be so easy to pick up exactly where they left off but now was not the time.

'I'm not ready, and at the moment I need to concentrate on my best friend's birthday, she's my priority today.'

'I understand,' he said, before squeezing her hand and laying down on the bed. No sooner had she gathered Layla's presents together than she heard his deep rhythmic breathing. She'd always envied his ability to fall asleep wherever and whenever he needed to. Right now, she was happy that he was on her bed and that they'd kissed.

She joined her friends in the living room.

'Sorry about that but happy birthday, beautiful Layla,' she said, handing her a gorgeous pink and silver gift bag overflowing with goodies.

Cassie reached down the side of the bed and pulled out a pretty gift bag with a butterfly print on it and pink-ribboned handles. Poppy went to the fridge and opened a bottle of champagne which she poured into three tall glasses. The sofa bed was soon strewn with torn tissue paper as Layla opened her presents. Cassie had bought her a new Bobbie Brown make-up set which she was delighted with and a mani/pedi voucher. Poppy's bag contained champagne, chocolates, a scented candle, a book and finally, presented in a pretty silver box, she unwrapped a beautiful silver heart-shaped necklace with the words 'All you need is love!' engraved on it. She was so touched by the heartfelt gestures and hugged both of her best friends.

Poppy heard the post being delivered and collected it from the doormat.

'There's one with a Liverpool postmark, maybe from your mum and dad?' Poppy said with a hopeful smile. She was still concerned that Layla's parents hadn't contacted her at all, and Layla really didn't want to discuss the issue for some reason.

'It's from my brother, Stu, with a twenty-pound book voucher. That's nice of him,' she said. The card was a funny one which made her smile, but Poppy could see that Layla looked disappointed.

'So, have you got everything you hoped for on your thirtieth birthday?'

'It's funny, but I always thought that I'd be happily married and pregnant by thirty as it always seemed quite old and way off in the distance but actually, I'm enjoying my life and looking forward to partying tonight.'

She placed her cards on the mantelpiece alongside Poppy and Cassie's.

Cassie made bacon and avocado bagels for their breakfast, which they enjoyed before she headed off to work.

'I suppose you want him to come tonight now.'

'No, not at all, not if you don't want him there because this is your birthday.' She jumped as she saw Ed appear in the doorway.

'I promise I'll be good, Layla, if you let me come to your

party and I also want to tell you, as the closest person in the world to Poppy, that I will love her for ever and will never hurt her again. I promise you that with all my heart.'

Layla wasn't the sort of person to beat about the bush and so let him have it.

'Yes, and I remember you making the exact same promise to Poppy's grandad and you couldn't manage to keep that one.'

Ed looked taken aback by her forthrightness. 'I know, and I'll never forgive myself for that but I've learnt my lesson, I swear. I put my own needs before hers and I'll never make that mistake again.'

'Layla, it's OK,' she said as she placed her hand on her protective friend's arm. 'No, it's not alright, Poppy, it really needs to be said.' She took Poppy's hand, squeezed it and held their joined hands up in front of Ed.

'I love this girl with all my heart, and she deserves so much better than what you've given her so far.'

'Believe me, all this has made me realise how much I really do love you, Poppy. You're the best thing that's ever happened to me and I'm so grateful that you're willing to give me another chance. Layla, I know you mean everything to her so it would be great to have your blessing.' He looked from one to the other.

'I hope you mean that, Ed, because if you ever hurt her again, I will find you and I will kill you.'

He laughed a little nervously. 'Liam Neeson would be so proud of you, but you have no worries there. The thing is, Layla, I just panicked and ended up digging myself a big hole and sinking further and further into it. I can't believe I nearly lost the most important person in my life and I'll never let her slip through my fingers like that again.' He gave a little involuntary shudder. 'You honestly couldn't punish me as much as I'm punishing myself.'

'It's OK, Layla, really, he knows that this is his last chance,' said Poppy. She turned to Ed.

'You really did hurt me badly, Ed, but I found out who my friends are, and Layla and Gabe and Cassie have all come through for me. Now off you go to the hotel as we have to get ready for our pamper day.'

'I won't let you down, any of you. I'll just go and get my stuff.'

The doorbell rang and Layla took delivery of the most beautiful bouquet of flowers. Pink and cream roses were artistically arranged with pink gerberas, lilies and lots of foliage, in a beautiful crystal vase. There was also an expensive-looking box of pink heart-shaped chocolates and a bottle of pink champagne.

'Ooh they're gorgeous, who are they from? Your parents, maybe,' suggested Poppy.

Layla flushed.

'Someone has an admirer, I see,' commented Ed, as he kissed Poppy goodbye. 'See you later, ladies.'

'Hey, wait, what's that?' Poppy was looking admiringly at the flowers when she noticed there was something shiny in the bouquet that the sun was reflecting off. She jumped up and pointed to a silver rose in the bouquet. 'Oh wow, that is unusual,' she said.

'Hold on a minute, it opens,' Layla discovered. She carefully opened the beautiful silver rose-shaped head to see the most exquisite pair of rose-shaped earrings in white gold, studded with delicate diamonds in the centre, nestling on a soft purple velvety background. Her hand flew to her mouth as she saw them, they were so her.

'Cor, he's got a few bob too, hasn't he?' said Ed on a

parting note after hanging around to see what was in the box. Poppy shushed him as she oohed and aahed when Layla put the earrings in.

After Ed had gone, Layla opened the card whilst Poppy made coffee.

Dearest Layla
Happy 30th Birthday
Love Always
S x x x

'Are you going to tell me who "S" is, Layla?'

'Oh, it's just someone I met and it's really early days at the moment, so I don't want to jinx it.'

Poppy could see how red she had gone and so didn't want to push it any further; she just hoped it was someone lovely who could make her happy. He certainly knew how to spoil her, and she deserved to be spoilt. Layla never had much luck with men. The ones she had ended up with had been liars or cheats or gamblers or just arseholes in general. A thought crossed her mind. Maybe he was married and that's why Layla was being so hush hush about it.

'OK, but I have just one question. When did you meet this secret admirer?'

Layla shrugged. 'OK, just one. It was in Liverpool in a nightclub just before Christmas. We stayed in touch.'

'So, when you went on that spa weekend the other week, was that with S too?'

Layla nodded, her cheeks crimson.

'Do you know I thought you looked bloody invigorated when you came back from there. Don't tell me, let me guess, I'll bet he's a six-foot, Scandinavian masseur called Sven,' Poppy teased.

Layla laughed at her friend.

After a relaxing day being thoroughly pampered and having face, nails and hair done, they headed out to the trendy restaurant/nightclub, The Sparkly Spanner.

The ground floor of the place was a glitzy restaurant with black marbled floors and tables and silver and black chairs. The walls were decked with black and silver stripy wallpaper and huge mirrors, and oversized crystal chandeliers added a final touch of sparkle. There were five floors in the club, each with a different theme.

Starting from the bottom, the themes were indie rock, then disco, then Anything Goes, which was a gay bar, then the ballroom, which was where the serious ballroom dancers liked to frequent. The top floor was a rooftop garden called Horizons, which had an amazing view of the city, complete with a huge bar and a couple of hot tubs for the more adventurous guest. The venue was impressive with a real buzzing vibe and as soon as they entered, they could see lots of their group already waiting at the bar. A lively DJ was playing but the music wasn't too loud so they could still hear themselves chatting, unlike all of the other floors where chatting was not a priority.

The group cheered as Layla walked in with her friends. She waved excitedly and thanked them, everyone kissing everyone else hello. Poppy caught Gabe's eye and his face broke out into a huge smile, as did hers. Her heart sank as she saw Pixie tighten her grip on his arm, pulling it around her, which meant that Gabe could only air kiss Poppy hello. He squeezed Pixie, then loosened his arm from around her. He took Layla by the hand and gave a birthday girl twirl, spinning her around in his strong muscular arms, then gave her a huge smacker on the cheek, tickling her with his bristles as he did so.

'Happy birthday, gorgeous.' She giggled a thank you back at him. Poppy looked on and couldn't help wishing that she had been the birthday girl. She managed to sidle over to Gabe to greet him properly; her cheek tingled for ages after he had kissed it.

'Is your phone broken?' she asked him.

'No, why?' he replied.

'Well it's just that I've rung you a couple of times and Pixie has said you would ring me back, but you never did.' Gabe looked blank. Pixie quickly arrived back on the scene.

'Oh, I'm so sorry, Poppy, I must have thought you said you would ring him back. The thing is we've been so busy, haven't we, Gabe, what with the move to New York.'

'I understand, it must be so exciting,' Poppy said.

'Yes, but I'll miss this lot though,' he replied.

'It's only for a few months though, you'll soon be back,' soothed Pixie.

'Don't forget, Layla and I will be there for Christmas too and that will be amazing. We can't wait,' said Poppy, noticing that Pixie didn't seem too thrilled with this news.

'Are we on for our bike ride tomorrow?' asked Gabe, 'I feel like I haven't seen you for ages. Sasha and Kelsey were asking about you the other day too. They wondered if you had any holiday jobs for their kids who are back from uni. I gave them your number so you can expect a call. Or come and see them tomorrow.'

'But Gabe, I told you I couldn't make the bike ride to-morrow,' interrupted Pixie.

'Yes, I know, so it would be nice if I could go with a friend,' he replied firmly.

Poppy was about to say she couldn't do it anyway but just then she felt arms around her and Ed's face loomed into view as he kissed her cheek and hugged her from behind, resting his chin on her shoulder. She felt ridiculous as if she had two heads.

'Hi, I'm Ed,' he introduced himself to Gabe. Gabe flashed him a dazzling white-toothed smile. At least that's what Poppy thought he did. Of course he may have been baring his teeth like a wild animal warning off a predator.

'Ah, Ed, I've heard such a lot about you,' said Gabe.

Ed replied, 'And you are? I'm sorry, I don't believe Poppy has mentioned you at all.'

'I'm the one who picked up your girlfriend and carefully put her broken heart back together again piece by fragile piece, you fucking cheating arsehole.' That was what Gabe would have liked to have said, after he had punched his lights out, but what he really said was, 'That's no problem, there's nothing very interesting to say about me.'

'Gabe is one of the most interesting people I've ever met,' said Poppy, shrugging Ed off her shoulder. 'He's been a wonderful friend to me.'

'Ah, that's nice. We all need a wonderful, interesting friend, don't we?' He emphasised the word 'friend'. 'Anyway, Dave, it was good to meet you and thanks for looking after Poppy for me after our unfortunate misunderstanding.' He tried to lead Poppy away from Gabe. Ed seemed to be feeling threatened. Gabe was glad as there had been an unmistakable spark between him and Poppy when they greeted each other.

'I didn't do it for you, FRED. Poppy is a lovely girl who knows I'm always here for her,' Gabe said through gritted teeth. What on earth was Poppy doing with this utter arsehole? He was almost relieved when Pixie came to drag him away as he wasn't a violent person, but this idiot was asking for a smack.

★

Layla was relishing being made a huge fuss of. After they had all finished eating, the lights went down, and the waiters brought over a cake covered in roses made from icing with thirty candles on it. They all sang happy birthday and then Gabe made a little speech saying how much Layla meant to them all and as it was a 'special' birthday, they had all clubbed together and got her a special present. She was so touched that she cried when she opened it to find two hundred pounds' worth of travel vouchers. 'That's so lovely of you all, thank you,' Layla said happily.

After dinner they had five floors of clubs to explore. Every dance floor was heaving with happy, sweaty clubbers having a good time. At one point Cassie grabbed Layla's hand and sneaked her off to Anything Goes. There was a huge mix of people wanting to have a good time. From scantily clad men and women to those who were more conservatively dressed to flamboyant drag queens, people were just people, and they were happy and accepting.

They moved upstairs to the ballroom where everyone else from their group had congregated and for the rest of the night, they had such good fun swapping partners for the chachacha, rumba and tango. They had professionals dressed just like the ones on the telly in sequins and frills who danced among the partygoers. Sometimes partnering up with them, sometimes dancing together, Gabe pulled Poppy to him for the tango and they were trying hard to copy the pros without laughing but ended up in fits of giggles. The close proximity of Gabe had a strange effect on Poppy. The only way she could describe it was that she felt like she was more alive, as though her blood was champagne, coursing through her body and bringing with it a new energy. All of a sudden, she remembered the dream she had about him and, blushing furiously, she started giggling.

'What, what?' he asked, laughing at her giggles. She was quite tipsy at this point.

'Oh my word, Gabe, I had the strangest dream about you. I can't tell you what happened but phew.' She fanned her face with her hand and shrieked with laughter. He joined in.

'Oh no, why can't I have dreams like that,' he joked. 'I just dream that all my teeth are falling out or I'm sitting on the toilet in a shop window with everyone looking at me.' They laughed again.

The champagne had flowed pretty much all evening and Poppy felt more than a little merry. She looked around to make sure no one could see them, and noticed that Pixie was dancing with the professional ballroom guy and Ed was sitting at the bar with his back to her talking to some other guys; Cassie and Damon, the sound guy from BADS, were laughing as they tried to perform a rumba. She grabbed Gabe's hand.

'Come with me, I want to look at the moon.' He followed her up to the rooftop bar where cubicles were separated with sheer voile curtains with fairy lights sewn into them, each one offering a view of the night sky. She weaved her way in and out until she saw an unoccupied one then she looked up delightedly at the full moon.

'Did you know it's a blue moon tonight?'

'Yes, I had heard something about that,' he replied.

'It's not really blue though, is it?' she whispered. 'Not like your eyes.' He could see the light of the moon glinting in her eyes, which looked a little sad.

'Are you OK, Poppy?' He suddenly felt her lips on his, the softness, the sweet taste of cosmopolitan. The sight of her thick dark lashes on her cheek as her eyes closed dreamily, the touch of her soft hands on either side of his face. He relaxed his lips to allow the tip of her tongue to touch his.

His hands held her waist. He softly moved them up and down, just a couple of inches each way to feel the delectable curve of her. She shivered with anticipation; he had never realised just how intimate a woman's waist was.

Gabe had never felt the sensation that was stirring up inside him before; the only way he could describe it was like the whole of his insides were waking up after a long sleep. As much as he wanted to continue – and boy, did he want to continue – he knew that Poppy was drunk, maybe even thought she was back in that dream that she had told him about, but this was all too complicated for him to deal with. He softly took her hands and slowly slid them away from his face. She pressed her mouth harder on his, parting her lips and inviting him in. He used every ounce of self-control he possessed to cup her face in both hands and gently break the kiss with a few little pecks on her lips.

'Poppy, darling, we can't do this.'

'Why not?' she asked, pouting childishly.

'Because, my darling, you've had far, far too much to drink and it's not fair on other people. Remember Fred, I mean Ed, and Pixie?'

'I don't want to remember them,' she sulked.

She tried to reach those wonderful soft full lips of his again. She was very sleepy now, but she wanted that kiss to carry on. He blocked her mouth by putting his finger up against her lips, and she kissed it gently.

'Look at me, Poppy.'

'I am,' she said.

'No, not at my lips, look at my eyes.' She was obviously trying hard and eventually managed to focus enough to look deep into his eyes. He held her face more firmly so she couldn't look away, forcing her eyes to stay locked on his. He almost melted as he saw her pupils dilate.

'Please, your eyes are beautiful, so blue,' she whispered.

'Not like this, Poppy, I don't want it to be like this. Your boyfriend is probably looking for you now.' It broke his heart to turn her down but that's the way he was. He wanted nothing more than to pick her up in his arms and carry her home, but he knew it wasn't his place. He laid her gently on the sofa in the cubicle, took her phone out of her bag as she slept and sent a text to Ed.

'Ed, I'm on the rooftop, sleepy, drunk. Come and get me. X' He added a smiley emoji with a tongue hanging out for authenticity.

He waited for a few minutes then saw the reply. *'OK I'm on my way.'*

He saw Ed enter the top floor so hid in the curtains where he couldn't see him but where Gabe could still see Poppy.

'There you are, Poppy. I've been looking all over for you.' Ed managed to help her get to her feet and out to their waiting taxi.

Gabe found an annoyed Pixie waiting down by the front door.

'Where've you been?' she scolded.

'I bumped into an old friend, sorry about that. I'm shattered, shall we go?'

Chapter 27

A few days later Poppy lay in a bubble bath and reflected on what had happened. Nobody had been fit for a bike ride the day after Layla's party due to their extreme hangovers. Poppy had spent most of the day with her head down the toilet, much to Ed's disappointment. He'd obviously expected more when he'd taken her back to his hotel. He eventually dropped her off home when they needed to check out and she went straight to bed so he went back to Liverpool, promising to come and see her again soon.

She was indebted to Cassie, who had been a dream as she had managed to arrange for Sasha and Kelsey's son and daughter to come in for some training. Cath had asked for a few regular hours after spending more time with her husband. She'd admitted that retirement had seemed like a good idea until she realised that he got on her nerves and she was better just seeing him in small doses. So they had a reliable bank of people to help out now, which meant the three of them could start enjoying some free time.

Their hard work was paying off, especially for corporate catering. They had visited most of the buildings along the road where Recharge Accountancy was situated. Delivering leaflets and free tasters had really worked. They had invested in two more bikes with panniers on the front. Maybe one day they would have a fleet of them. The new bikes were much more modern than Poppy's one, but she refused to use them as she had grown very attached to hers, especially as it connected her to Gabe.

She felt mortified about what had happened with him. In fact she was blushing just at the thought of it. She couldn't believe she had done it; she so didn't believe in cheating on people. Cringing, she ducked her head under the water as if it could wash her shame away along with her hair conditioner. She blamed that hot dream she'd had about Gabe, mixed with the champagne and cocktails. She ran her finger slowly across her mouth, still remembering the feel of his lips on hers. They were so soft, in sharp contrast to his spiky bristles. She remembered the frustration she had felt because he didn't kiss her back; she wanted him to crush her lips with his own and hold her tightly. The thought of the intimacy of his hand on the curve of her waist made her nerve endings tingle but he obviously didn't feel the same about her.

So many thoughts ran through her head. Why was she feeling like this? Did she feel like this with Ed? Did she just want something she couldn't have? She wished she could have talked her feelings over with Layla but then she was only just beginning to rationalise them herself.

Poppy thanked her lucky stars for her friends. Without Gabe, Layla and Cassie, she really wouldn't have been able to achieve all that she had so far. She looked at the sterling silver charm on her bracelet, the little bicycle with the pannier. It was so cute, and it meant such a lot to her. She loved the fact that Layla had bought all three of them one as it showed they were a team. Cassie fitted in really well with her and Layla and was a huge asset to the team. She was the sort of person who whirled in, got the job done, increased efficiency, showed everyone else how to whirl and then whirled out again. She had been amazing, but Poppy knew that Cassie was very much a free spirit and wouldn't be sticking around for much longer. However, she also knew they would all be friends for life. Cassie was awesome, there was no other word for her.

She then noticed the other charm that Ed had put on her bracelet. It was quite sweet really, a little cupid firing a bow with a heart on it. It was quite light compared to Layla's one and didn't seem to be stamped, but that didn't matter as it was the thought that counted. He'd admitted to her that his plan to present it to her was probably more romantic in his mind than how it had actually happened. He had been hoping for a picnic with a bottle of bubbly, but what she actually got was him telling her he loved her and attaching it to her bracelet, as she sat hunched on the floor next to the toilet.

He had brought up the subject of her moving back to Liverpool again when they spoke on the phone, but she absolutely loved her life in Bramblewood and she had commitments there now. Also, she hadn't yet decided whether she wanted to get back with him yet, despite him introducing himself as her boyfriend the other night. She turned on the hot tap as she had a lot more contemplating to do.

Chapter 28

Poppy's heart danced when she and Gabe found time to reinstate their bike rides. Neither of them had mentioned what had happened the night of Layla's birthday so Poppy was hoping that Gabe had forgotten about it. If he did mention it, she was going to pretend that she had no recollection of it, but she doubted he would.

Pixie seemed a little more relaxed about them seeing each other occasionally, probably because she had now met Ed and knew that Poppy's boyfriend wasn't imaginary; he was in fact very real. Although Poppy hadn't quite agreed with the boyfriend status, she hadn't corrected him when he'd introduced himself as such to the BADS crowd.

'Guess what?' said Poppy as they cycled along. 'The Posh Pannier has been nominated for the Bramblewood Business Awards, which is apparently run by the local newspaper and some established local businesses. We're up for Best New Business.'

'That's brilliant, Poppy, well done. You really deserve to win. I loved seeing the article in the paper with the three of you talking about your achievements.'

'Likewise with the one about you and *Three Wishes* going to almost Broadway. I thought it was fab.'

'I saw Kelsey and Sasha the other day and they asked for my autograph.' He laughed. 'What are we like, hey, two kids that done good,' he said in a New York accent.

'I can't believe that you'll soon be going to America, and you'll be gone for ages.'

'I know, I'm going to miss you and this; I doubt I'll have time for bike rides when I'm there.'

'Well, if you do, make sure you think of me when you're whizzing round Central Park.'

'I will do, I promise. Talking of whizzing, come on, it's freezing; I'll race you to the pub.' She screamed as she pedalled as fast as she could to try and keep up with him. She wanted things to get back to how they used to be with Gabe before he got annoyed about Ed. Gabe really didn't like him, and the feeling was obviously mutual judging by how Ed spoke to him.

After eating their meals at the pub, they sat in a corner with a red wine each.

'So have you been practising your lines, Mr Genie Man?'

'I haven't had a chance to yet, but I think I can just about remember them.'

Poppy got out her phone and pulled up the script. 'I'm going to help you then.'

'OK, you be the Fairy Godmother,' said Gabe, smiling.

Poppy found the lines she needed, and they worked their way through the play with Gabe only needing prompting once or twice. 'By Jove, I think he's got it.' She clapped and he pretended to bow.

'We've had some wonderful times, haven't we?' he said, putting his arm around her shoulder as they left the pub.

'Yes, and we'll have plenty more of them as soon as you get back.'

'Oh, I don't know though. Things change, don't they? I mean I might come back and find you've legged it back to Liverpool to get married or something and well, the thing is, I've kind of got used to having you around.' He gave her a little squeeze.

'Well, I've kind of got used to being around, and there's no chance of that happening. I've got responsibilities here now and friends and a life and you.'

She stopped walking and he wrapped his arms around her. She looked up into his eyes. 'You are right though, things do change. I mean, what if you become a famous producer or actor and end up moving to LA? I might never see you again.'

'Oi, I thought I was the one who wrote the fairy tales around here? There is no chance of any of that happening. I'll be back before you know it.' He leaned in to kiss her gently on the cheek. Poppy closed her eyes, worried that he could see straight into her soul, see how much she longed to kiss him properly but was fearful that he would reject her again. She swallowed; her throat felt dry.

She looked at his face. This man was an Adonis. The kiss melted away the cold and burned its way to her heart, which fluttered erratically. He winked at her, and a slow smile unfurled on his mouth; she felt it was just for her as though they shared a secret.

'I couldn't bear to lose you,' she said, 'you mean far too much to me for that.'

'That feeling is muche,' he said, as they unlocked their bikes.

'What's muche?' she asked, puzzled.

'You know, it's short for mutual.'

'Oh, I love it,' she laughed. 'I'm going to use that from now on.'

'No, you can't,' he replied. 'It's my word.'

'Well, you won't know if I do because you'll be away,' she teased. 'And anyway, you stole "love muffins" from me.'

'Ha,' he boomed, 'you're right, I did. OK, you can use it but only occasionally.'

'Yes!' she said, throwing her arms up. Their laughter filled the air as they rode home.

As they approached the trees near the pub, Poppy realised that they had gone through full circle since she had first moved here. The bare winter branches had given way to an abundance of pink blossoms like a candy floss coating covering the trees, petals dropping like confetti onto the heads of children playing below in the spring sunshine. Summer brought forth luscious leaves of emerald green before turning to shades of sienna and gold as autumn cast its spell.

Chapter 29

Poppy answered the phone as soon as she saw Gabe's number pop up. He didn't normally ring her when she was at work, so her heart beat a little quicker than usual.

'Hi Gabe,' she said as she continued to type an email with one hand.

'It's me, Layla.' Poppy could immediately hear the distress in her friend's voice.

'Are you OK, what's happened? Why are you on Gabe's phone?'

'It's my dad,' she managed to say through tears. 'My mum's just rung me to say he's had a stroke, he's in hospital and it's really serious. Gabe is taking me to Liverpool. I ran home first to get a few bits and I've left my phone there, but I didn't want you to worry.'

Poppy's heart was pounding, and tears filled her eyes. She knew how much this would be hurting Layla, especially as her parents hadn't been speaking to her.

'I'll jump on the next train up.'

'No, really, you don't have to do that, I'll be fine honestly. I'm meeting my mum and Stu at the hospital and just to let you know It's a Wrap is fine as everyone is helping out.'

'Oh, don't be worrying about that, you just get there safely. Oh, wait what about Sven? You're meant to be going away with him, aren't you?'

'Yes, but the fight hasn't landed yet, so I've sent a few texts explaining everything.'

'OK, well if there's anything you need me to do then please just let me know and if you want me there, I will drop everything and be on the next train.'

'I know you would, thanks, Poppy, but I'm fine for now.'

'OK, I hope everything is OK. Take care. I love you.'

'Love you too. Bye.'

Poppy couldn't concentrate so asked Tania to cover for her while she went home. She raced back and pulled down an overnight bag from above the wardrobe. She needed to be with Layla. As she sorted out her toiletries, she could hear Layla's ringtone coming from the other room. She raced to it but was too slow. She saw a missed call from 'S', called the number back and a woman with a foreign accent answered, 'Layla, my darling, how are you? How's your dad?'

'Oh hi, I'm Poppy, Layla's friend. Who is this please?'

'Hi, I'm Selina, I've just landed in England and seen all the messages. How is she?'

'She's still on her way to Liverpool, I'm just going to get the train to see her.'

'Would you like a lift? I'm about half an hour away from where you live. I'd like to be there for her too.'

'Yes, that would be great as long as you don't mind.'

'Not at all, I'm on my way.'

Poppy had just finished sorting everything out when she received the text from Selina to say she was here. She raced down the stairs and through Market Square to the high street where she had parked. Selina waved to her and Poppy got in the car and placed the two travel cups in the cup holder.

'Hi, I'm Poppy, I made you a coffee.'

'Thank you. It's nice to finally meet you but I wish it

hadn't been under these circumstances. Layla has told me so much about you.'

'Oh yes, we go way back. Poor Layla, she's supposed to be going away with her new man this weekend. She'll be devastated if anything happens to her dad as they had fallen out and I'm not sure why.' Poppy couldn't help noticing that Selina was looking a little shifty.

'Hey, wait a minute ... are you the mysterious S?'

Selina looked awkward as though she didn't know what to say for the best.

'Look, Layla wanted to tell you herself but yes, I am and think I can probably clear the other point up for you too,' answered Selina as she drove off.

'What other point?' asked Poppy.

'The reason why her parents aren't talking to her. It's because of me.'

'Oh no, that doesn't sound good. What happened?'

'Why don't I start at the beginning seeing as we have a long journey.'

'That sounds like a good idea,' said Poppy.

'We met at a club in Liverpool, I wasn't looking for anyone as I'd lost my girlfriend almost three years ago and we were very much in love.'

'I'm sorry to hear that,' answered Poppy. 'That you lost her, I mean, not that you were very much in love.'

'Thank you. I stayed in touch with her brother as he had agreed to be a donor for us at one point but that was obviously not meant to be. We both miss her so much. He pointed Layla out to me and when I saw her, I quite simply couldn't take my eyes off her and she said the same about me. She came back to my house and we kissed outside my front door; unfortunately her brother's friend saw us and filmed it on his phone to wind him up. When her brother was being told off by their parents for something, he showed the video to them in front of their friends.'

Poppy held her hands to her mouth. 'Oh no, I take it that didn't go down very well.'

'It didn't. Her dad kicked her out and her mum stood by and watched it happen. They wouldn't answer her calls or anything. She came to me for the night and that's when we … you know. I hadn't realised she'd never been with a woman before. We had such a special night and she managed to find a special place in my heart that I thought would lie dormant for ever. I had to go back to Spain just before Christmas and she came to visit you then moved in with a friend. We both accepted at the time that it was a lovely moment but because I was moving away, that was all it could ever be.' She paused. 'However, I couldn't stop thinking about her and we met up again when I came over. I'm hoping to get a transfer to London so we can be together.'

'It sounds like such a wonderful love story. I had no idea that she was a lesbian but then I've been so selfishly wrapped up in my own problems. I feel terrible. What sort of friend am I?'

'I don't think anyone can be as shocked as Layla is herself. I would say she's bisexual. It shouldn't really be me telling you all this, but she was going to tell you after this weekend because we've realised we are serious about each other. And as for what sort of friend you are, you're her best friend and she loves you.'

Poppy looked at Selina whilst she was driving. She was stunning, and she could completely see why Layla was drawn to her. The way her lips formed each word she said was mesmerising and her long dark hair bounced around her shoulders as she turned her head occasionally to look at Poppy as she spoke.

'I'm so happy for her to have found you. You seem so lovely, and she's definitely been glowing since she met you. I thought you were a six foot two Swede called Sven.' She laughed and Selina joined in.

'Yes, she told me you said that. I know how close you are and I promise you I will do everything I can to make her happy and to help her get through whatever she has to with her father.'

'Thank you,' said Poppy as she squeezed Selina's hand.

When they arrived at the hospital, they could see Layla and her mum and brother in the room with her dad laying in the bed connected to various machines. Gabe was sitting on the chair outside and greeted Poppy with a hug.

Layla looked at them through the window and her hand rushed to her chest as she saw who Poppy was with. Poppy could see the anguish in her eyes. 'It's OK,' she mouthed to her, 'everything's fine.' She blew her a kiss and Layla nodded. Poppy saw Selina say, 'I love you' and saw Layla's eyes light up as she replied, 'I love you too.'

Then Layla's body language seemed to change. She held her back straighter and she sat on the chair next to her dad and spoke to him. He eventually took hold of her hand and they could hear the monitor beeping a long monotonous tone. The nurses and doctors rushed in and Layla held on to her mum and brother as though they were life rafts in an ocean.

Eventually Layla came into the waiting room and joined them, her face void of colour. Poppy ran to her and embraced her tightly. Gabe enveloped both of them in one of his legendary bear hugs while they cried together. Poppy's tears were for Layla and her dad but also for her beloved nan and grandad and the mum she had never known. Being here evoked painful memories.

Selina hung back as though she felt superfluous and didn't want to get in the way. Poppy could see that Layla wanted to go to Selina, so she released her from her embrace.

'I see you two have met,' she said shyly.

Poppy replied in a gentle tone, 'Yes, we have. Layla, why didn't you tell me? We're best friends and you know you can tell me anything.'

'I was so scared. After Dad's reaction I couldn't bear the thought of losing you too. Poppy, you know you mean the world to me; I love you so much. The trouble is that the longer it went on, the more I worried that you would be annoyed so I ended up in a catch-22 situation.'

'I would never be annoyed at you, Layla; I love you and always will.'

Layla slowly walked over to Selina, who opened her arms widely, surrounding her with love. Layla looked at home in those arms.

'I'm sorry about your dad,' said Selina, as she stroked her hair.

'Thank you. Saying goodbye wasn't easy but I told him some home truths. He was upset because I didn't marry his friend's son, but on the couple of dates we went on, he mauled me like a piece of meat. He wasn't interested in my personality, my hopes or dreams; he was only interested in himself. When I was with him, I didn't feel good about myself. I asked him, "Would you really rather I ended up with someone like that? Somebody that would make you happy, and me miserable." And he shook his head, so I told him, "I have a beautiful girlfriend, I'm the happiest I've ever been in my entire life and I can't live a lie to keep a promise to you. I'm sorry if I've disappointed you. I love you, Dad."

I sobbed and went to leave the room, but he took my hand and said sorry and that he loved me.' Her shoulders shook and Selina hugged her tightly. Poppy and Gabe had heard everything, and he hugged Poppy a little bit tighter.

An ashen-faced Muriel, Layla's mother, and a sobbing Stu joined the group. Poppy and Gabe paid their respects, before Muriel extended her hand to Selina.

'Pleased to meet you although I wish it could have been under happier circumstances.'

Selina shook the older woman's hand and offered her sincerest condolences.

'I know how much Layla loves her dad and her family.'

Muriel nodded her thanks. She didn't look Selina in the eye but added, 'I'm so sorry for, you know.'

'Don't worry,' said Selina.

She had booked a hotel for the night and told Layla that she understood if she wanted to spend the night with her family. They agreed that they would spend the rest of the evening with her mum but would spend the night in the hotel.

Gabe drove Poppy back home to Bramblewood and she relished the alone time she spent with him.

'I feel as though Pixie hates me being near you; whenever I'm there she just grabs your arm and tries to pull you away. What's got into her?'

'Well, she thinks I'm in love with you,' said Gabe.

'What? That's ridiculous.' She burst out laughing and nudged him, expecting him to join in. He'd come to a standstill behind the other traffic so used the opportunity to look at her, but he still wasn't laughing.

'I've been really stupid, Poppy.'

'What do you mean? What have you done?'

'I really hurt Pixie before when we were a couple. I wasn't

over Chris and I should never have gone out with her, but I did. Then I finished with her and to spite me she went with Marco and I just couldn't go back to her after that. She was heartbroken. Then the night of my party we got closer, and it was just like old times. But she's moved into Marco's room temporarily whilst he's in America and now I feel I'm in a relationship I don't want to be in and I have feelings for someone else.'

'Who?' asked Poppy, and he looked searchingly into her eyes.

She felt her face burn. She couldn't believe she tried to kiss him on Layla's birthday when he had feelings for someone else but at least she now knew he didn't love Pixie.

'Oh, no one you know. So, what's the latest with you and Ed? Is he treating you any better yet?'

'Well he did buy me this charm after he saw the one that Layla got me. See?' She waved her wrist in front of him and the two charms jingled together. 'That's two of my wishes come true now thanks to you.'

'Is that cupid one meant to have bits of brown on it?' he asked.

'No, it's not,' she replied, trying to rub it. 'It did make my wrist go green the other day.'

Gabe tutted.

'Why are you tutting?' she asked.

'I didn't tut.'

'Yes, you did, you did a big huge tut like this.' She tutted as loud as she could.

'OK, maybe I did tut and I probably did an eye roll as well.'

'But why?'

'Because I wish I hadn't made that wish come true. The

guy is an arrogant arsehole. I just can't see what's in this relationship for you, Poppy. You deserve so much better.'

Tears sprang to Poppy's eyes. She knew that Gabe was talking a lot of sense. 'It's a long story, Gabe. He's apologised for that and I've promised him a second chance. He knows if he puts one foot wrong again then he is out.' She sniffed back her tears.

'Do you love him though, Poppy?' asked Gabe.

She couldn't answer.

Chapter 30

Since Gabe had moved to New York, he facetimed Poppy regularly and their conversations would often get pretty silly; Layla joined in sometimes too. Still grieving for her dad, her emotions were very up and down.

'Hey Poppy, Layla, I have a question.'

'What?' they both shouted; Layla was stood at the ironing board ironing their clothes.

'In the light of Layla's new announcement, does this mean I am officially not your gay best friend anymore,' he laughed.

'Oi, you cheeky sod!' Layla laughed as she threw a balled-up pair of socks at the computer screen. He saw the missile approaching and ducked out of the way, which made them both laugh hysterically.

'He's right though, Poppy, you finally got the gay best friend you always wanted,' Layla replied with much affection, 'although I'm not all that into shopping?' she laughed.

'I know it was very stereotypical of me but I get the best of both worlds as I guess you're both my GBFs now.'

'I'm happy with that,' said Gabe as he popped his head back up on the screen. 'So how is everyone over there?'

'All good, thank you; Cassie is enjoying house-sitting for you. She's relishing having more space. Also, some gossip for you. She got together with Scarlet from BADS, you know the girl who's in the band?' said Poppy.

'Oh yes, I know who you mean. Ah, good luck to them,' he replied.

'They look great together,' added Layla. 'It's good to see them so happy … So, how's things going over there? Is that the new loft apartment?'

'Yes, it is.' He moved his phone around the room so they could get a good look. They both oohed and aahed in all the right places. 'Marco did well to arrange for us to have a room in the massive loft apartment he shares with a couple of friends. It's only a couple of blocks away from Times Square. Marco has settled in really well and *Latino* is getting rave reviews.' Gabe picked up a magazine. 'Ah, here it is. "Sexy, passionate and full of life." Sounds just like Marco if you ask me,' he laughed.

Sounds very much like you, thought Poppy.

'Have you met the new cast yet?' asked Layla.

'We have and I'm so impressed with the energy they'll bring to the show. The lady who's playing the fairy god-mother will be working with me the most. She's a beautiful girl called Cindy, extremely talented and really making a name for herself having starred in a few shows on Broadway. The critics loved her.'

'I bet Pixie doesn't,' muttered Poppy under her breath.

'Sorry, didn't catch that,' said Gabe.

'Oh, the cat just scratched me. So are you happy Gabe?'

'I really am, the rehearsals are making me feel alive again. I love the adrenaline rush from dancing around on the stage, singing and generally being paid to enjoy myself. This is the life I've always dreamt of having. Actually, no strike that, this is the job I've always dreamt of having. My personal life, however, is not, but then we can't always get what we wish for can we? Anyway, must go, bye.'

'What did he mean by that?' asked Layla after his face disappeared from the screen.

'I'm not sure but I don't think Pixie is the one for him.'

'I always thought he had the hots for you,' said Layla as she put the ironing board away.

Poppy's stomach flipped.

Chapter 31

'I've got great news,' said Ed when Poppy answered the phone to him. 'I know how hard it is for you to leave everything you love down there so I've decided to move down finally to be with you. I've already uprooted you once so it's my turn now. The job I've accepted is not as good as the one I've been doing but I'm prepared to sacrifice that to be with you. Besides, the rent will be a bit cheaper between four of us, won't it?'

Poppy's heart felt like it had just dropped an anchor. 'Oh wow. Yes, I suppose that is great news, isn't it? What a surprise, I wasn't expecting that.'

She was very surprised, especially as she was planning on telling Ed that she wanted to just be single for a while. Her feelings for Gabe had escalated over time and although she knew he was spoken for, she also realised that there was so much more to life than what Ed had to offer. Even the charm he bought her was going a funny colour and kept making her wrist go green; it reminded her of their relationship.

Gabe made her heart pound and the blood race around her veins with a passion. He was gorgeous, sexy, hunky, intelligent, immensely talented and beautiful inside and out. She wished she had taken Layla's advice and gone for him instead of Marco when they first met, but the truth was, neither she nor Gabe had been ready for a relationship then and she was drunk and had just wanted rebound sex. Thank God she hadn't, as she would have regretted that so much. Marco was just a player and going with him would have destroyed any chance of ever getting together with Gabe.

She didn't quite know whether she could break it to Ed. After all he was making a huge sacrifice to move down to be with her and as they say, better late than never. She supposed she'd made her bed so she would have to lie on it … she just wished she didn't have to lie on it with him.

At Gabe and Pixie's leaving party, Poppy had been talking to Holly and Franco. They'd asked her about her day job and whether she would be leaving it any time soon. She explained how much she hated it and told them about Burger Breath Brian and his bra-twanging habits and that Tania was keeping a file in case they needed to put a complaint in against him.

'You should have put the complaint in because then HR would have a record of it but you're doing the right thing by keeping track of any incidents,' said Franco. 'I worked on a case where a woman was being sexually harassed and eventually left the place because she couldn't put up with it anymore. She had a very good case against this boss and some really good evidence, but she lost the case and it cost her fourteen thousand pounds in costs.' Poppy was shocked by that.

'The law really is an ass,' she said. Franco agreed with her.

'Even if you take out a grievance on someone, it ends up sapping all of your energy and does make some people physically ill with stress. Bullying and sexual harassment is despicable but sometimes it's just not bad enough, in the eyes of the law, to back up a complaint.'

She really didn't want to work there anymore so maybe this was the little pep talk she needed to encourage her to hand her notice in. She loved The Posh Pannier and It's a Wrap, along with the freedom of being her own boss. Old Burger Breath gave her such stupid piddly things to do, things that Britt couldn't be bothered to do because she was too busy giving him a seeing to and it was really unfair. She wanted to leave in a positive vein, not wait until she was driven out by idiots. She made a decision there and then. On Monday she was going to hand her notice in. Relief flooded her body, and she was floating on air by the time Monday came round.

'I can't believe you're finally leaving work,' said Layla over breakfast.

'I know, me neither, it's been a long time coming. Typical that it should be when Ed finally moves down so we could have been working together. By the way, did I tell you he's being put up in a hotel for the first week so I'm going to stay there with him so you and Selina will have the place to yourselves.' Poppy felt a warm glow inside as she saw Layla's whole face light up.

'Oh, that will be nice. Although if he starts acting like an idiot then you get right back here. I still don't trust him, Poppy, I'm sorry.'

'I know, but I've said I'll give him another chance and he's promised he'll make more of an effort. He's even taken a demotion so he can move here. Let's face it, this is what I originally wanted, it just so happens it was almost a year later than I originally planned.'

'Isn't there a saying, be careful what you wish for?' said Layla. 'But actually, when you think about it, it's been an amazing year for both of us.'

'Yes it has. I mean it started off really, really badly and I was a total wreck but then it improved a hundredfold; I've got amazing friends, a fantastic business, a fit and healthy body, my boyfriend back and—' she hesitated after seeing Layla's face, 'OK, don't look at me like that; I know he's still got to prove himself to be loyal but there's no way he'll go back on his promise to you, Layla, he's terrified of you. Maybe a handsome boyfriend? Yes, he's definitely handsome in an arrogant sort of way. But that's not a bad list of things to have going for you.' She checked her watch and gulped down her tea. 'Gotta go, see you later.'

Tania hugged Poppy when she told her she was leaving.

'I'm so pleased for you. It was such an honour for Dan and I to be your guinea pigs for The Posh Pannier and we are so proud of you. I can't believe first Dan left and now you – I'm going to be all alone.'

'Well if you want to come and work for us, you'll be very welcome, I promise.'

Time flew by whilst working the month's notice. Poppy had a huge smile on her face every day. She had never been happier and wished she had left months ago, although she couldn't have afforded to then.

On her last day she was busy tying up some loose ends with various emails when she sensed someone near her. The hairs on the back of her neck stood up in warning, like little meerkats who've just spotted a predator. Her computer screen showed the reflection of Burger Breath creeping up behind her, no doubt to twang her bra strap for one last time.

Before he got the chance, she forcefully pushed back in her wheeled office chair with all the strength she could muster and knocked the bastard flying. There was a loud crash, bang, wallop as he hit the floor in a heap and a deep grunt as all of the air was knocked out of him.

'Oh dear, Brian, I'm so sorry, I was just pushing my chair back to clear my desk, but you must have been very close to my chair. Did you want me for something?'

'No, don't worry, I just dropped my pen on the floor behind your chair,' he lied, spluttering as he tried to get up. Rubbing his head, he made his way over to his office. Britt chased after him to see if he was alright, offering him a tissue for his nose, which was bleeding. 'You've really hurt him,' she grunted on the way past.

Poppy looked at Tania and a few of the other ladies who had come into unpleasant contact with the creep and winked at them. She was greeted with fist pumps as they all tried not to laugh.

'Hopefully he won't try that again,' she said. 'I had an exit interview with HR this morning and I told them all about his pervy antics so hopefully all you ladies will be safe from him now.'

Her leaving do was in the pub a couple of doors away from the office. Even Britt came for a drink and said a pleasant goodbye. Poppy opened her leaving gift of a beautiful silver watch and one hundred dollars to spend in New York on her Christmas holiday.

'Thank you so much, everybody, that's so thoughtful of you,' she gushed, giving Tania an extra hug as she knew she would have chosen the gift.

She handed a small gift bag to Britt. 'I guess I won't be needing this anymore as I will soon be there to see the real thing.' She looked in the gift bag and saw the snow globe they had given her last Christmas.

Having the grace to blush, Britt apologised to her. She added, 'You must have been going through a terrible time and I made it worse. I'm not a horrible person really, it was meant to be a joke.'

'It just obviously wasn't very funny,' said Tania.

'I'm sorry,' said Britt, 'and I was wondering whether I could put my order in for The Posh Pannier for lunch from now on as I've been dying to try it.' Poppy delved into her bag and gave her a couple of order forms.

Leaving Recharge Accounting had given her a wonderful sense of freedom. She knew it was hard work and a lot of responsibility having her own business, but she was in charge of her own destiny now and that made her heart sing.

At two o'clock on Sunday morning she was woken by a loud shrill ring. She grabbed her phone and realised it was a facetime call from Layla who was in Spain for the weekend with Selina; they had been taking advantage of bargain flights.

She answered the call. Ed had looked around to see what the commotion was and then covered his head with the pillow when he realised it was girly chat.

Layla and Selina's faces came into view on the screen. Layla was crying, big fat tears rolling down her face, but she didn't look miserable. She was smiling a huge Cheshire cat cheesy grin.

'Poppy, I'm sorry it's late but I want you to be the first to know.'

'What is it? What's happened? Have you won the euro millions or something?'

'It's much better than that,' she replied excitedly. 'Selina has asked me to marry her.' Layla burst into tears again, so full of emotion.

'Ah, that's such lovely news, I'm so happy for you! But wait, what was the answer?' she teased.

'YES, yes, yes!' said Layla, kissing Selina all over her face.

'This calls for a celebration,' said Poppy. She got out of bed and went to the kitchen where she opened a bottle of Prosecco, poured herself a glass, took some strawberries out of the fridge to munch on and balancing the phone on the cruet set in the centre of the table, she pulled up a chair.

'Come on, then, tell me all about it. I want to know every single detail.'

The happy couple excitedly told her what had happened, sometimes both talking at the same time and giggling lots.

'Well apparently, Selina was going to propose the weekend when my dad passed away. She's since been waiting for the right opportunity, but something always seemed to go wrong. As it was, we were at a housewarming party, all of her family were there and so she just did it. She got down on one knee, told me how much she loved me, couldn't live without me and asked me to marry her.'

'Let me see the ring then.' She could see the delight on Layla's face as she held her beautiful heart-shaped diamond ring up to the camera. It took Poppy's breath away and tears sprang to her eyes, 'Oh Layla, it's amazing, I'm so, so happy for you both, congratulations, I love you.'

'Thank you, we love you too,' they both shouted. Poppy clinked her glass of fizz to the screen and they did too. Then they rang off. She drained the last mouthful from her glass then went back to bed. She suddenly felt an insatiable need for something. The true love she saw in the eyes of Selina and Layla showed her that something was seriously missing from her life. She knew that there was only one person in the world who had ever looked at her like that and sadly he wasn't lying in her bed waiting for her.

She woke Ed. 'We need to talk.'

Chapter 32

'I love a whirlwind romance,' whispered Cassie to Poppy as they walked down the aisle behind Layla, who was holding onto Gabe's arm.

'Me too,' whispered Poppy. 'I can't believe they've arranged it all in just a couple of weeks. I'm so pleased that Gabe managed to get special permission from the theatre to come to the wedding as he wouldn't have missed it for the world. Look at how proud he looks.'

'Yes, and Marco is a good sport for standing in for him. I suppose he knows the role off by heart.'

Selina stood at the top of the aisle with her father giving her away. She had walked up the aisle just before Layla, with her sister and her friend as bridesmaids and her little niece as a flower girl.

The two brides looked beautiful, both in white lace and silk dresses with fresh flower bouquets and headdresses. Layla's was made up of pale pink, cream and dusky pink roses, while Selina had chosen traditional Spanish flowers, and they each wore a traditional long Spanish lace veil. The contrast of Selina's long dark hair and Layla's natural blonde looked stunning, both styled in loose curls. It was such a beautiful sight, like a scene from *Midsummer Night's Dream*. The photos looked spectacular, especially those with the bridesmaids. Their sheer dresses were each in a shade of the flowers from their headdresses, and all of the bridesmaids wore their hair up with a flower in the side to contrast with their dress. The blend of colours worked beautifully.

The ceremony was a tearjerker; Layla and Selina had written their own vows and declared their love so openly, honestly and beautifully. Layla only cried a couple of times. The brides' mothers both wept tears of joy, Muriel confiding in Poppy that she also wept tears of sadness, not sure whether she was happy or sad that her husband was missing this. She knew he loved Layla, but she thought he would have found this hard to accept. She, on the other hand, wanted a happy daughter and this vision of loveliness before her was what she wanted; she couldn't believe she'd nearly lost her.

It was the prettiest wedding Poppy had ever seen. One of Selina's handsome cousins came to talk to her as soon as she was free from bridesmaid duties.

'Hello, I'm Antonio, and you are?'

'Hiya, I'm Poppy.' She smiled as he kissed her cheek and caught a glimpse of Gabe behind him. Gabe averted his eyes quickly and turned his attention to Pixie, who was calling him over to the reception area to prepare for the announcement.

Once everyone had managed to find their places, Gabe boomed out in his baritone voice. 'Ladies and gentlemen, can you please stand for our beautiful brides, Mrs Selina Rose-Belasco and Mrs Layla Rose-Belasco.' Selina and Layla walked in, hand in hand, with smiles from ear to ear. Everybody cheered and tapped spoons on their glasses to welcome the newlyweds in.

When it came time to throw the bouquet, some of the single girls realised that there was an increased chance of catching it due to the fact that there were two of them. Poppy caught the first one thrown by Selina, and Pixie caught Layla's. Giggling, they looked up and both looked at Gabe. He didn't seem to notice Pixie but by the look on her face she'd obviously noticed him looking straight back at Poppy.

Poppy broke the gaze as it was doing strange things to her insides; she could also feel the death stare coming from Pixie. She hid her burning cheeks by holding the flowers to her face and inhaling the fragrance, wishing for things she couldn't have.

The wedding venue, a beautiful Spanish country house which belonged to a friend of Selina's uncle, had enough bedrooms for all of their guests to stay in. It also had a chapel area for the ceremony and a huge ballroom for the entertainment in the evening, which in this case was a couple of live bands and a disco. A lively mariachi band entertained the guests too, which was lots of fun.

In the evening Gabe made a point of dancing with all of his special girls, which now included Selina as well. He saved Poppy till last and whirled her around the dance floor expertly. Her head rested on his chest and she could feel his heart beating at a steady rhythm, which quickened as he squeezed her tighter.

'You look and smell gorgeous. I'm getting a hint of strawberry shampoo and fresh roses.'

'Oh, thank you, you don't look so bad yourself.'

'Thank you. It's been such a busy day I can't believe this is the first chance I've had to speak to you.'

'I know, and I've missed you so much. So, how is my favourite genie? Is the show still going well?'

'I'm good thanks and it's brilliant,' he said. 'Standing ovations every night and the critics have gone wild about it. Things are looking great. The Hollywood guys are waiting to see how successful the run is before making a decision on a Christmas film.'

'Wow, Gabe, that's fantastic news! Well done, you, you deserve every bit of success and happiness you get. How does it feel to perform on almost Broadway?'

'Well, there is simply only one word that can describe that sensation and that is extraordinary!' he replied.

'Oh that reminds me that you still have one of my wishes to complete and that is for me to do something extraordinary, so you have your work cut out for you on that one,' she laughed.

'Well, you won that new business award and now have a nice trophy sitting on your counter in work – isn't that extraordinary enough for you?'

'No, it's not. It's fantastic but not extraordinary so you best get working on something good,' she teased.

As they laughed, he took a selfie of them with his phone.

'Just capturing another special moment with my little Popsidaisy before you fall asleep on me again.'

She laughed, feeling very cosy on his broad muscly chest.

'Falling asleep on you that time was one of the best moments of my life. I would love to be able to turn back time.'

'Why, what would you do differently?' he asked.

'Oh, now that would be telling,' she winked. 'But I would never in a million years have expected a chance encounter with a magical genie to have changed my life so much.'

'For the better, I hope,' he smiled.

'There is absolutely no doubt about that.' She stared deep into his eyes, which were filled with love and tenderness. He returned the gaze and pulled her into him. She closed her eyes and cuddled into his warmth, her special place.

'By the way, just so you know I need a refund on one of my wishes.'

Gabe held her at arm's length so he could see her. She noticed little frown lines appear on his forehead. 'What do you mean?'

'Ah, there you are,' Pixie's voice broke the spell. 'Come on, Gabe, our taxi's waiting.' Gabe released Poppy but not before kissing her on the top of her head. She said goodbye and watched them get swallowed up in the crowd. Every inch of Poppy that had touched Gabe now felt freezing as his warmth had been pulled away. She wished she had been brave enough to tell him how she felt about him.

Selina and Layla honeymooned in the villa which they had previously stayed in; Selina's father had presented it to them as a wedding gift. They would have to live apart for the time being until Selina could arrange her transfer to London. However, when Layla came home two weeks later to the miserable rainy English winter, she had a long heart to heart with Poppy to ask her if she would mind her going back to Spain.

'Well, I'm sure we can sort something out,' she said. 'How long for?'

Layla looked down nervously at her hands.

'Oh, I see, you want to go for good.'

Layla nodded. 'Not for good. Selina is still going to apply for a transfer as she would like to live in London for a bit. But leaving her was the hardest thing I've ever had to do, Poppy; we were both in a right state. I'll still keep my investment in the business but what do you think?'

Poppy threw her arms round her tightly.

'I want you to be happy, Layla, don't worry about anything else. You can be a silent partner in the business, or whatever you want to be. Now get yourself back to that beautiful wife of yours. I don't know how I'm going to cope without all my best mates around me. Thank God Cassie is just around the corner and comes on my bike rides with me. Now give my love to Selina, won't you?'

'I will, Poppy. She doesn't know anything about this, you know, she thinks the next time she sees me will be New York. So if she calls looking for me then just tell her I'm at work or something.'

Chapter 33

At last the time had come to go to New York. This was the first time she had ever flown alone so she was a little nervous. The Posh Pannier and It's a Wrap were in safe hands with Cassie and all of the new crew. Sasha and Kelsey had also offered to help out if they came unstuck. Cath was enjoying spending more time there as it wasn't her responsibility anymore, so she didn't have the stress to deal with.

She couldn't believe that in just eight hours she would be meeting Layla and Gabe again. She had facetimed and skyped Layla lots of times, but it would be lovely to see her in the flesh. She got the odd text from Gabe every now and then, which usually made her laugh and she was looking forward to one of his gorgeous bear hugs. Cassie had given her some post to take for Gabe and Pixie.

As the flight took off, Poppy turned on her Kindle to read Gabe's latest script for the crime series he had planned, as this was the first chance she'd had to read it. She could never sleep on the plane but managed to close her eyes for a little bit in between eating the weird food they served on aeroplanes. She'd hardly noticed the time as she was so engrossed in the script.

When she arrived at the airport, she laughed to see Layla and Selina holding a sign up saying Poppy Kale. They had arrived just a few hours before. They hugged and kissed each other hello. Layla looked even more beautiful than usual, tanned and gorgeous from the Spanish sun; she and Selina were such a stunning couple. They each grabbed Poppy's cases and led her out to find a taxi.

New York was just as she had pictured it, covered in a smattering of snow, although some parts had received a huge dump with three feet falling in just a few hours. Christmas trees were everywhere, covered in twinkling fairy lights and the place was buzzing. As the taxi made the journey to the hotel, she could hear the horns beeping practically non-stop. The three girls chatted excitedly, pointing out landmarks and catching up on gossip. Their hotel was in Park Avenue, which was much quieter and ideal for providing them with a good contrast when they wanted to get away from the hustle and bustle.

Poppy checked in and found her room was right next door to her friends'. The room was small but opulent, as was the rest of the hotel. The bathroom didn't have a bath in it as there was only room for a shower, toilet and sink, but the view from her window was straight onto Park Avenue. She quickly freshened up and knocked for the girls.

'Right, in order to tick off as many sights as possible, we might as well do Grand Central Station as it's just at the bottom of this avenue,' Layla suggested. They walked down the avenue past countless coffee shops with people looking out of the window watching the world go by, then past huge elaborate office buildings with groups of people standing outside chatting and stamping their feet to keep warm whilst having a smoke.

They entered Grand Central Station and stopped in shock when they saw two poster boards advertising the Random Theater. One was for *Latino* with a close-up of Marco looking damn sexy and the other advertised *Three Wishes* with a picture of Gabe as one hot-looking genie.

His arms were folded, which revealed all the contours of his muscles. He had a six-pack that made you want to run your hands and face up and down. He wore a black silk bejewelled waistcoat that matched the turban on his head. The blue of the stone in the turban emphasised his gorgeous sapphire eyes. They both had beards. Gabe's was a goatee, so his deep dimples were still visible as was his dazzling smile.

'Wow, Gabe is looking hot,' said Selina, pretending to fan herself. Layla explained that Marco was his cousin. They hadn't realised how alike they were until they saw these posters.

'They look like brothers in this except one is the devil and one is the angel,' Layla added. 'These Americans don't half know how to sex people up, they both look hot, hot, hot!'

Poppy could only manage, 'Wow!' Her heart and other parts were fluttering.

They posed for lots of photos with the posters, kissing them and generally being silly, then they texted them to Gabe for a laugh. He replied with a pic of him and the fairy godmother in full costume ready to go on stage, with the message, '*See you tomoz x*'

Poppy felt a little disappointed that she wouldn't see him until the next day, but he would no doubt be exhausted after the show and she guessed the cast and crew often had to talk through scenes and generally come down together after the hype of the show.

The three girls walked around Grand Central Station in complete awe of the complex architecture. It was lit up with a golden glow as it was getting dark outside. They looked at the fascinating three arched windows and were captivated as they changed colours from purple to red, green and blue.

'Ooh look, the Christmas light show,' they heard a woman telling her child. They marvelled at the steps they had seen in many films but mainly in *The Untouchables*, the famous scene where the pram goes bouncing down the stairs. They stopped for a cappuccino in one of the many delicious-smelling coffee shops in the dining court and simply watched the world go by.

After the short walk back to the hotel, they decided to try the Japanese restaurant in the hotel next door to theirs. The grand building had a huge Japanese flag hanging outside. Downstairs in the restaurant the waitresses wore authentic Japanese outfits, and the restaurant was sectioned into cubicles. The food was amazing, especially the pork tonkatsu. They tried a sip of sake, which they weren't too sure about, except Selina, who liked it quite a lot, not realising how strong it was. After their meal they were pretty exhausted and headed off back to their hotel.

'You do realise that it's four in the morning for us, don't you?' Poppy yawned. 'Let's get some sleep.'

She slept as soon as her head hit the pillow; she relished having such a big bed and lay in a star shape all night.

The next morning, they slept in quite late due to the blackout lining in the curtains. Poppy realised she had a few texts and missed calls from Gabe. She quickly texted Layla, *'It's gone eleven!'* before jumping in the shower and quickly brushing her teeth. She sent another message to say she'd be in the lobby and made her way down to the ground floor where she could help herself to some complimentary coffee and a pastry. As she bit into the delicious flaky cinnamon swirl, she heard the unmistakable boom of Gabe's voice.

'Step away from the pastry. Vacuum alert, lady with very messy pastry crumbs all around her face. Do not approach.' Poppy brushed the crumbs from around her mouth, cheeks and chin then used a napkin to wipe her greasy hands. She saw the three smiling faces of Gabe, Marco and Pixie. She ran over, straight into Gabe's arms. He swung her around kissing her on both cheeks and squeezed her hard, it felt so good. She then hugged and kissed Pixie and Marco. They helped themselves to coffees and sat in the luxurious leather armchairs and couches. They were soon joined by the newlyweds and Gabe embarrassed them by announcing their arrival into the lobby as he had done at their wedding reception.

'So, our lovely Layla is living in Spain now – how are you enjoying that?' he asked.

'Loving it,' she said joyfully. 'I never knew happiness like this existed.'

Marco was introduced to Selina. He took her hand and kissed it. 'Now I know why I could never melt the heart of the ice maiden Layla; how could I compete with such beauty?' he said in his sexy accent.

Selina pretended to swoon over him, which made everyone laugh. The happy couple joined them for coffee then they were off to see the sights.

They had lunch outside the Rockefeller tower, in the café overlooking the ice rink, jumping every time somebody crashed loudly into the barrier surrounding them. The frosty air mingled with the sound of Christmas songs being played. Skaters wrapped up in warm coats with bobble hats and Santa hats glided across the rink, their happy faces adding to the festive atmosphere. They couldn't resist having a go. Poppy hadn't skated since she was a teenager so was a bit like Bambi at first, legs splaying everywhere. Gabe and Marco held each of her hands until she was steady enough on her feet then Pixie dragged Gabe off to do some impressive moves.

'Don't you just hate it when some people are just so good at everything?' Poppy laughed. She loved that she had such gorgeous, talented friends. She looked at Marco; he was helping young ladies who were having a bit of difficulty. They obviously recognised him from the show because they were in awe of him and giggling.

She liked Marco. He was in his element here because let's face it, he just wasn't the settling down type, he simply wanted to have fun. This time last year she had had such a huge crush on him but it had been affected by the bad place she was in so she forgave herself for being so stupid. There were no hard feelings between them but probably because it had never gotten serious.

She could only imagine how Pixie must feel; she had slept with Marco when Gabe had finished with her, completely on the rebound, although they all seemed to be getting on OK now.

She was so pleased she hadn't slept with Marco as she was sure it would have affected her friendship with Gabe and she probably wouldn't have felt comfortable mixing with him today either. After the skating session they sat down in the café again and ordered massive hot chocolates topped with whipped cream and mini marshmallows with a huge chocolate flake sticking out of the top of it.

Even though she was wrapped up warm, the cold air had got to her and she felt chilled to the bone, so it was a wonderful feeling as the hot chocolate warmed her from within.

Gabe took a phone call as they stood up to go. It was the director of the show, Nathan O'Brien, saying that he would like to meet with him later that afternoon regarding an important matter. They would meet at five after rehearsals.

'Ooh I wonder what that's about,' said Pixie.

'Maybe Hollywood has snapped up your show and is making it into a film and they need four beautiful stunning girls to be in it,' Layla laughed as she grabbed the other three girls in her arms, and they all looked up at him, blinking flirtatiously.

'Ah Pixie, Poppy, Layla and Selina, I have a question to ask you. Do you know four beautiful stunning girls that I could use for my film?'

'Oi you,' they shouted, slapping him playfully. 'You know you can't handle this much gorgeousness,' added Layla.

They kissed each other goodbye and arranged to meet at seven at the Random Theater as they had tickets for *Latino* and were really excited about seeing Marco perform.

Poppy, Selina and Layla spent the afternoon traipsing the length and breadth of Fifth Avenue, which they loved. Laden with shopping bags, they headed back to the hotel for a quick nap before the show, setting their alarms before they did so as they would hate to sleep through it. Apparently these tickets were like gold dust and tickets for *Three Wishes* were also sold out.

Seven pm arrived and the girls pulled up outside in their taxi. They found Pixie in the foyer area but no sign of Gabe. An excitable buzz filled the air in the small theatre. Some people dressed in their finery and others casually in jeans and sweatshirts. Poppy, Layla and Selina turned several heads as they entered the building, dressed in full-on glam.

'Girls from Liverpool don't do casual,' Poppy explained to Pixie.

'You always look glam too, Pixie, and Selina is an honorary Scouser now as well as a Spanish bombshell,' Layla said.

'You have to make an effort for Broadway,' said Poppy.

Pixie laughed. 'Everybody is staring at you. I think they think you're celebrities.'

Gold-framed pictures adorned the red velvet-covered theatre walls. Most of the pictures were Berry's dad posing with various artists who had performed there over the last few decades, when they were lesser known of course. Berry had obviously carried on the tradition as the more recent ones were of her with various famous people, some they didn't recognise who would no doubt be stars of the future.

'Hey, look, isn't that your friend Marco?' observed Selina, pointing to a picture which had obviously not long been up there.

'Yes, it is,' Pixie laughed. 'And look, here's Gabe too.' She pointed to another picture. Poppy squealed and took a picture of it with her phone.

They headed to the bar to buy some drinks and to pre-order some for the interval. Pixie had tried ringing Gabe, but his phone was switched off. She left him a voice message then turned to Poppy.

'We're going to have to go in without him as the lights will go down in a minute,' she explained.

'Oh that's a shame, I suppose his meeting has gone on for longer than they expected. Let's hope they are working it into the contract so that we all get exciting parts and we can move to LA and be fabulous,' Poppy laughed.

They took their seats in the centre of the fifth row, the best seats in the house, Pixie told them. The first half was amazing and blew them away. All of the girls fell in love with Salvatore; he was amazing, loving, handsome, sexy and passionate. Poppy whispered to Pixie, 'If only Marco was like this in real life.' Pixie laughed and agreed.

The story evoked a whirlwind of emotions; by the time the interval arrived they had laughed, cried, become angry, happy and turned on. Poppy loved how the story unfolded and remained very true to the original script and the dancing was passionate and hot, hot, hot.

Sipping their interval drinks in the bar, the bell rang for the start of the next performance. They were given plastic glasses to tip their wine into and made their way back to their seats. As she sat down Poppy felt her phone vibrate in her bag. She checked the phone and realised she had a text from Gabe. Her brow furrowed with concern and she told the others she needed the toilet.

'Damn the timing of my bladder,' she said. 'I'll be back in a bit.'

It was dark now and she had to excuse herself many times to get past the other people sitting in the row, some were polite, but others tut tutted her. When she finally got outside, she read the text again, it simply said.

'*Poppy I need you! X*' Her heart was doing somersaults – what on earth could have happened, there's no way he would have missed seeing the show with them if it wasn't serious. She called him but got no answer, so she sent him a text.

'*Are you OK, where are you?*'

'*An Irish bar near your hotel. Come alone.*' A separate text followed with the address.

She went outside and hailed a taxi. Within ten minutes she was nervously walking through the doors of the bar, she had sent a message telling Layla she was back at the hotel with an upset stomach. Layla had offered to come back with her but she assured her she was fine.

She saw Gabe straight away when she walked in. His face was as familiar to her as her own was in the mirror, except normally his face was plastered with a smile and this was not a look she recognised. He was drained of all colour; she had never seen him look so pale. His hair was sticking out at funny angles where he had been dragging his hands through it, his blue eyes dulled and bloodshot and the skin around them puffy. He was sitting at a table in the corner with a half-drunk pint of Guinness in front of him and a whiskey chaser. There was a glass of rosé wine waiting for her too. She hurried over to him.

'Gabe, what is it? What's happened?' He looked up at her, his eyes brimming with tears. He put his head in his hands, elbows leaning against the table and he sobbed. He didn't make much noise, it was mostly silent, but his body wracked with the pain that was coursing through him. She put her arm around him tightly and managed to rest his head on her shoulder. He gripped her tightly and she kissed him gently on the top of his head, his soft jet black hair tickling her lips. He eventually managed to stop after she stroked his hair for a while but his grip around her was still so tight.

She handed him some napkins to blow his nose. She looked at him; her big, strong Gabe looked so childlike and fragile. She was desperate to know what had happened but didn't want to rush him. He drank the whiskey in one gulp, grimacing as the sharp tang hurt his throat. He then started on the Guinness while Poppy took a gulp of wine.

'Gabe, is it your family? Is everyone OK?' He answered the questions as she asked them by shaking his head then nodding in response. He went to talk but then the emotion hit him again and he went through the same process. She was patient, holding him tightly. So far no one except for a passing waitress had noticed as most of the customers were sitting up at the bar watching sports.

The waitress mouthed to her, 'Is he OK?' and Poppy nodded to her.

'Gabe, are you OK here, or do you want to go to my hotel?' He nodded and stood up quickly, downed the rest of the Guinness and threw some money onto the table to cover the drinks.

He held her hand tightly and they walked the couple of blocks to her hotel in silence. She opened the door to let him in and went to the fridge in the room which contained a few bottles of wine she had bought yesterday. She opened a rosé and poured each of them a glass. He downed his in one so she topped it up again. He went to do the same but she gently put her hand on his arm to stop him. She had never seen him like this before. He couldn't speak, and he looked like he was going to explode and maybe punch a hole in a wall or something. She didn't feel scared though as she knew he wouldn't ever harm her, or anyone for that matter.

She took a sip of her wine and he took a huge gulp of his. He had obviously had a few whiskeys as she could smell it on him.

He put his drink on the table and took hers out of her hand. He then cupped her face in his big strong hands and his mouth fell on hers with such passion, it hurt her lips. His tongue was in her mouth, and her hands reached around his neck to pull him even closer. He stroked up and down her body, pressing himself against her. She could feel his longing for her, hard and crushing against her body. Desire swept through her, leaving her weak to temptation. His hands cupped her breasts, making her gasp with pleasure. He kissed down her neck, lifted her top up and ran his fingers over her breasts so delicately he hardly touched her but the shockwaves she received from his almost-touch shot through her body, awakening every nerve-ending. His mouth reached back up to her mouth while his hand continued to caress her. He gasped into her mouth, 'I want you so much. I've wanted you from the very first moment I saw you.'

Poppy drew on every bit of self-control she possessed and she pulled away from him.

'Gabe, not like this. You were right. I don't want it to be like this. We have been cheated on in the past and we are not cheaters.'

'You are just trying to get me back because I said that to you,' he whispered huskily in her ear, making her tremble with desire.

'No, I'm not, Gabe, I promise. I swear to God I want nothing more than to roll around in this bed with you, but not like this, not when it would hurt other people and not while you are so upset. We need to talk about what's happened, and you need to at least tell Pixie that you're OK because she's worried about you.'

He knew she was right but stole one more kiss from her anyway. Her eyes closed, and she reluctantly pulled away.

'I'm making you a strong black coffee.' She filled the kettle and put it on.

They sat down in the comfortable velvet armchairs and Gabe explained what had happened.

'As you know, Nathan invited me to his home office for a meeting. He welcomed me in and brought me a coffee and some iced water. The office was in their huge garden and had a completely separate access from the main house. It was a huge annexe which Nathan said was his man cave.'

He took the coffee from Poppy and thanked her.

'Anyway, he told me that things are looking great for *Three Wishes*. The press coverage has been fantastic and the show as you know is sold out. They've also had interest from other parties to make it the next big Christmas comedy film.'

'Gabe, that's fantastic. Oh my God, I'm so proud of you.

Here, that deserves a biscuit.' She ripped the packet open and offered him one, but he shook his head.

'Yes, thanks, it will take a while, but negotiations are going well so far apparently, so, as you can imagine, I was chuffed with this news. It was exactly what I wanted to hear. I thanked him for the amazing experience and for giving my Pantomusicalay, as I called it, a chance.' Poppy felt her stomach knot about what was coming next as she could see his hand clenching and unclenching, and she felt it must be bad to have got him in such a state. She put her hand on his forearm and stroked it. 'Just take your time.'

'He told me that his wife had a lot to do with the marketing of the show and that she knew me. Then I heard a familiar voice that I hadn't heard for years.'

'Who was it?' asked Poppy, who was about to take a sip of her drink and nearly spilled it.

'To cut a long story short, it was Christina, you know, Chris, my ex.'

'What? How—'

'I know, I couldn't believe it. She left me years ago because she'd been offered a part in a film. The trouble was she was pregnant at the time and we had planned to get married. She mentioned having an abortion, which broke my heart. The thing is, the night before she left, she had a miscarriage. We both just cried and cried, and I told her she should be happy now because that's what she wanted.'

'Oh dear,' said Poppy.

'I know, believe me, I'm not proud of myself. It certainly wasn't my finest hour and I've regretted that a lot since then. But it was because I'd found a receipt for the morning after pill, which she swears she didn't take. As you know I was a wreck at the time and my family were so worried about me. That's when Marco came to live with me.'

'Gabe, I'm sorry that this all happened, and it must have been awful for you … but did something else happen because I've never seen you like this?' She offered him a box of tissues and he took a couple and blew his nose.

'She apologised and told me that she had wanted to tell me straight away, but I wouldn't open her letters, which is true and now I could kick myself for that. She did get the part in the film and that's when she met Nathan.' He took a deep breath and exhaled slowly. 'But something happened, and she had to drop out.'

Poppy was bursting to know and patted him on the leg.

'It seems that when she had the miscarriage, she never had a check-up at the doctors as she was so early on in the pregnancy, but a few months later she found out she was pregnant. She'd been having twins and the other one survived.'

Poppy gasped.

'Poppy, I've got a son, and he's called Joey and he's just beautiful.'

Poppy burst out crying and hugged him tightly. He retrieved a small photo album. The front cover said, 'For Daddy x'. The first couple of pictures were from the scans, then as a first born and right up to a picture taken of him just the other day.

Gabe wept when he looked at the pictures of the little boy with the dark hair and the golden skin, the big blue eyes and those huge dimples in his cheeks.

'He is the image of you, Gabe,' said Poppy. 'How old is he? And why didn't she tell you?'

'He's three, or she said if you ask him, he'll say three and a half,' he smiled. 'She had another son with Nathan and was frightened as time went on that by telling me, their happy little bubble would burst. But knowing I was here, the guilt eventually got the better of her. Anyway, I'm just glad that I know now. I asked if I could meet him, and she said of course.'

'This is amazing news, Gabe.'

'I know, I just can't believe it. Sorry for having a breakdown, the emotion just took a hold of me. I asked her if she just picked up my show out of guilt, but she said no, that she'd always believed in *Three Wishes* from the moment she first read it.' He took a swig of his coffee and pulled a face at the bitterness of it before continuing.

'I'm not sure I can concentrate any more. All I can see in my mind is that little boy in the photographs looking back at me. He's so beautiful and has made my heart completely melt. I can kind of understand why Chris did it, but I so wished she had told me straight away. I've missed out on him being born, being a baby, learning to walk and talk. Nathan said he had compiled some videos of all of those moments to give to me so I could at least see what it had been like. That was a small consolation. But the missing out is what has ripped me to shreds.'

'I can imagine it is, Gabe, but do you know what, you're the most positive person I know, so you stand up tall, Mr Genie, and make sure you make all your little boy's wishes come true in life. You're going to be the most amazing daddy and you and Joey have a wonderful future ahead of you. You're a lucky man.'

'I am, aren't I? I'm also a very hungry man – can we order some room service?'

Two club sandwiches with fries were delivered with more coffee and a couple of choc chip cookies.

Poppy forced Gabe to text Pixie to let her know he needed to take some time to get his head around something, so to please let him have some space.

She texted back, 'OK, I love you.' He shook his head but didn't reply.

'What about Ed?'

Poppy put her head in her hands and scrunched her hair through her fingers.

'It's over with Ed. I realised I didn't love him at all and that he didn't love me. I want someone who looks at me the way Selina looks at Layla or Franco looks at Holly. Or the way you ... oh, never mind. I've decided I need to be on my own. I just felt guilty that he moved two hundred miles to be with me.'

'But don't forget, Poppy, you moved two hundred miles to be with him and look how well he treated you.'

'I know, I guess you can't just switch off from being a nice person.'

'How did he take it?'

'Not very well, we'd only been back together a week. It was after Layla and Selina got engaged; I realised he wasn't what I wanted. He asked if there was anybody else, I told him no and he said he wasn't going to give up proving his love for me. He mentioned something about a grand gesture.'

'What sort of a grand gesture?'

'I've no idea. But I told him I'd made my mind up. He asked if we could stay friends, and he rings me now and then. In fact, he messaged me the other day to say that Burger Breath Brian had been sacked after everyone came forward with complaints.'

'Well, that's great news. Well done for reporting him when you did.'

'Yes, it's a great result but anyway, enough about them, what about Pixie?' Poppy's eyes filled with tears. 'She's such a lovely person. I feel terrible because she loves you so much.'

'I feel awful about her too and I did hope that we could

make a go of it but when we got over here, we had a really good chat and we've decided to just be friends. I felt like a right bastard for upsetting her again but she's doing OK.'

'What, so you're not together anymore?'

He shook his head. 'We never really did get back together properly, to be honest, we were taking things really slowly anyway because of the upset from the time before. The last thing I wanted to do was to hurt her. But she and Dean, one of the producers, are getting on really well.'

'Well, that's good, isn't it? For her I mean. I really don't think Pixie likes me.'

'She does like you, but I think she thought I was interested in you, I told her we were just friends, but I think she kind of wanted you out of the way.'

Poppy felt a stab to the heart on hearing he'd friendzoned her to Pixie.

'As soon as I found out about Joey, there was only one person that I needed, that I wanted and that was you, Poppy. Even now that we're not together, I know that Pixie would be devastated to know that, and I do still care about her a lot.' He looked down at the empty coffee cup in his hands. 'Look, I'm so sorry about how I acted earlier. It wasn't fair on you for me to act like that. It was stupid of me and could have complicated matters even further,' he said.

'If I'm honest,' she replied, 'I realised a long time ago that I had feelings for you Gabe, but our friendship means so much to me that I simply can't risk losing that for anything. I just feel so confused about everything, but one thing I know for certain is that I love you. You're the first person I think about when I wake up in the morning and the last face I see when I close my eyes at night. But if we got together and it didn't work out then I would have lost everything. I just can't take that risk.'

241

'I would be devastated to lose you too, Poppy, and at the moment with the news about Joey, my head is all over the place. Things were much less complicated when I was your gay best friend. Weren't they?'

'They certainly were and I guess we can't always have what we want, can we?'

Gabe slept in her bed, he kept his boxers on, and she wore her pyjamas.

Occasionally she felt the bed rocking and would realise he was sobbing again, too much drink on top of all of that emotion was not a good mix. He had his back to her, the dim bedside light shone on his smooth skin and cast even more of a golden glow on it. She spooned him tightly to comfort him, then when his sobbing subsided, he turned to face her. They looked deep into each other's eyes and stroked their faces gently with their fingertips. They caressed each other softly down their arms, backs, waists. They knew the out of bounds areas and avoided them completely. In some ways this felt more intimate than actually having sex.

'I've never been this deep into anyone's soul,' he said.

'I have,' she replied. 'The night I met you, I felt that your soul touched mine and I definitely came away with a piece of yours inside me. I fell in love with you that night, I just didn't realise it at the time.'

They hugged tightly. Poppy felt that they deserved medals for being able to respect each other's boundaries. Neither of them wanted this night to end but it did and in no time at all it was morning.

Layla was knocking on the door. 'Rise and shine,' she shouted, 'hope you're feeling better.'

Poppy panicked for a minute. She opened the door and registered the shock on Layla's face as she saw Gabe sitting at the side of the bed in his boxers. She explained that it wasn't what it looked like. Gabe had had a shock and needed some space today, so she needed to be with him. She told her that she would explain later.

'Are you sure, darling, because we can wait and do the Statue of Liberty with you tomorrow if you like?'

'No, don't worry, you go on with your plans. We'll be fine.'

Waking up to Gabe in bed with her was an amazing feeling; they had always had such a wonderful unique connection since the moment they met. This must be what people mean when they say they have met their soulmates. It's just that these two soulmates were strictly friends with complications.

Chapter 34

Gabe arrived with Poppy at Nathan's house. His dog Molly Malone yapped at them, wagging her tail to welcome them into her home. Gabe introduced Poppy as his best friend. Nathan and Chris welcomed her and Gabe warmly. 'Hello Poppy,' said Chris. 'I hear we have you to thank for sending off *Three Wishes* and *Latino*. Well done for that, I always knew the former would be a hit. I couldn't believe it when Nathan showed me it in the submissions and *Latino* is mind-blowing.'

'Gabe has made history as the only writer in thirty years to have two shows running concurrently at the Random Theater,' said Nathan.

Poppy studied Chris's delicate features and tried to imagine her and Gabe together but couldn't. Possibly because she suited Nathan so well, they were an attractive couple.

'Hi, it's nice to meet you and wow that's amazing but then Gabe is a very talented guy. I loved *Three Wishes* when I saw it last Christmas. I saw Marco in *Latino* last night, and I thought he really brought Salvatore to life magnificently.'

'Oh yes, he's magnificent but wait until you see Gabe in this version of *Three Wishes*, he's incredible.' Poppy glanced at Gabe and could see a slight flush to his cheeks.

'You've seen me?' he asked.

'Yes, I sneaked in the back of the theatre the other night. Anyway, I won't be a minute.'

Chris left the room and they sat nervously waiting on the couch; Poppy had butterflies in her stomach as she knew how much this meant to Gabe. Chris soon came back in holding hands with the most beautiful little boy Poppy had ever seen; he was the image of Gabe, especially when he smiled and his huge dimples cut hollows in his cheeks. Gabe's hand tightened around Poppy's when Joey walked in the room.

'Hello Joey,' he said weakly. 'I'm very pleased to meet you.' He shook his tiny hand, and Joey looked up into Gabe's big blue eyes.

'Two daddies.'

Gabe looked at Chris for reassurance and she nodded.

'Yes, that's right Joey,' he said, 'You've got two daddies, you're a very lucky boy. I'm so looking forward to spending some time with you.'

Nathan and Chris went into the kitchen to make some drinks and after taking coffees to Gabe and Poppy and juice for Joey, they stayed out there to give them a chance to get to know each other. Gabe had lots of fun crawling along the floor playing with the train set and doing some Batman and Spiderman puzzles.

'Joey, I've got a nephew called Luca and he is your cousin. He loves Spiderman. Would you like to see a picture of him?'

Joey nodded and sat on his knee to look at the photos on the phone. He saw one of Gabe in his genie costume and asked who it was.

'That's me,' he said.

'Wow, Genie. I have wishes.'

'Joey, you are my son and I promise you that I will spend the rest of my life making all of your wishes come true.' His voice shook and lip trembled as he spoke. His heart was aching and felt like it was quite literally bursting with love for this precious little boy and he had a lot of catching up to do.

Joey ran to the kitchen and shouted, 'Mummy, Daddy, genie give me lots wishes.'

The visit couldn't have gone any better. When he had asked if there were any toys that Joey would like, Chris had asked him not to bring presents as she wanted him to get to know Gabe with no distractions. She didn't want him just looking forward to getting presents, she wanted him to look forward to seeing his daddy. As they were leaving, Joey gave them both a huge hug. Poppy had taken lots of photos of them both together which Gabe wanted to get printed as soon as possible. There was a perfect one of Joey cuddling Gabe tightly, their faces right next to each other; same colouring, same mouth, same dimples and same eyes.

'Your family are going to love him so much. They'll be so glad they decided to spend Christmas with you,' said Poppy.

'I know, I'm so excited. I need to keep him a secret for a little while longer, though, as I don't want to tell them on the phone. Hey, I still don't feel up to facing people so I might see if I can book a hotel room.'

'Are you sure because you can stay in my room if you want.'

'Are you sure?'

'I'm as sure as I've ever been about anything in my life.'

Gabe worried that the revelation had been such a distraction that he wouldn't be able to remember his lines, let alone put in a whole performance.

'I'll go through them with you if you like,' said Poppy. 'I've got so much adrenaline running through me at the moment, it would be good to release it somehow.'

'Can you remember them from our bike rides?' asked Gabe.

'Well, we'll soon find out won't we?' she replied.

They went through them until the early hours.

Gabe was in awe of his son and had printed out a few pictures of the two of them and framed them for Christmas presents. He'd kept one for himself, which he put on the bedside table next to Poppy's bed. He couldn't take his eyes off it.

'You really are two peas in a pod,' Poppy said softly in his ear. She kissed his smooth shoulder and stroked his hair to get him to sleep. Well, actually it was because she wanted to stroke his hair, but he went to sleep anyway.

The next day was Christmas Eve and the rest of Gabe's family were arriving. What a beautiful surprise they had in store. Poppy decided to make the most of her time with Gabe. Maybe if she didn't go to sleep then the morning wouldn't come, so she tried to lie there with her eyes open for as long as possible.

'How gorgeous is this boy?' he would say, showing her the picture and she would reply, 'He's very gorgeous, just like his daddy.' Then he would squeeze her arm lovingly and she would cuddle him tighter. It was heaven.

Christmas Eve was Gabe's next performance as the genie in *Three Wishes*.

Poppy was dying to kiss him but couldn't, so spent the night tossing and turning and not being able to sleep. He felt the same. When she awoke the next morning, he was looking at her.

'Morning, darling, how are you?'

'Tired,' she replied, wanting to close her eyes again but at the same time wanting to keep them open so she could continue to look into his amazing eyes. He kissed the tip of her nose gently and sprung out of bed. He started booming out one of the songs from his show. He felt elated, his wounds were healed, he was now determined to make the most of every minute he was able to spend with his son. He tickled Poppy awake as she was drifting off again.

'Thanks for looking after me, Poppy.' She sat up in bed, rubbing her eyes, and he gave her one of his immense bear hugs. 'You really are the best friend a genie could ever have. I love you.'

'I love you too. You'll always be my GBF.' She felt that secure warm feeling again. Wrapped in his arms was her favourite place to be.

'By the way, Gabe, happy birthday,' she said. 'I'll give you your present later.'

'Ah thanks, babe. I've got to go so I suppose I'll see you later at the show.' He picked his photo up and put it in the bag with the others; he would wrap them later and give them to his family.

'Of course, you will,' she replied, 'I wouldn't miss it for the world.'

They both knew that their little bubble was bursting as everyone would be there the next time they saw each other.

They kissed at the door, lips closed but locked together for some time, breathing in each other's scent as they hugged.

When he had gone, Poppy knocked at Layla's door. They were still in bed, but Layla scooted over to make room for her best friend. She told them the whole amazing story about little Joey, and showed them the pictures she had taken. They cooed over him, saying how cute he was.

'How is he?' asked Layla.

'A lot better today, but he was so broken, Layla, it was awful to see. My lovely big strong GBF was so weak and vulnerable. Also, we nearly ... you know.'

'Whaaaat,' shouted Layla. 'About bloody time too, can't you see you two are made for each other? I told you that you should have gone for him. Wait but what about Pixie?'

'It turns out they're not together anymore but she would be hurt if we got together as she always suspected there was something between us. He's just had this massive bombshell dropped on him and he's really not in the right place for a relationship,' Poppy said, tears springing to her eyes. 'It feels like a hopeless situation.'

'I'm so sorry, babe, maybe one day things will work out. The timing's just never been right.'

Poppy couldn't hold back the tears. Lovely memories flashed into her mind of all the great times she had had with Gabe. Most of the memories were fun, his happy face smiling, then an annoyed one when she had told him she was taking Ed back. Then right up to watching his heart break in front of her over missing out on his baby son's first years, to the elated look this morning when she realised that he had a wonderful future as Joey's dad.

Layla held her as the tears flowed.

'I'm sorry,' she said. 'It's just been really emotional. It really hurt me to see him so sad.'

'That's because you're in love with him, Poppy. Heart and soul, you have fallen for him.' Layla kissed her.

'Come on, let's go to the Statue of Liberty. We didn't want to go without you yesterday.'

They got ready and had a fun day. Although they had to queue for a little while to get on the boat, there were plenty of entertainers to amuse them. They bought foam Statue of Liberty crowns on the boat which they wore for the rest of the day and they lunched on Liberty Island. It was great fun.

'Remember that snow globe?' said Layla. 'Well, you bloody showed those bitches, Britt and Mandy.'

'I know,' said Poppy. 'Did I tell you that she apologised? I gave it back to her in a gift bag on my last day.'

Layla laughed. 'No, I didn't realise. Good for you and I'm glad she saw sense in the end. So now is probably a good time to give you this.' She handed a gift bag to her.

'Oh, this is heavy,' said Poppy. She opened it to find a beautiful snow globe depicting the landmarks of New York, including Times Square and all the theatres.

'Look you can even see the Random Theater on there, and ice skaters and the Rockefeller Christmas tree. It plays a song called "Christmas in New York".' Poppy wound it up and listened to the jolly tune. Layla pressed a button and the Christmas tree lit up and spun round.

'This is amazing, Layla, and much nicer than the other one. I'm going to treasure this, thank you.'

Chapter 35

Gabe had met all of his family at the hotel they were staying at in Times Square. It was right in the centre of all the activity, and they were all booked into the hotel's restaurant for Christmas dinner the next day.

Holly, Franco and Luca had arrived from England and Rosa and Stanley from the Caribbean; they were all in Holly's huge suite when Gabe arrived. After hugging and fixing drinks, wishing Gabe a happy birthday and giving him presents, Gabe excitedly gave Holly and Rosa a beautifully wrapped present each.

'This is just a little early Christmas gift,' he said. 'Mum, can you sit down when you open yours.' Intrigued, two of the most important women in Gabe's life opened their presents.

'Ah what a lovely picture,' said Rosa. 'You are so clever how you have taken a picture of you when you were little and merged it with one of you now. Technology is a wonderful thing.'

'Er no, Mum, that's not what I've done.' His eyes welled up again and he took a deep breath. 'You see, this is my son Joey, I've only just found out about him.' Rosa and Holly looked at him, Rosa's eyes blinking rapidly.

'What do you mean? I don't understand. Stanley, did you know about this?' She looked at Stanley and he shrugged his shoulders and shook his head.

Stanley joined his wife to have a closer look at the picture.

Rosa stroked the glass that covered the beautiful little boy's face. Tears began to splash onto the mirrored frame.

Gabe continued, 'When Chris had the miscarriage, it turns out she was having twins. She lost one baby but the other carried on growing. He's your grandson and his name is Joseph Stanley. They live here in New York.' Happy noises filled the air as Holly, Rosa, Franco and Stanley all hugged Gabe.

'What wonderful news.' Rosa sniffed into a tissue as she hugged her son to her soft cushiony chest. 'I can't believe it. When can we see him?'

'Chris has said she will bring him over later to see you all.' They couldn't wait.

'We need to go shopping for Christmas presents for him,' said Holly. She stooped down to Luca's height and said, 'Did you hear that, darling, you have a new little cousin to play with.' The little boy nodded happily and gave his uncle Gabe a huge hug.

As promised, Chris dropped in with Joey. Gabe was delighted to introduce his son to his nana, grandad, auntie, uncle and cousin. Rosa and Holly cried when they hugged him, Stanley's eyes were moist in the corners.

'He looks so much like you, Gabe,' he said.

'This has to be the happiest hotel room in the whole of New York,' Holly said to Gabe, her voice heavy with emotion. Gabe hugged her. His heart melted even more when he received a homemade birthday card from Joey with Daddy written on it in his childish scrawl. He had also drawn a picture of Gabe as a genie holding a little boy's hand.

Chapter 36

Once again, the theatre was bustling. Christmas songs played in the foyer, and the air buzzed with excitement. Having pre-ordered their interval drinks, the group had taken their seats. Chris had allowed Gabe's family to take Joey to watch his daddy as a genie. He was sitting with Luca on his left and Rosa on his right. Joey was in awe of Luca and Rosa was in awe of Joey. Layla, Selina and Poppy all sat with Gabe's family, Joey excitedly waved a hello to Poppy when he saw her, and she waved back and blew a kiss to him.

The show started and adrenaline rushed through Poppy's body. She sang along as she knew all of the words. The audience were lapping it up, laughing and shouting, it was an interactive experience. Having seen the show before, Poppy and Layla knew when Gabe appeared with a puff of smoke and they were waiting for it nervously. Here it came, whoosh, a bang and a huge puff of smoke appeared. As it cleared, the girls expected to see the funny performance they saw back home but as the smoke cleared, they saw Gabe standing in his silk baggy trousers, his bejewelled waistcoat open revealing his smooth skin. Poppy drifted into a daydream of putting squirty cream on his contoured abs and licking it off. She mentally slapped herself. His muscular arms and handsome face seemed very well received by the audience judging by the wolf whistles and whoops. The campness of the UK performance was gone and he used his natural booming voice to make the audience jump when he first spoke. He had such great stage presence and looked so damn sexy.

'Wow, even I fancy him,' whispered Selina to Layla and Poppy, making them giggle.

Gabe gave a sneaky wink to Poppy who was sitting with his family and friends when a little voice shouted out from the crowd, 'My genie daddy!' The audience laughed, and Rosa cuddled her little grandson. Gabe continued to perform with the sparkle of a tear in his eye.

The show was even better than before and had the desired effect on the audience. During the interval the group were milling about having drinks. Luca chased Joey around the bar area, tickling him and making him laugh. They ran back over to Rosa and she gave them an ice cream each.

Poppy was shocked to hear an announcement over the loudspeaker.

'Would Miss Poppy Kale please come to reception.'

'Did I just hear that right?' she asked Layla.

'Yes, you did, and you'd better go and see what they want.'

'OK, can you mind my bag please?'

Poppy tentatively went to reception and was met by Pixie, who grabbed her by the arm and led her down a corridor.

'Oh, thank God, Poppy, you know the lines for the fairy godmother, don't you?'

'Well, I have practised a few times with Gabe. Why? What's going on?'

'You didn't have prawns at lunch, did you?'

Poppy stopped walking. 'No, why?'

'Well because Cindy did, along with about a quarter of the cast and let's just say they didn't agree with them.' She grabbed Poppy's hand and broke into a run.

'Wait, what? You can't seriously expect me to perform on stage. Can't her understudy do it?' she gasped.

'Prawns,' shouted Pixie.

'Well, I'm assuming that her understudy has an understudy—'

'Prawns, prawns and prawns,' replied Pixie, 'they've all had the bloody prawns. I promise we wouldn't ask if we weren't desperate.'

'Well, can't you do it?'

'I can't, I've got to be in the ensemble, and I don't know all the lines.'

'Damn my photographic memory,' muttered Poppy.

Gabe appeared, still in his finery and grabbed her hand.

'Oh brilliant, thanks Poppy. You're a lifesaver.'

'Nope, no way.' Poppy shook her head and wagged her finger at him. He put a reassuring arm around her. 'Come on, just imagine that we're on our bikes cycling along the River Bram with the wind in our hair. It will be just like old times.'

She sighed in resignation as he dragged her off backstage and sat her in the make-up chair while the experts transformed her in minutes to the Fairy Godmother, complete with beautiful Cinderella-style dress, blonde curly wig in an up do and a magic wand with a crystal star on the top.

'You owe me big time for this, Gabe,' she shouted after him.

'Right, we just need to attach the harness now,' said the dresser. Poppy suddenly remembered one of the reasons she was reluctant to do this – the fairy godmother had to fly in! This was not good.

Before she could say anything, she was abruptly hoisted to the ceiling as the curtains opened. Her stomach lurched, and she screamed loudly, much to the amusement of the audience. Instead of flying gracefully across the stage to where Gabe stood, she couldn't help flailing her arms and legs about, causing her to swing to and fro and land in an ungainly heap on the floor.

Gabe had to stifle a giggle as he tried to catch her, but she flew past him still screeching. The audience were nearly wetting themselves with mirth; most of them thought it was meant to happen like this.

She felt less worried when she saw Nathan watching from the sidelines laughing hysterically. She wondered if he'd write it into the show.

When Poppy stood up and brushed herself down, she was amazed at how quickly all of the words that she'd rehearsed on their bike rides and just the night before came back to her. Despite her heart nearly beating out of her chest, she seemed to enter a dreamlike state as though her mind had left her body. She followed Gabe's lead and tried to forget that she was playing to an audience and just concentrated on him.

Layla and Selina sat there open-mouthed when they realised it was Poppy on the stage but soon joined in the laughter, especially when they could see that Poppy was beginning to enjoy it.

She was backstage enjoying a twenty-minute break before she was needed again. She sipped water from a paper cup wishing it was vodka and one of the cast members gave her a throat sweet. She managed to gather her breath and then, all of a sudden, was hoisted back in the air. She tried not to flail too much this time and her entrance was a lot smoother although she did still have to shriek a bit as she flew.

They got to the part where she had to grant the genie his final wish for the woman he loves to love him back.

'My dear genie, I would grant you any wish that you

pleased but to wish for someone to love you is one I cannot fulfil. Love is the most precious gift and must be given freely, and—'

'But it's you I love. It's always been you,' he interrupted.

They moved closer and looked into each other's eyes. Poppy's heart fluttered as Gabe smiled at her in encouragement.

'Those are the words I've longed to hear, so this wish I do grant you but not with my magic and my wand. It is with my mind, my heart, my soul. I'm yours for ever.'

The genie enveloped the fairy godmother into his strong arms and kissed her passionately. The audience whooped their approval loudly. The whole cast joined in the final song of 'Christmas Wishes'. Joey and Luca were in their grandparents' arms clapping and singing along with the audience. The curtain went down to rapturous applause, then raised again and the cast sang a medley of all of the songs from the show, their colourful costumes making such a pretty spectacle on the stage. Normally the genie and the fairy godmother joined in at this point but were still kissing passionately in the middle of the stage with the rest of the cast dancing around them. Poppy felt as though fireworks were going off inside her as Gabe's kiss overwhelmed her.

The curtain went down again, and everyone took a bow. The genie and the fairy godmother reluctantly broke off their embrace, held hands and bowed, the audience whistled and cheered and whooped. Gabe bent to his knees and held his arms out to his little boy in the front row, Rosa handed him to his daddy, and he waved delightedly to the audience. Layla knew it was naughty, but she took a photo of the genie holding his son and with his arm around the fairy godmother. They looked like such a happy family.

★

Poppy walked past the gift shop on her way to get changed and bumped into Selina.

'Ah just the person,' she said. 'I got you this as you've now fulfilled your last wish.' She handed Poppy a gift bag.

Poppy opened it and gasped as she saw a tiny silver charm of the joined theatre masks. 'Well it did feel very extraordinary, that's for sure. Thank you, Selina, I love it.'

'Here, let me clip it on for you.'

'Ah there you are,' said a breathless Layla as she emerged from the crowd.

'What's up?' asked Poppy.

'Ed's stolen your bag.'

'Ed? What's he doing here?' she looked behind Layla.

'I don't know. He wants you to meet him at the top of the Empire State but don't worry, I'll go and get it back.'

Poppy was already moving towards the door.

'No, it's fine, I need to sort this out once and for all.' She got outside and hailed a cab. Layla jumped in after her and told the driver their destination.

'How did he know where we were?' said Poppy.

'He mentioned Facebook, I checked in here earlier. I'm so sorry, Poppy, he just appeared out of nowhere and was begging me to get you there because he wanted to surprise you. I said no. Then he recognised your bag, snatched it and jumped in a cab.'

Gabe was outside signing autographs and posing for selfies when he saw Selina looking troubled.

'Hi darling, are you alright? Where's the others?'

'They're on the way to the Empire State, Ed's here and he's stolen Poppy's bag. You don't think he's going to propose, do you?'

'What the hell?' Gabe's stomach sank and he put his head

in his hands. Pixie had heard the whole thing and witnessed his reaction, and guilt overwhelmed him as he saw the hurt on her face.

'Go to her,' she said.

'What do you mean?' He looked shocked; his heart was flipping like a pancake.

'Gabe, ever since I met you, I've wanted you to love me but the fairy godmother was right, that love has to come freely. I wish that you could look at me the way you look at her, but I know you can't. I know you love Poppy, and I can tell she loves you too. Go after her.'

Gabe hugged her.

'I do love you, Pixie, very much, but as a friend and I always will, I promise you that.' He kissed her on the cheek and ran to a taxi. Selina joined him.

It was only when they were in the cab that Gabe realised he was still in his genie outfit, but he had to get there fast and tell Poppy exactly how he felt about her.

Poppy was getting some unusual looks due to the fairy godmother costume she was wearing. She made her way through the crowd to Ed. He smiled a radiant smile, he did look handsome but really, he did nothing for her anymore.

'Where's my bag, Ed? This really isn't funny,' she said firmly with her hands on her hips.

'I'm sorry about that, but desperate times call for desperate measures.' He gestured to where it sat on the floor and grabbed her hand as she went to retrieve it.

'Poppy, please wait, just for a minute.' Her stomach sank as he dropped to one knee.

'Look, I know I don't deserve you but you mean the absolute world to me and my life is empty without you in it.' He took her hand and she pulled away from him.

'Poppy Kale, will you marry me?'

As he asked the question, he took the ring from the box and held it up to her, like a priest offering communion.

Poppy, a little shell-shocked, felt a sense of relief seeing Gabe make his way through the crowd.

He moved towards her. 'It's OK, I've got this,' she said.

The crowd around them was getting bigger and included some of the security men, who seemed intrigued by this live theatre show that was unfolding.

She spoke slowly and meaningfully, drawing strength from within.

'Thank you for the lovely proposal, Ed, what I wouldn't have given to have experienced it this time last year. You were all I ever wanted, you know, but you put your own needs before mine.' She gently pushed his hand away. 'So, thanks but no thanks. As my grandad always said to me, "Never settle for second best."'

'Come on, Poppy, think of all the good times we've had. You don't want to give up on all that! We're great together. I want a future with you, that's why I moved all that way to be with you,' Ed answered.

'But it wasn't though, was it?' She shook her head, her lips pursed. 'You lied. Tania told me that you were demoted, that's why you moved away, not because of me. And these grand gestures, tickets to Paris and proposals on top of buildings, they're lovely but it's the little things that matter, the knowing that someone is there for you all the time no matter what. That's what counts and that's what love is.'

He had the decency to look shamefaced and mumbled something.

'Actually, Ed, there is one thing I will always be eternally grateful to you for.'

He looked hopeful. 'What's that?'

Poppy looked at Gabe now, his blue sparkling eyes focused on hers.

'The fact that you encouraged me to move two hundred miles away from home, away from all of my friends and everything I'd known. Because, if I hadn't have done that, I would never have met this man. He can reduce me to tears of laughter with one little look or word, he knows my favourite dessert and with the aid of some Batman plasters has helped to put me back together again.'

She turned back to Ed. 'I'm sorry, Ed, but it's really over.'

'I guess the best man won,' he said before sloping off to the sound of the crowd booing him.

Her eyes found Gabe and her face broke into a smile. He stepped towards her, arms wide open and she ran into his bear hug freely and without any feelings of guilt. Gabe crushed his lips against hers and she welcomed him passionately. 'I love you so much, Genie Man,' she said, breathless from his kiss.

'Oh wait, before I forget.' He put his hand inside a little hidden pocket in his waistcoat and pulled out a tiny silk drawstring bag. He handed it to Poppy.

She opened it and clasped it to her chest. 'Oh, it's perfect, thank you. I guess I don't need a refund on that wish after all.' He clipped the small gold genie lamp to her bracelet.

Snowflakes began to fall like glitter in a snow globe against the backdrop of the midnight blue sky. Poppy lifted her arm up and wiggled her wrist, the three charms tinkling together and sparkling in the moonlight.

'You did it, Gabe. You made my Christmas wishes come true.'

'That's the bit you don't get, Poppy, you achieved those things yourself. They didn't come easy, you worked bloody hard and deserve happiness and success. You brought me back to life. Without you I wouldn't be here in New York and who knows, I may never have found my son, so thank you for that. I know you're scared of losing our friendship, but I promise we can have both. I've loved you from the minute I saw you and for the rest of our lives your wish will always be my command.'

'Do you know what I'm wishing for now?' she asked, her face lifted towards his.

He answered her by pressing his lips against hers and pulled her into one of his legendary bear hugs. Poppy melted into his kiss, feeling safe and at home in his arms. The small crowd cheered and clapped and whooped and whistled. Some were filming it on their phones. Gabe stopped kissing for a second to announce, 'Aaaaaand, it's a wrap.'

Acknowledgements

Poppy's Christmas Wishes was the first book I wrote but my third published novel. Having wanted to write a book for most of my life, I had the problem of not really knowing what to write about; I'd tried a few times when the children were young but nothing really came to me. Then one night I was out on a works Christmas do and heard the most amazing laugh; my friend and I got chatting to the man behind the laugh and he told us he was sporting a goatee as he was playing a genie in Aladdin. That gave me an idea that I sat on for another five years until I plucked up the courage to write it and another five years before it was published. So I would like to say a huge thank you to the lovely Orion Abbott-Davies for providing me with that initial spark of an idea, which started me on my writing journey. Strangely this book is being published by Orion Dash, is it just a coincidence or a sign that it was truly meant to be? I'm really grateful to the whole team at Orion Dash but especially to my editor Rhea Kurien, who works so hard and is brilliant at bringing out the best in a novel, and my cover designer, as I've truly never seen such beautiful covers and they keep getting even more gorgeous, which I didn't think was possible.

As I was writing this book, I would pass fifty pages at a time over the garden fence to my bestie who lives at the back of me and as we did our regular walk along the river, we would talk about the characters and the story. That was the first time I felt that amazing feeling when someone gets your writing and the characters become your mutual friends, so thank you to Kay Davies for being my first reader and an amazing support from the very beginning. I soon confided in my Auntie Margie Morris and one of my other besties, Sandra Woods, and they both fell in love with the characters too. This gave me the encouragement I needed to keep on going and that's what I did. My friendship with Sandra is what inspired the amazing friendship between Poppy and Layla as we had great fun on our nights out in Liverpool and she's been such an amazing support to me over the years, especially with my writing, so thank you both. Thanks also to my other wonderful BFFs and early readers, Carolyn Mead, Katie Nash and Barbara Stone. I love you all.

I would like to thank the fabulous author Heidi Swain for the gorgeous quote she supplied for *Poppy's Christmas Wishes* as it was such a fun book to write about strong friendships and I think she captured the essence of it perfectly. I've watched Heidi's author journey from the very beginning and she's a wonderful inspiration and lovely friend.

Huge thanks to my gorgeous writer friends 'The Muses', Lucinda Lee, Julia Wild, Lynne Shelby, Paula Fleming, Melissa Oliver, Alison French, Sophie Rodger, Kathleen Whyman and Giulia Skye, thank you for being there for the happy times and the painful times of writing a book. You're all brilliant and such wonderful support and great fun to be around.

Thank you to all the fantastic authors and book bloggers who have supported me both as a blogger and an author: Vicki Bowles, Kirsty Clifton, Karen Cocking, Dawn Crooks, Linda Hill, Milly Johnson, Debbie Johnston, Karen King, Claire Knight, Lara Marshall, Julie Morris, Kim Nash, Lynne

Shelby, Sharon Wilden, Babs Wilkie and last but definitely not least Anne Williams.

I will be forever grateful to my family for all their support and encouragement and for believing in me. My husband Johnna, sons Jake and Damon and especially my daughter Lydia for her amazing advice and editing skills, which have been invaluable.

I would also like to thank Lydia and Damon for the wonderful surprise Christmas song they wrote for me, inspired by this book. It's called 'Christmas Wishes' and is on Youtube and Spotify and absolutely blew me away.

Huge thanks also to each and every one of you for choosing my books. I hope you enjoy reading *Poppy's Christmas Wishes* as much as I enjoyed writing it. Merry Christmas!

Annette xx